FATED
Cinderella's Story

Destined Series, Book 1

KAYLIN LEE

For information contact:
Kaylin Lee
http://www.kaylinleewrites.com

Editing by Kathrese McKee of Word Marker Edits
Cover design by Victoria Cooper Designs

ISBN: 1973806193
ISBN-13: 978-1973806196

CONTENTS

There's more to the story...

Sign up for Kaylin Lee's new release email list at http://smarturl.it/torn-freebie and get the free prequel to *Fated*, a 12,000-word novelette called *Torn. Torn* is a short story set two years before *Fated* begins and can be read before or after *Fated*.

For my parents, who taught me to love stories, listened to my own crazy stories, and somehow always had time for another trip to the local library.

Everyone sees what you appear to be, few experience what you really are.

Machiavelli

Chapter 1

"Ella, they've set a date for Prince Estevan's selection ball. It's this summer!" Alba spread the Procus Society pages of the *Herald* across the breakfast table.

I dragged my attention away from my exam notes. "Already? Didn't he just have one of those?"

My stepsister ran her finger under the words. "It's right here. 'Crown Prince Estevan is set to welcome all the young ladies of good Procus families in a summer selection ball, sure to be an extravagant affair, if last year's selection is any indicator.'"

I sat at a rusty table with my family on the rooftop terrace above our bakery. Honey scones and coffee cups crowded together on the old white tablecloth, sharing the small space with inky pages of today's *Herald*.

My stepmother Zel and my other stepsister Bri ate their scones and ignored Alba. They had both been quiet all morning, so I answered Alba again. "But I thought the whole point of a selection ball was that he's supposed to choose a wife and be done with it. He's not supposed to have a ball every year."

"You can't force true love, Ella! The prince just didn't meet the right lady last year." My twin stepsisters were not quite thirteen, but to hear Alba talk, she was an expert on love. "He needs another ball so he can have a chance at true love. Even you wouldn't begrudge him that, would you?"

I bit back a smile. "Even me, hmm?"

The gossips at the Royal Academy whispered that the prince had found true love with at least six beautiful Procus ladies since last year's ball. I didn't want to wipe that sweet smile off Alba's face, so I didn't elaborate. She went back to drooling over the paper, and I returned to my notes.

I made it through a few more minutes of studying before I dropped my notes on the table, leaned back in my chair, and groaned.

"What's wrong, El?" Zel nudged me.

I rubbed at my tired, burning eyes. "What's the point? It doesn't matter how well I do on the final exam. I'll never belong at the Royal Academy, much less in a government apprenticeship. I don't know why I'm trying so hard."

Zel squeezed my hand. "Never say never. Besides, it'll be that much sweeter to prove them all wrong, won't it?"

I had to laugh. "True." Zel had been the one to encourage me to apply for the scholarship when they first opened the Royal Academy to commoners. But it was one thing for my own stepmother to believe in me. It was quite another to convince my professors and classmates that I was worthy of a government position. "Even so, I wouldn't mind being descended from a Procus line. Or at least looking like a true Fenra."

Zel snorted. "There's no such thing as a true Fenra. Ignore them, El. I'm serious. You're beautiful. I wouldn't change a single thing about you."

Heat spread across my cheeks. "Not even these green eyes?" I kept my tone light, but from Zel's gentle smile, she saw right through me.

"Definitely not the green eyes."

I was fortunate to have the dark hair and bronze skin of the Fenra ruling class who had founded Asylia centuries ago, but I'd also been cursed with the light-green eyes of a Kireth descendant—the eyes of a mage. I was well past the age when any magical tendency might manifest itself. Without doubt, I was not and never would be a mage. But my green eyes suggested a different story to everyone who saw me.

Zel must have guessed my thoughts. "Even if you looked full Kireth like me, you still might not have inherited mage powers. Those Procus fools at the Royal Academy need to learn not to base everything on appearance. Besides, if you truly were a mage, you'd already be in the Mage Division, and they all know it."

I nodded and leaned back in my chair. She was right. Anyone who did have mage powers—a natural tendency to either absorb or expel magic—was required to enter government service or Procus patronage. It was a public safety issue, as every Royal Academy student knew. The city government couldn't risk letting mages roam free. I had to stop letting my classmates get to me.

Zel sipped her coffee and went back to her section of the *Herald*. I listened to Alba with half an ear as she rambled on about Prince Estevan and his ball.

"The article talks all about last year's ball—who was there, what they wore, and which beautiful ladies the prince favored. Oh, I would give anything to be there!"

And I would do anything to avoid such a spectacle. Good thing neither of us would ever attend a royal ball.

I stretched in my chair, tired from studying for the final exam all morning and most of last night. Fragrant herbs and raised, wooden vegetable beds filled the rooftop so tightly we barely had room for a table, but it was warm and breezy in the late spring sunshine. The scent of lemonburst and mint nearly blocked out the smell of rotting garbage in the street below.

"The gowns, the music, the food … Did you know that last year they invented a new drink, just for Prince Estevan's first selection ball? It's called chry … chro … chrysos, I think. Sparkling liquid gold that tastes like sweetened frostberries. Can you imagine?" Alba feigned a swoon in her seat.

I made a face at Alba, and she giggled. Then I shuffled my notes together and shoved them to the side to make room for a second honey scone on my plate.

"Oh, Ella, do you mind that I borrowed your ribbon?"

"Ribbon?"

Alba fingered her long, wavy black hair and bit her lip.

Ah, that one. She'd tied a glossy red ribbon around her head, and it was quite pretty, setting off her rosy cheeks and lips and highlighting her soft, pale skin. I thought about saying so but kept quiet. Her pale skin was the only thing that kept her from looking Fenra, and she read enough of the Procus Society pages to know that everyone who was anyone wanted to have bronze-colored skin. "That's not my ribbon," I said instead.

"But I found it in your room. It was right there on your bed this morning when I went to put away your washing."

I raised my eyebrows and gave the ribbon a closer look. "Definitely not mine. I don't have anything like that." All of my possessions were either serviceable, stain-hiding brown or part of the Royal Academy uniform. There was no place for a red ribbon in my life.

Alba looked confused. "But it was right there, on your—"

"Don't worry about it, Alba. Wear it if you want to." I stood and picked up my plate. "I have to make a few deliveries before school, so I'm going to go get ready now. Have a good day."

"Be careful!" Alba waved the newspaper at me. "There was another Crimson Blight attack yesterday."

"On a trolley?"

She shook her head. "A market in the River Quarter."

"Well, in that case, I'll be fine." I blew her a kiss and smiled to reassure her. Alba gave me a troubled smile. Zel waved to me but didn't speak, and Bri only glanced at me before returning to her breakfast. Everyone was feeling off today. Maybe they'd feel better by the time I came home after school to open the bakery shop.

~

Back in my cramped bedroom, I changed out of my house dress and put on my worn school uniform. The shirt was as white and crisp as I could make it, and the navy skirt, let out too many times to count, hung just below my knees. The length was barely within dress code regulations. Good thing I hadn't grown much in the last two years, and that I only had to wear it a few more days.

I splashed water on my face and hands for a makeshift bath and twisted my hair back into the neatest bun I could manage, then paused for a moment in front of the small mirror above my sink. A tired, green-eyed girl stared back at me, her dark hair already sticking out from her bun. I grimaced.

At least my hands and face were clean of cinderslick's telling golden glimmer. Who had time for the three hot water washings it would take to remove the sweet, fiery odor of cinderslick from my hair? I rolled my eyes at my reflection. Certainly not me. My time was better spent studying and working.

I slung my battered book bag over my shoulder, walked into the kitchen, and shoved my school texts and pencils out of the way on the big wooden work table. The loaves were ready to go, neatly wrapped and waiting for me on the kitchen shelves, but the scones still needed wrapping now that they'd cooled.

I took a long whiff of the fresh, buttery scones, but then the distinct scent of burnt cinderslick made me cough. Cheap, government-made cooking fuel. As I baked and studied in the early hours of the morning, the smell of cinderslick would cover me, clinging to my hair, skin, and clothes the rest of the day.

My Procus classmates at school hated the smell. After all, I doubted any of them had ever set foot in a kitchen, and their families certainly had no need for cheap cinderslick rations. Quality cinderslick didn't have such an overpowering smell.

They claimed my stepmother hated me so much, she refused to heat my bedroom and forced me to sleep in front of the kitchen oven to soak in warmth from the cinderslick. Cinderella, they called me. As if I cared.

I shouldered the canvas delivery bag, careful not to squash the wrapped loaves inside, and stepped into the front shop, only to stumble to a halt. A young man stood by the door with Zel. My stepmother never spoke to strangers. Had we been discovered?

I surged forward to rescue her, forcing myself to take slow breaths and trying not to appear as tense and terrified as I felt. "Stepmother, Alba has been asking for you upstairs," I said. It was the script we'd planned years ago, but my voice wavered as I pushed the words out. I kept my eyes downcast subserviently like I was the defeated, weak-willed stepdaughter everyone assumed me to be. "Please allow me to help this gentleman with whatever he may need."

Instead of leaving me to deal with him, Zel said, "Ella, I'd like you to meet someone."

I dragged my gaze from her to the man. Disaster.

He had to be a mage. He appeared to be a little older than me, and was tall and broad-shouldered, with blond hair hanging over his forehead and nearly reaching his gray eyes. No one with such clear Kireth heritage and fine, rich garments could be anything other than a mage. But where was his gold mage service armband? His brown slacks and plain white shirt were crisp and clean, and he wore the latest fashionable cut. His head had an arrogant tilt as he looked me up and down.

A mage, right here in our bakery. We were in trouble. I nodded a greeting as he took my small hand in his large one. Something about his gaze had my cheeks growing hot, as though he liked what he saw and wanted to keep looking.

What was wrong with him?

"Weslan, this is my stepdaughter, Ariella. Ella, this is Weslan Fortis," Zel cast him a smile and looked back to me. "He's going to be staying here and helping you with the bakery now."

He was— Wait, what?

I dropped his hand like a hot stone and glared at my stepmother. "I don't need any help."

"You're about to graduate from the academy, and who knows what your apprenticeship will be like? Don't you think it will be nice to have someone to help with the baking and deliveries so you don't have to do it all yourself?"

I willed Zel to understand, so I wouldn't have to say anything that might give us away. "But that's beside the point, Zel! Do you really think that someone like … him … should be here with us?"

Zel only smiled at me and placed a calming hand on my bare arm.

Weslan took a reflexive step backward. Did that mean what I thought it did?

"Weslan is exactly the right person to be here with us."

I stared at her, silently begging her not to speak the words I had dreaded hearing for so many years.

"He knows."

Chapter 2

The floor rocked under my feet. How could she have told him?

"Weslan's mother knew that your father sometimes used the bakery to shelter mages who found themselves in need, like I did so many years ago." She stared at me meaningfully. "Weslan has found himself in a difficult position, so his mother sent him here until things ... get sorted out. And I've told him he can stay."

It was clear there would be no more disagreement on the matter. Beside us, Weslan shifted back and forth on his feet.

I shook my head, dumbfounded. "I've got to get to school." I gripped my bookbag's strap with the tight fingers of one hand and clutched the delivery bag with the other hand. Keeping my eyes fixed on his broad chest because I couldn't force myself to meet his eyes again, I said, "If you're going to be helping, I guess you could start by sanding down the front door. Someone left me a little note this morning."

Zel flinched.

Guilt washed over me, but I shouldered my way out the door, averting my eyes from the CINDERELLA IS A TRAITOR carving that had appeared this morning. I had sacrificed so much to protect Zel's secret, and now she was flinging the doors open for some conceited, blacklisted mage? Nothing made sense anymore.

~

When I was eight and the girls were almost three, Zel was nearly captured by the trackers.

I'd been watching the twins for her in the living quarters above the bakery, making play houses with bedsheets and tall towers with Zel's books, anything to distract them from the hunger in their little toddler bellies. Zel had left early that morning, hoping to reach the market and return home with more victus before the twins woke for breakfast. The gritty, clay-like porridge created by the city's healer mages to feed common families tasted horrible, but at least it was free. Unlike the cinderslick, we didn't even need a rations certificate to pick it up at the market. Toward the end of the plague years, before things got better, picking up more victus meant waiting in line if you didn't arrive at the market before dawn. But she'd been gone for hours, and I was worried. I didn't understand the magnitude of her secret back then, but I knew keeping it was more important than anything else.

A loud thud came from the ceiling over our heads, and the door to the roof swung open. Zel rushed down the narrow stairway, her eyes wild and her hair in a halo of tendrils around her long, golden braid. "Ella," she'd said, her voice shaking. "Downstairs. Now. I want you to clean the whole kitchen and the shop. The stairs to the living quarters too. Every inch of it, with liquid expurgo and a brush. Scrub it well, do you hear me? And don't come upstairs until you're done."

I stared at her, frozen and confused, as the twins ran toward her, crying and shouting to get her attention. But instead of looking at them, she met my eyes steadily, her face a mix of fear and sorrow. "Now, Ella. I'll stay here and feed the girls. You can have victus when you're done."

"Y-yes, Zel," I said. I paused, wondering if she would explain or offer to help me, but she was silent. I'd walked toward the stairs in a haze, turning back once to see tears glistening on Zel's cheeks as she watched me go. From that moment on, everything had changed.

I walked down our narrow lane, dodging overloaded merchant carts and unfriendly glares from anyone who recognized me as Ariella Stone, the unwanted stepdaughter at the traitorous Golden Loaf Bakery. I ignored them all.

When my father was alive, they'd hated him for his intellectual ideas and thoughtful gaze. "Grasping," they'd called him. "Thinks he's better than us." My father was descended from a long line of merchants. Our little bakery in the Merchant Quarter had been in his family for generations, but he had loved books far more than bread, especially the imported books from the West.

I remembered only bits and pieces from when my mother was still alive. My clearest memories were sitting down to dinner, listening as my parents hotly debated mysterious questions I didn't understand, and hosting the occasional forlorn-looking guest—cast-off mages too weak to be useful to the city, I later realized—who would sleep for a few days in the little pantry off the kitchen and then disappear.

When I was four, Mother died, and Father's world dwindled to a tiny circle of friends—primarily Gregor, the jovial spice merchant two doors down from our bakery. Then Zel arrived, pregnant with twins and desperate for shelter at the bakery. The plague took the city by storm three months later and my father was one of the first victims. Though she would have been safer outside the city, Zel had stayed with me. In the chaotic height of the plague, no one had questioned my insistence that Zel was my stepmother, though no marriage certificate existed. Thanks to Zel, I'd survived and kept the bakery instead of being lost to the River Quarter like most of the other children orphaned by the plague.

Three years later came Zel's near-miss with the tracker mages at the market.

For weeks afterward, the trackers had paced the twisted streets and alleys of the Merchant Quarter, certain she was hiding somewhere in the city. But she'd stayed hidden upstairs, and I'd scrubbed the bakery downstairs clean of her trace, and eventually, they'd given up looking for her. We'd never risked Zel's exposure again. We couldn't. Zel was my stepmother and I loved her, but she was also a powerful weapon. If she were caught, she'd be forced to do horrible things. I'd do anything to keep that from happening. Laboring at the bakery day and night was a small price to pay for her freedom.

"Hey, hey, Cinderella, what's that awful smell-a?" A chorus of childish voices rang out behind me.

My shoulders stiffened. Not those obnoxious chants again.

"Cinderella, Cinderella, that nasty bread you sell-a, it's full of worms and dirt."

Now that one didn't even rhyme! Ridiculous. Besides, our bread was better than that of any other bakery in the district, thanks to Gregor's high-quality flour and my family's cherished recipe book.

I ignored them. I'd heard it all before. The group of children jostled past me on their way to school, and I breathed a sigh of relief when they turned the corner ahead of me.

At first, our neighbors in the Merchant Quarter had pitied me, the poor orphan girl, pushed to the status of a servant by her cruel stepmother. Pity had turned to hatred the moment we began to use imported flour. They thought I was wrong to risk bringing the plague back into the city with flour and yeast imported from Lerenia, never mind the fact that Prince Estevan had instituted a system of inspections by purification mages that ensured every import was safe. For many Asylians, though, the plague had taken too much, and they couldn't think rationally about trade. Any risk at all was simply too much.

These days, for all their loyal talk, I didn't know of many bakers who still used flour from the expensive Asylian wheat that grew in meager crops outside the city walls. Flour made from Lerenian wheat was softer, more flavorful, and only one-fifth as expensive. I'd begun buying it from Gregor's spice shop as soon as the city gates were unsealed and imports resumed. Though I'd paid dearly in other ways, I'd never regretted the decision. I'd done whatever it took to stay out of poverty, continue at the Royal Academy, and keep my family safe. No one knew Zel's secret—I had endured years of taunts and mockery to keep it that way.

Why, oh why, had she risked everything to bring a mage into our home and our business? And what possible reason did she have for telling him the secret I'd give my life to protect?

My eyes burned, but I refused to cry. I had to keep studying and working. One day, things would get better. I'd get a good government job, and we'd never be this vulnerable again.

I rubbed my arms as I walked, shivering in the dank air. Our lane was still shady and cool this time of day, hidden from the morning sun. I passed a small pile of garbage outside the tavern and held my breath until it was behind me. Ever since the plague, no one could be bothered to clean up the Merchant Quarter—not even the Sanitation Ministry. I frowned and turned my eyes away from the stinking gutter. Wasn't it their job? Of course, the Procus Quarter and main roads were always perfectly clean.

I made my way to each business in the Merchant Quarter that had a standing order with our bakery. Since I went to school during the day, and Zel and her daughters couldn't risk being caught downstairs in the bakery shop, we survived by delivering orders. Thick, crusty loaves went to the taverns. Scones and honeybread went to the coffee houses. Hearty rye loaves went to the shops that needed to feed their workers. But I always kept a few items at the bakery for after school, in case the occasional shopper wandered inside.

I finished the deliveries, crammed the empty canvas bag into my bookbag, and made it to Grand Procus Avenue just in time to see a magic-propelled trolley barreling toward me. Finally, something was going right today. The coach was overflowing with passengers inside, but I took a running leap and jumped on the outside, using the latticework side of the trolley as a makeshift handle.

The trolley sped through the Merchant Quarter and into the River Quarter at a breakneck pace. No one lingered on the broad, clean-swept River Street, but if I peered through the openings in the latticed trolley walls, I could see bodies in the shadows of the narrow, uneven alleys that led off from the main promenade deeper into the River Quarter. It was hard to see the unmoving bodies without wondering which ones were lost in the questionable ecstasy of aurae and which ones had been taken by death.

The high city walls had been formed in a rough circle immediately after the Fenra revolution against the mages seven hundred years ago, when the founding families, now called the Procus families, put the Kireth mages to work for humans, instead of the other way around. They'd divided the area within the walls into four quarters—one for the founding families, one for the common laborers, one for those commoners who knew a trade, and one for farmland, by the river. As the city population grew, the walls had stayed in place, so we built ever higher, crowding into our inherited quarters like narrow, tall stalks of wheat. Now the River Quarter was full of laborers squatting in abandoned warehouses and crowding into rickety tenements.

I turned away from the dark alleys of the River Quarter and kept my eyes to the right, catching glimpses through the crooked streets of the Royal Precinct, its gleaming, stately government buildings clustered around the massive Royal Palace at the city's center.

Solemn government bureaucrats walked the wide, well-swept avenues, deep in conversation with one another. The occasional mage appeared too, wearing the golden arm band of a service mage. My thoughts returned to the mage at the bakery this morning. What was his name again? Weyland? Wesley? At least I wouldn't be the only one who reeked of cheap cinderslick anymore. Was he glad to be cast off? *Weslan.* That was his name.

He might be glad. Now Weslan wouldn't be pressed into government service or forced to live as a pet for a Procus family that acted as his patron. But mages with patrons got to live like kings, and even government mage laborers got a steady monthly stipend. I sighed. I sure wouldn't mind having a stipend of my own.

Young government apprentices in navy blue uniforms raced through the streets clutching bundles of paper and important-looking brown packages. One day soon, if all went according to plan, I would be one of them. My best bet was to do as well as I could on today's final exam. A commoner like me couldn't depend on connections or reputation to get an apprenticeship. I'd have to prove in numbers that I was the best. I couldn't let this morning's events shake me.

So what if Zel had spilled our secret to an unknown mage? Who cared that this mage would be invading my space for a while? That couldn't matter to me. Everything depended on me getting a government job—making a monthly stipend, providing for the family, and saving up to maybe one day get us all out of the city to a place without so many trackers. I'd been working for this for five years. I couldn't afford to lose focus now.

~

I braced myself as the trolley approached the corner of Government Avenue. When the trolley slowed to make the turn, I leapt off and jogged forward to maintain my momentum. Getting off here meant a few extra blocks to the Royal Academy, but I had less chance of twisting my ankle. The trolley always used to stop for passengers. These days, the lazy Transportation Ministry mages couldn't even be bothered to do that. They just got the trolley's running and let them race around the city at a breakneck pace, and we commoners tried to keep up.

I straightened my uniform and adjusted the strap of my bookbag on my shoulder. I resisted the urge to fix the loose bun on the top of my head. No matter what I did, more prodding and pulling always made it worse.

I hurried down Government Avenue, slowing when I crossed the Procus Quarter's guarded boundary and the Royal Academy came into view. I ignored the widened eyes and averted gazes from those I passed. After five years traveling across the city every day for school, I was used to the discomfort among Procus Quarter residents when I walked through their precious corner of the city as though I had a right to be there.

The Procus Quarter was clean and peaceful, with no wild trolleys or greasy food carts to disrupt the serenity. I passed a thick, iron gate with uniformed guards at the entrance— the Falconus family compound. Trying not to attract the guards' attention, I peered through the slats in the fence. There had to be at least a dozen towering stone villas in their compound, one for each family in the clan. A lush garden grew inside the front gate. I'd heard they'd purchased grower mages from the Lerenian government and brought them here to tend their famed goldblossom garden. The sweet, spicy, floral scent permeated the compound and tickled my nose as I walked past. Did anyone really need to live in a permanent cloud of perfume? Procus families were so strange.

The wide, ornately carved doors of the Royal Academy appeared on my left and a flutter of nervous energy whirled in my chest. Final exams. I'd been up half the night studying, and now there was nothing more I could do. Either I would place well enough to get a coveted government apprenticeship, or I would be stuck in the kitchen forever. No pressure or anything. I climbed the steps, wiped my clammy hands on my skirt, and swung open the door.

"Excuse me," said a cold female voice behind me.

I started and backed out of the way. "I'm so sorry, Lady Argentarius," I said, lowering my eyes and gesturing for her to go first as I held the door. "I didn't realize you were there."

Belle Argentarius swept past me with her beautiful head at a regal angle.

I rolled my eyes at her back. We'd been classmates for five years, and consistent rivals for the top marks in the class, but to Belle, I would never be anything more than a kitchen girl.

She sniffed, coughed, and waved her hand in front of her face as though she'd smelled something foul. Like cinderslick.

I gritted my teeth. Just for that, I'd stick extra close to her on the way to the exam.

My ears rang with the chatter of nervous students, all making their way upstairs to the exam rooms at once. They dodged frantically out of the way for me and Belle. Was it their aversion to my smell or their terror of her? By the annoyed look she cast me, she wasn't too sure. I smiled.

My heart thumped in my chest as we arrived on our floor. Clutching the strap of my bag as it dug into my shoulder, I followed Belle around the corner and into our classroom. The wooden desks were arranged in neat, tightly clustered rows stretching to the back wall. I took my usual spot on the far edge of the room.

"Miss Stone?" Professor Jace beckoned me to his wide, paper-strewn desk at the front of the room.

I walked over, hoping my face expressed confidence. "Yes, Professor?" In a few more days, I would be out of the academy for good. There wasn't much they could do to me now.

He smiled thinly at me, as though he knew what I was thinking, but instead of speaking, he simply held out his hand.

I stared down at it before looking back at him, confused.

He nodded toward his hand, so I reached forward and reluctantly shook it. Then he pulled me toward him and bent his head close to mine. "Whatever happens today, know that you don't belong here. You never will."

Heat flared across my face.

"If it weren't for the plague, you'd still be holed up in a stinking common kitchen like the servant girl you are." His voice was low and thick with spite, and face twisted in an ugly sneer.

I tried to yank my hand from his grip, but he held me even tighter.

"And there are those in government who will never allow you to take the place of a deserving Procus candidate for your apprenticeship. So don't for a moment think you might compete with your betters."

We stared at each other, but I said nothing. What was the point? I'd heard worse.

He leaned back and raised his voice. "Good luck with your exam, Miss Stone."

Finally, he let go, and I retraced my steps as though he hadn't even spoken. That would have to be my answer.

Belle stood a few feet away, frowning at us, but when I met her eyes, she looked away.

I took several deep breaths to calm myself as I searched for my seat. I couldn't allow anyone to take me off course today, no matter what they said or did.

The classroom had nearly filled since I'd entered, but I found my seat at the edge of the classroom and slid into it. I got out my pencil and squared my shoulders as I looked forward, waiting for Professor Jace to hand out the exams. To my surprise, Belle slid into the seat in front of me. Normally she sat as far away from me as possible. I looked around. The other seats were taken. Poor Belle.

"Good morning, class." Professor Jace's greeting sent the stragglers hurrying to their seats. "Nothing much to say to you today. I can only hope a few of you have retained some small amount of knowledge after this year, since we are all about to find out for sure how many of you have been sleeping in my class all year."

A titter of awkward laughter swept the room. My mouth was so dry I couldn't laugh even if I had wanted to. I couldn't wait to get this test over with.

"So without further ado, here are your exams." He placed a frighteningly thick sheaf of papers face down on each desk, and my fingers twitched, desperate to flip them over. When every exam had been passed out, he stood at the front of the classroom and smirked. "No use in putting it off any longer. You may begin."

There was a rustle as thirty students all flipped their exams over at once followed by a deafening silence as everyone read the first page of the test. I held back a smile. The first question was from a short unit we had studied at the beginning of the school year. I had reviewed the material last night. I had a feeling my indolent Procus classmates were going to struggle with this test. Lucky me.

If the Procus children weren't so idle and the plague hadn't decimated the ranks of government bureaucrats, there would be no open government positions and Royal Academy scholarships for commoners like me. Those with good Procus connections could always survive low test scores, of course, but a solid final exam score would be a powerful asset for a commoner. I hoped.

I wrote methodically to make sure I didn't miss anything. I couldn't shake a thrill of satisfaction as I finished the last question on the first page and realized I was the first person to give off the telltale rustle of a page turning over. All my studying was paying off.

I stopped to stretch out my right hand and glanced absently around the room before diving into the second page of the exam. Then I swung my eyes back up. There, in the corner of the room closest to my seat, sat a weathered book bag. Strange. I shook off the distraction and turned back to the test. It wasn't my fault my classmates couldn't be bothered to put their bags away neatly.

A small movement at the corner of my eye caught my attention. Why was I so easily distracted today? All my classmates had their heads bent over their exams and were writing furiously. Professor Jace was at the far wall by the door with his back to me, looking for something in the bookcase. Through the window of our closed classroom door, I noticed someone loitering in the hallway. Perhaps a student was tardy?

But he wasn't racing past our classroom. He just stood there. As though he felt my eyes on him, he pressed his face to the little window in our door.

I froze. This was no student. His hair was obscured by a black hood, and a blood-red mask hugged his features like a glove.

It couldn't be. Why would they … What could … The Blight? Here?

I stood and screamed a wordless warning, but my voice was lost in the chaos when a sudden wave of heat and noise overtook the classroom. Something sharp hit the side of my head, and everything went black.

Chapter 3

"I don't understand why you can't just—"

"Young man, for the last time, get out of my way."

The male voices arguing with each other hovered high in the air, far over my head. My eyelids were so heavy I couldn't get them to budge.

"I'm not leaving until you take another look at her. There's no reason a victim of—"

"I don't have to explain myself to a blacklister like you. If you don't have the money to pay, we are done here. See, she's waking from the sopor already. Collect her and be on your way before my assistant comes to change the bed linens, or you'll be charged double for wasting hospital resources."

The other voice uttered a string of curse words. Two strong, warm hands came under my back and lifted me to a sitting position.

I tried opening my eyes again. This time they fluttered, but I squeezed them shut again against the painful blaze of light.

When I tried to speak, only a small croak came out. Why was my voice so rough? It felt as though I hadn't spoken in ages. Pain seared the right side of my face. "W-what's happened?" I forced out.

"Shh," said the voice. "I've got you." He lifted me into his arms.

I groaned as my head throbbed and the pain on the side of my face burned even hotter. I forced my eyes open, then blinked and stared up in shock. Golden hair, strong jaw, worried gray eyes, mouth flattened in a line as he stared down at me—it was the mage. Weslan? Why was he with me? And where was Zel?

"What are you doing here?" I croaked. "Where are we?"

"You were hurt at school," he said, his frown growing deeper. "You were knocked unconscious in the blast, and they brought you to the hospital to be healed. Zel sent me here to deal with the healers and to bring you home when they released you." He stared at me meaningfully. "You know she can't very well come here to get you herself."

I knew that. I had just forgotten, for a moment, I supposed. What else had I forgotten?

I grunted—that was the closest to nodding I was going to get. "I want to walk."

He tightened his lips but set me down without question.

My legs buckled immediately, and he caught me and held me upright while I got them straightened enough to bear my weight. "How long was I unconscious?"

"A week."

A week? That couldn't be right. "It took me that long to heal? What happened to me?"

"You had a serious head wound. They sedated you with sopor to give it time to respond to their healing. But they needed your cot for another patient, so they took you off the sedative a few minutes ago." He darted a glance out the door and swore under his breath.

I looked blearily around the sparse room, realizing for the first time that two other patients lay unconscious in cots next to mine. I recalled now that the first voice had been ordering us out of the room when I woke up. But if I was well enough to go home, why did my face still hurt so much?

"Am I all better?" I didn't know what else to say.

He hesitated. "You have some … scarring where a piece of a desk hit your head." He pointed to my temple but didn't touch my face. "And along the side of your face." He gestured down to my jaw.

Hesitantly, I touched the side of my face that was burning with pain. I fingered the cloth bandage that covered my skin as a sick feeling welled in the pit of my stomach. "Scarring?"

His eyes met mine. "The wound has not fully healed, but the cost to fully heal the scar is very high. Zel sent them everything she had saved up, but it was only enough to pay for the healing they've done so far. They did save your life, after all. The rest, your body will have to heal on its own."

The words echoed in my throbbing head. What was he saying? I didn't understand.

Weslan glanced at the door again. "We need to leave. They said we had to be out by the time the healer's assistant comes to change the bedding for the next patient, and he could be here any minute now."

I nodded numbly. I noticed I was wearing a thin white gown with no shoes. "I need to change into my dress, and then I can go." I didn't know how my legs would support me the whole way home, but all I wanted was to throw myself into Zel's arms.

Weslan handed me a folded work dress and a pair of worn leather shoes. The shoes were the ones I'd stopped wearing last year because of the widening holes at the place where the sole met the leather. "Your school uniform was ruined in the blast," he said. "But Zel gave me these. I'll block the door while you get dressed."

I took them and put them on while he waited outside the room. I probably should have cared that I was changing in a room with two unconscious strangers. The healer's assistant could come and push past Weslan at any moment, but I was too overwhelmed to worry. I would be scarred forever. What had happened? Who had done this to me? My brain felt like it was in a fog.

I slipped my feet into the unlaced shoes and tapped Weslan on the shoulder. "Ready." My body shook, my face throbbed, and I couldn't think straight. "Just get me home, please."

"Come on then." He took my arm, and I leaned on him as we shuffled down the hall. We passed a series of cramped rooms filled with patients. Every bed was occupied, and we wove between harried-looking healers who glared at us. At the end of the hallway, we reached a small, noisy waiting room packed with families. No one took notice of us except a young secretary who frowned and nodded his head at the door as if to hurry us along.

I gripped Weslan's arm a little tighter and angled my head away from the secretary, hoping I didn't fall over before we escaped from this place.

We exited to the bustling street, and I shut my eyes against the flood of sunlight with a moan of pain. I nearly sat down then and there. When I opened my eyes, the world spun around me. People bustled every which way, jostling us as we stood there in the middle of the footpath. I closed my eyes for another long moment and took a deep breath. I could do this. All I needed to do was get home.

Gripping Weslan's arm like my life depended on it, I let him lead us down the street, away from the hospital. Ten steps later, I stopped short, taking note of my surroundings for the first time. "Why are we in the River Quarter? We're only a few blocks from the Royal Academy. How are we going to get back to the bakery?"

Weslan gave me a grim look. "We're walking. No money left for a hired coach, and you're in no shape to make it onto the trolley."

I bit my lip. As much as I didn't want this mage around, I had to admit none of this was his fault. "Let's get out of here.".

We'd been creeping along for several minutes at a snail's pace when my legs began to shake like jelly. What had that healer been thinking, sending us out into the city minutes after waking me from sopor-induced sleep?

A fomecoach burst around the corner, taking the turn too narrowly and veering onto the footpath. Weslan threw us out of its way, pulling me with him and twisting as he landed on the ground so that his body cushioned my fall. The Procus driver swerved back into the street without a word of apology, ignoring a chorus of boos and insults from the commoners on the footpath.

Weslan helped me to my feet, but my legs gave out as soon as I straightened them. I collapsed against him, landing heavily as his arms went around me for support. My body was done. I rested my forehead on his chest as I tried to collect myself, my breath coming in gasps. I was too exhausted to feel embarrassed. No doubt that would come later.

"This is ridiculous," he muttered.

I craned my head to peer up at his face. He clenched his jaw and stared behind me in the direction we'd come.

"I'm sorry." I hated this feeling of helplessness. Why wouldn't my legs move? I tried to push away from him and stand on my own again, but he tightened his arms and held me still. I wished I was too tired to notice the heat from his hands burning through my dress.

"It's not your fault." I found an odd comfort in the rumbling of his chest as he spoke. "You, of all people … I just don't get it. None of this should be happening."

I leaned against him, my thoughts whirling. Why did it feel so good to be held by him? He was a mage. I barely knew him. What was I doing?

He looked down and raised an eyebrow at me, and I felt my cheeks heat up. Had he guessed what I was thinking?

"I don't think you can walk any further," he said. "If I bend down, can you reach around my neck and ride on my back?"

Apparently he hadn't.

"I can try." There was no point in fighting for dignity now. He turned his back to me and bent low. I reached for his shoulders and pulled as hard as I could. My arms were so weak, I barely got off the ground.

"Sorry," he said.

"What?" The next thing I knew, he reached his arms around behind him, placed his hands firmly under the backs of my thighs, and hoisted me smoothly to his back. I sputtered in protest.

"Can you hold on now?" His voice sounded suspiciously like he was smiling. Rude!

"Yes," I managed, injecting as much spite as I could into my voice. I'd gone from intrigued to humiliated in about two seconds. I wrapped my arms around his neck and scowled. "Let's go."

Weslan wove through the busy street traffic, dodging coaches, cart vendors, and beggars that lined the River Quarter's narrow streets. Then he cut through the Royal Precinct, where mages in gold armbands roamed the streets alongside bureaucrats and apprentices.

I wondered if Weslan had been one of those mages. Perhaps he wasn't the type to take a Procus family as a patron the way I had assumed. What had happened to get him kicked out of the Mage Division? I hadn't heard of that happening since before the plague. These days, they needed every mage they could find, and they kept them all confined in the barracks of the Mage Division, a gated area made up of several blocks in the Royal Precinct. The only way out was to take a patron and move into a Procus compound. At least, I thought they kept every mage these days, even the weak ones. But Zel's actions yesterday—last week, I mentally corrected myself—proved that I didn't know as much as I thought I did.

I tried to hold tight to his shoulders to keep my weight from becoming too much, but my strength soon gave out. Exhausted and unable to stop thinking about the pain on the side of my face, I rested my head heavily on his shoulder and let him carry me home in silence.

~

Weslan shouldered open the door to the bakery and helped me slide to the floor, keeping one hand on my waist as I swayed. We'd taken at least an hour to reach the bakery. My legs were cramped and aching, and the wound on my face felt like someone had set fire to it.

Weslan looked down at me, his face strangely apologetic, and drew in a breath, but a shriek cut him off. "Ella!"

A series of thumps followed, drawing our attention to the staircase. Bri and Alba raced down at a breakneck pace, huge smiles on their faces. Weslan stepped back as they grabbed me in a bone-crushing hug.

I closed my eyes and leaned into them. My stepsisters. They'd nearly lost me this week. What would have happened to them if I'd perished in the attack? What would have happened to Zel? Everyone depended on me. I clutched them to my chest, burying my face in Alba's soft hair.

Zel followed behind them, descending the stairs with hasty steps. She reached the bottom as the twins released me, and she ran to wrap me in her arms. Neither of us spoke, and I nearly collapsed with relief. Home. I'd made it home.

Finally, Zel pulled back and supported me to a chair in the kitchen. "Get Ella some water," she said to the twins, and they jostled one another as they raced to the sink. Weslan stood by the door, like he didn't know what to do with himself now that we were home.

"Zel," I said, my voice cracking, "What happened?"

Zel took my hand in hers with a sad smile. "Let's just talk about that later. Right now, I just want to be happy that you're home."

I pulled my hand back and frowned. "Please. I need to know what happened."

She bit her lip. "Your school was attacked. Trackers found the remains of a suffio bomb afterward, and it wasn't far from where you were sitting. They said you're lucky to be alive today."

I leaned back in my chair. Why would anyone attack a classroom, of all places? I shook my head but regretted the motion when my head throbbed and the room swam in front of my eyes. I was forgetting something important. "Attacked? By whom?"

Zel shook her head. "No one knows. But it was most likely the Crimson Blight, even though it doesn't fit their model. The Quarter Guard seems certain it was the Blight, anyway. Something about the compound used in the bomb—the same mix of suffio as the last few attacks."

"Was anyone else hurt?"

"Several students were injured, but only you and one other student were hospitalized. Thankfully, no one was killed."

"Who else was hospitalized?"

"Belle Argentarius." The worry lines around Zel's eyes creased as she spoke. "She was the one closest to the bomb when it went off. The last we heard, she was still unconscious, but the healers expect her to make a full recovery. They're keeping her asleep to give her more time to respond to their healing without pain."

Huh. I put a hand up to the painful, unhealed wounds on my face, then dropped it to my lap. Jealousy wouldn't bring me any healing. Belle might not have been kind, but she was smart and hardworking in her own way. I wouldn't wish this on her. But what if someone had? What if she was the target? Why would anyone want to hurt Belle?

I sipped the water Alba had placed before me. My mouth was dry, but I sipped slowly, not wanting to overdo it.

"So when do I have to retake my final exam?" I looked at Zel expectantly. It hurt to think about taking a test when my wounds weren't even healed, but perhaps it would help me to move forward if I could get back on track soon.

Zel slid her gaze away from mine, toward Weslan's. I looked at him and then back at Zel. What was going on?

Weslan cleared his throat and stepped toward the kitchen table, his arms crossed. "The term is over. They … ah … won't be offering another chance to retake the exam. All the other students retook it last week, while you were in the hospital."

My heart sank, and I slumped in the chair. So much for that idea. "I'll just have to retake the year then. That's fine. My apprenticeship can wait another year." I didn't love the idea of spending another year working in the bakery kitchen while going to school, but at least I had already learned all the material.

Zel shook her head. "Honey, I'm so sorry. So very sorry."

I stared at her. "What are you talking about?" When she stared at me with tearful eyes and shook her head again, I turned to Weslan. "What is she saying? Why is she sorry?"

He unfolded his arms and then folded them again. "I've been to every higher academy in the city. There are no more scholarship places left. There's no place for you to retake the term."

I stared at him, hating the naked pity on his handsome face. "You're wrong." I spat the words at him, shocked by the venom that had suddenly filled me. This couldn't be happening.

"No, Ella." He looked at me without flinching, his voice level, his brows furrowed. "I spoke to every government official and school administrator I could find. All the scholarship spots for the final grade have been filled by upcoming students from the lower grades."

I wanted to slap him. I bolted to my feet and swayed. My head swam dizzily.

Zel was by me in an instant, her arm at my back keeping me from falling over. "Sit down, sweetheart. You need to rest."

I pushed weakly against her, but she didn't budge. "But … I've worked so hard … I don't understand! How could they just shut me out?"

"The fact remains that they have." After her tenderness and concern, the finality in her voice grated against me. "And you need to lie down and rest. You've been asleep for a week, Ella. You can deal with this later." My face burned with pain and the room tilted again. I could not make sense of her words.

"So that's it? I'm just not going to graduate? This is ridiculous!" My chest seemed to be collapsing, like someone was sitting on it. "This isn't happening. I was so close to graduating. What am I going to do? I'll never be able to get a government job. I'll never get any kind of job at all. I'll never be able to leave this stricken bakery!"

Zel's hand dropped from my back, and I heard two identical intakes of breath from the twins. Oh. My stepsisters and my stepmother would never be able to leave the bakery either. I pressed my lips together and shook my head in a silent apology. Then I turned to go and fell.

Weslan rushed forward to lift me into his arms yet again. He carried me to my little bedroom off the kitchen. Neither Zel nor her daughters followed. As he placed me gently atop my bed, I kept my eyes closed to avoid seeing whatever pity or condemnation might be on his face.

As I lay back on my familiar lumpy pillow, the pain on the side of my face became more than I could bear. Throwing pride to the wind, I cracked open my eyes. "Did the healers give me anything for the pain before we left?"

"No." He frowned down at me. His voice sounded tight. "We spent all the money we had to pay for the healing, remember?"

"Oh. Right." I rolled to my side so my back was to him, the good side of my face pressed into the pillow while the side covered with bandages and searing pain faced the ceiling. "I guess I'll just sleep it off, then," I lied.

I sensed him lingering over me. After a moment, he placed one strong hand on my shoulder, gave it a gentle squeeze, and left the room, shutting the door softly behind him. I was alone.

I pressed my eyes shut as the tears came, drenching my pillow and hair with hot, salty pools. I shook silently in my bed for several minutes. Then, as quickly as they'd come, the tears were gone. I took a few deep breaths and focused on the comforting, familiar feel of my bed. But the pain in my face kept me tense, an inescapable sign that nothing would ever be the same again. I'd lost everything.

How was I supposed to go on? I'd worked five years for this, dreaming of leaving the bakery, getting a stable government job, making a steady income, and not having to rely on rations anymore. I would have been able to provide for Zel, Alba, and Bri, with plenty left to spare. Maybe even one day, I would have saved enough to go to another city, one without so many trackers. Some place where we could live in peace without fear of getting caught.

Now I was eighteen years old without a higher academy certificate much less a Royal Academy diploma. There was no way I'd ever be able to find a decent job outside the bakery. We would be eating cold victus for the rest of our lives. And that would be only if nothing else went wrong.

~

I walked through the hallways at school, admiring the beautiful antique molding and intricately carved door frames. I loved this building—its creaky, polished wood floors, the papery smells, the thick, wavy glass windows. The Royal Academy was the one place where I truly came alive, as though only in this building could my mind become what it was meant to be. I heard the distant laughter and shouts of my classmates, but here in the dim hallway, I was alone.

Someone dressed in dark clothing hurried ahead of me in the hallway. He turned the corner, and I followed. He rounded the next corner further down the hallway.

I walked faster. Something about him wasn't right. I had to find him. I had to warn my classmates.

Even when I ran to catch up, he was always just ahead of me. I ran faster, and so did he. We raced through endless corridors until the last hallway ended in a blank wall. The man stood there, facing the wall, his back to me. He wore a black hood.

I opened my mouth to shout a warning to my classmates, but what would I say? Slowly, he turned toward me. His face was gone, replaced by a pool of dripping blood. I screamed.

He stepped toward me. One step, two.

I should run. But something had trapped my legs, and I couldn't make them move. A wave of unbearable heat and pain washed over me. Was this it? Was I going to die?

I woke in a fever, sobbing, and gasping for breath with my legs tangled in the sheets of my own bed. My skin was slick with sweat, and my face throbbed like someone was hitting it again and again with a club.

The golden-haired mage sat on my bed, his hand on my shoulder. His image wavered before my eyes. He held out one hand with three small blue pellets in it. "For the pain," he said.

I grabbed his hand and ate the blue pellets off his palm like an animal. Shame filled me. But who could remain human in the face of such pain?

Chapter 4

The blue pellets kept me in a hazy, dreamy, painless state for days. I wasn't sure how many. Occasionally, gentle hands lifted me from the bed and pressed a spoon of warm broth into my mouth. Voices spoke over my head—a gentle, concerned female voice, and a terse male voice. Zel and Weslan? Why did they sound so worried?

Then one day, I felt a little more alert, and the next day, even more alert.

The next time Weslan brought a bowl of broth, I was awake. His clothing and hair were rumpled, and the skin under his eyes was dark and heavily creased. I couldn't bear to ask where he had gotten the little blue pellets that had alleviated so much of my pain.

He held up a bowl of steaming broth, and I took it from him, whispering a raspy "Thanks" that didn't seem to cover it one bit. He nodded and left without a word.

I inhaled the broth, hungry for the first time in days. Then, with a full, warm belly, I curled up on my side with my back to the door and slept the rest of the night.

~

When I woke next, the familiar smell of cinderslick was heavy in the air. The scent that had only vaguely bothered me before now made me want to run upstairs to the bathroom and retch. It wasn't only the smell of cheap fuel. It was the smell of shame, of dependence. The smell that told me I'd never be anyone other than Cinderella.

I got up and exchanged my sweaty, wrinkled dress for the old work dress hanging on the rack in the corner of my room. My skin crawled as I slid it on. Putting a clean dress on skin this dirty was just plain wrong, but I was too hungry to draw a bath now.

A dull ache plagued the side of my face. Zel had removed the bandages in the last few days. I remembered that much. Now I felt only a long area of sensitive, raised skin that hurt to touch. I didn't dare look in the mirror. Didn't know what I would do if I saw it right now. Best to face reality with a full stomach.

Part of me longed to cover the scar with my hair or a scarf of some kind, but I ruthlessly squashed that desire. I twisted my hair up into a tight bun. This was how I looked now. There was no point in trying to hide it.

I opened the door to the kitchen and stopped short. There, in front of the oven, Weslan sprawled on a pallet, snoring as though he had not a care in the world. I stepped closer, eyeing his tousled blond hair as it spilled over his forehead. He was so obviously Kireth, with his long, broad limbs and light coloring. But his skin held hints of Fenra heritage too. A bit of a tan colored his hands and cheekbones, and a smattering of brown freckles—the telltale mark of Fenra blood—clustered on his knuckles. I stepped closer, wondering if I should wake him.

He'd cared for me with great gentleness while I was recovering. I could remember now—little glimpses of his face, his hands feeding me broth and wiping my brow. He'd brought me those small blue pellets again and again, and he'd somehow eased them out of my system at just the right time. Perhaps he was a good man. Perhaps he could be trusted.

No. I knew better than that. Asylian mages were nothing but lazy, greedy leeches. Not every commoner thought so, of course. Some coveted the mages' magical powers and secure, comfortable positions in government. But I wasn't one of them. I wasn't so naïve. Besides, he was too attractive to be trustworthy.

The next moment, as though he sensed me standing over him, he opened his eyes and sat up blearily. "Ella? What are you doing up?"

I fingered my dress, inexplicably shy. "I suppose it was time," I said. "I feel better. Pretty hungry, actually." I steeled myself. I had to thank him for all he had done. It was almost too humiliating to put into words, but I couldn't let his actions go unacknowledged. Even I wasn't that harsh. "Weslan ... I ... well, I need to say ..." I faltered as he got up and turned the dial on the luminous that lit the kitchen.

He stretched, and I saw the exact moment he caught sight of my scar, revealed by my severe bun. Shock and revulsion twisted his finely sculpted face. He dragged his gaze away from my scar and met my eyes. "You were saying?"

My chest tightened. "I just wondered if you've already put in the baking for the morning, or if you were too busy napping on the kitchen floor to do it."

He glared at me. "It's already in," he ground out. "Not that you'd know, after doing nothing but sleep for days."

"Fine," I said. "Glad to hear you're at least good for something besides making pretty dresses for rich girls." I'd gone too far. I knew it as soon as I said it.

The next moment, he threw on his jacket and stomped out the back door, slamming it shut with a crack that echoed through the kitchen.

I sucked in a deep breath and let it out. I couldn't think about some lazy mage and his bad temper right now. I needed real food in my stomach and a bath. Everything else could wait.

~

"Sorry about your ribbon, Ella." Alba hovered at the door to the kitchen, twisting her fingers in her skirt. "I've looked everywhere, and I just ... I can't find it ... I really don't know what happened, but I'm so sorry—"

I wiped my floury hands on my apron. "Alba, I've told you before. It's not my stricken ribbon. Forget about it."

Her face blanched at my tone, and tears glistened in her eyes.

I should apologize. I knew it. But I couldn't stand the sight of her perfect, beautiful face and flawless skin. "I have work to do." I went back to kneading the dough. Her little sob and the pitter-patter of her slippers echoed from the stairway.

My face throbbed in rhythm with each push on the dough. My scars were still tender to the touch, and I fought off constant headaches. Zel thought the headaches were connected to the original head injury, but knowledge didn't make them any easier to bear. I desperately wanted more of those little blue pellets. I was too embarrassed to beg Weslan for more, and I had no idea how he'd been able to find them. Besides, everyone kept reminding me that we were completely out of marks thanks to my healing expenses.

I tried to make peace with Weslan when he returned to the bakery in the evening. "Thanks for sanding down the front door," I said quietly. "It looks good. You can't tell the carving was ever there."

He barely spared me a glance, his voice cool and distant. "What are you talking about? There were no carvings on the door."

I knew he was mad at me, but that was no reason to call me a liar. So much for trying to be nice.

We spent the rest of the evening eating cold victus and navigating around the kitchen with a cold wall of silence between us. Later that evening, Zel hinted gently at me to be nicer to him.

Right. *He* was the one ignoring *my* attempts to be nice. Also, who was the one recovering from a head injury?

Before dawn the next morning, I finished kneading another batch of dough and covered it to let it rise. I'd make the winterspice rolls later in the morning. First, we needed breakfast. There had to be something in the larder that I could cook up. I averted my eyes from Weslan's suspiciously empty and unrumpled pallet by the oven and grabbed the little vial of cinderslick from the shelf by the oven.

Hold on—it was much lighter than it should've been. I opened it up and peeked inside, scowling as I realized it was almost empty. Had Weslan not picked up the new rations? I blew the loose strands of hair out of my face. Unbelievable.

I bundled up in my slim jacket against the cool early morning air and slipped out the back door into the dark alley. Dawn would be here soon, and if I made it to the market as it opened, I could be back with enough cinderslick to finish the baking in time to make our deliveries.

I patted the thin fold of quarter marks from the kitchen stash in my pocket and made my way through the cramped, winding streets of the Merchant Quarter. Although most families like ours relied on the government rations issued once a week for cinderslick, if you were willing to pay, there would always be more to be found.

At the closest cinderslick vendor's booth, I put my quarter marks on the counter, but he shook his head. "Not enough," he said gruffly. "Prices going up. Nothing I can do."

I stared at him, uncomprehending. The next ration day wasn't until two days from now. How were we supposed to survive until then? And how on earth had Weslan used up a whole vial of cinderslick in five days?

The next three vendors' prices were the same. I stormed back to the bakery and up the stairs. Dawn had broken, and Zel had to be awake by now. If she wasn't, I'd wake her myself. I knocked on the door to the living quarters she shared with the girls.

She opened the door and stood wrapped in her thin robe, her golden braid mussed and hanging down around her shoulder. Her eyes looked wary.

I bit my lip. I knew I had been difficult to be around the last two days, but try as I might, I couldn't keep the bitterness from my voice. "We're already out of cinderslick. I just went to the market, but the price has gone up. I need more marks to buy more cinderslick because right now, we don't even have enough to make breakfast or do the baking for the day." I realized I sounded impatient, but I couldn't help it. At least anger kept me upright, still moving forward, still working.

Footsteps echoed on the stairs behind me. Weslan approached, scowling. "Oh, so you finally decided to start paying attention."

My temper rose to meet his. "That's right," I said, folding my arms. "I went to the market to try to get more cinderslick because we're already out, even though it's only been five days since ration day. And guess what I found out? The prices are going up. I can't even buy another vial for two marks. I need more money. Otherwise we're all eating cold victus from now until ration day. And good luck baking any bread for our customers without cinderslick!"

"Listen, Ella." Weslan glowered and stepped onto the landing toward me. "I told you a thousand times. We spent all Zel's money to pay your healers. There's nothing left. We sold part of last week's rations to finish paying the bill. That's why we're already out."

I took a step backward. "Well ... ," I faltered, hunting for words to say. Nothing made sense anymore. "Well, there must be something we can do."

"Nothing," Weslan said, gritting his teeth. "There's nothing we can do. We'll just have to wait until the next rations day."

"What do you have to say about all this, Zel?" I put my hands on my hips. "Is everything Weslan's decision now?"

Zel stepped out of her room and shut the door softly, and it occurred to me belatedly that she might not want the twins hearing our argument. She tried to put her arm around my shoulders, but I sidled away from her.

"I'm gone for a week, and suddenly this mage takes over the bakery I've been running for years. What's going on here, Zel?"

"Now, Ella," Zel said reprovingly. "Weslan is doing his best. He's done nothing but help us since your accident."

"My accident?" I scoffed. "Is that what we're calling it? It's not like I got clumsy and fell. I was attacked." I spat the words out. My voice was ugly and harsh even to my own ears, but I couldn't seem to rein it in.

"There's no need for this kind of anger. Weslan is not your enemy. He's lost a lot too. He's trying to make the most of it and help us out at the same time."

I considered Weslan, and for a moment, all I could think of were his warm hands behind my back as he lifted me out of the hospital bed and carried me home. Guilt gnawed at me, but then I noticed his broad shoulders and square jaw, his confident bearing, and his annoyingly perfect hair. He'd lost everything, had he? Then why did he look like he was still on top of the world?

As if he knew my spiteful thoughts, he sneered. "You know, I'm surprised they charged us that much for your healing, given that you still look the way you do."

Chapter 5

Given that you still look the way you do. Weslan's words echoed in my ears. I flinched as though he had slapped me and put up an involuntary hand to touch the scars on my face.

I shoved past him, ran down the stairs, and scurried back to my room where I sat on the bed, hunched over, my head throbbing. I pressed my hand to my scars, feeling the raised, wrinkled flesh and the soft ache. If only I could push the skin down and smooth it back into place, like I would a jagged edge on a ball of rising dough.

My light-green eyes used to be my only problem. My father called them beautiful. They shone in the mirror, a bright, stark contrast to my bronzed skin and dark hair. But I'd known since I was small that green eyes were no good. Adults would avert their eyes when they saw me, and children would shove me in the back and call me an ugly Kireth girl.

As I got older, I realized nearly everyone in Asylia had mixed Kireth and Fenra blood. Our people had lived together in this land for a millennium, and occasionally, a Kireth and Fenra couple would have children. Most of the time, though, all anyone cared about was whether your Kireth blood showed. And my green eyes, beautiful or not, certainly showed. Now I had scars to make me even less desirable.

I stood and kept my eyes averted from my mirror. I didn't care what anyone thought. I couldn't care. That had to be enough. The front door slammed shut. Weslan must have left. I was on my own to make breakfast with barely any cinderslick, yet again.

I entered the kitchen and looked around. We wouldn't be able to bake bread, and the bakery would have to close for a couple of days. There was nothing I could do about that. But there was a bit of aging fruit in the bowl on the counter and some leftover day-old bread on the shelf. We could eat that for breakfast. I sliced the fruit and the bread and took the last of the cheese from the larder, arranging it all on a tray. It could be my peace offering to Zel. Tomorrow, we would make due with victus.

I was slicing up one more piece of fruit when a flash of red caught my eye. I paused, the knife still in my hand. A scrap of red fabric was fluttering down beside me, as though someone had been standing there and accidentally dropped it.

Was that the ribbon Alba kept going on about? It landed softly on the floor and my heart skipped a beat. Had someone been in the kitchen with me, watching me? Why would Alba or Bri do such a thing? If not them, who? The knife in my hand slipped, slicing into the soft tip of the index finger on my left hand. I yelped, threw down the knife, and pressed a dirty dish towel to my finger to stop the flow of blood.

Zel arrived a few seconds later. "Are you well?"

"I'm fine." I turned my back to her, wishing I could take back the sharp words. She was trying to help. Everyone was always just trying to help.

There was a terrible crash, and I threw myself to the ground, placing protective hands over my head. The man with the face of blood hovered in my mind's eye. Was he real?

My body shook as I clutched my head. I should run. I should lead the attackers away from Zel and her daughters. I felt a hand on my shoulder and flinched.

"Everything's fine," Zel said gently. "I just knocked some pots off the shelf."

Zel stood over me, holding a stack of pots in one hand as she gripped my shoulder with the other. She set the pots on the counter, clearly trying to make as little noise as possible.

Of course. Now I looked like even more of a lunatic. I got to my feet and wiped blood onto my dress. With a groan, I grabbed the towel and pressed it to my finger again.

"What happened to your hand? You're bleeding everywhere." She grabbed a clean linen cloth from the shelf, took away my dirty dish towel, and pressed the clean cloth to my hand.

"The cloth will be ruined."

"Doesn't matter," she said. "All that matters to me is that you're safe." She pressed the cloth against my finger until the bleeding stopped, and then she bandaged it with a clean roll of gauze from the shelf beside her. "Don't worry, I really believe we will find the money to pay for ..." She shook her head. "We will find the money, and things will get better. One way or another. I promise."

"Money to pay for what? Cinderslick?"

Zel hesitated. "You know it's almost summer. Inspector Cyrus has been by to ask for our tax."

A chill went through me. "And you used money set aside for the tax to pay for my healing."

Zel nodded once. "Yes."

I swayed and grabbed the counter for support. Our annual merchant tax cost hundreds of marks. We saved all year to be able to pay it. Without that savings, there was no way we would be able to pay our tax. If we didn't pay the tax, the Merchant Quarter had every right to kick us out of the bakery and suspend our business license.

Our livelihood—the safe oasis for Zel and her daughters—was in jeopardy because of me. And we'd be lucky if we found a spot in the Common Quarter. Most likely, we'd end up in one of the rickety tenements in the River Quarter. Zel and the girls wouldn't last a day before the trackers found them. "Why did you do that? What were you thinking? You're going to lose everything. After all that I've done to keep you safe, how could you risk it all for me?"

Zel grabbed me by the shoulders, her beautiful face more serious than I had ever seen it. "You matter to us." She looked me unwaveringly in the eye. "You matter. We couldn't have let you die, not when the healers had the power to save your life and we had the money to pay for it." She let go but didn't step away. If anything, she looked even more fierce. "I have no regrets. And neither do the girls. It was the right decision. And I know you would've done the same for any of us."

I couldn't argue with that. But still—I had given so much to keep them safe, and now they had risked it all to save my life? It didn't feel right.

I straightened. "Well, we'll just have to get the money somehow."

She took my hands in hers. "We'll be fine, Ella. We're going to find the money, and I don't want you to worry about it. We'll have more bakery orders with the prince's selection ball in a couple of weeks. So just hold on until then. Everything is going to work out."

I squeezed Zel's hands and forced a hopeful expression onto my face to match hers. I wanted to believe that things would work out. I did. But honestly, what chance did we have? We were two steps away from disaster, and with a secret like ours, we wouldn't last much longer. "Fine, Zel. You win. I'll hope for the best."

Once Zel left the kitchen, I got back to making breakfast. As I put the last dish on the tray, I glanced around the room. The scrap of red fabric was gone. Had I imagined it? Was I going beyond mere paranoia, imagining that someone had physically been in the room beside me? Zel had to think I was going crazy.

Maybe I was. I was terrified all the time. I didn't know what to think. How would I ever feel safe again? Every time I closed my eyes, I saw the nightmare man with the face of blood. Who was he? A construct of my imagination? A response to learning the Blight was likely behind the attack? A product of my head injury? Had my mind not yet fully healed? The questions made me jittery and unsure. How was I supposed to live like this?

Weslan didn't come back for breakfast. Or lunch. Or dinner. Perhaps I'd antagonized him enough that he was willing to abandon us. But would he betray us?

After all, mages in Asylia were opportunistic to their core. They might be forced into service, but they had no problem living like parasites off the Procus families, exploiting their magical powers for gain and wasting their lives on absurd luxuries. Who knew where Weslan had gone, or what he would do when he decided to cross us?

Late that night, I woke with a start to the sound of someone fumbling around in the kitchen. I tensed. There was a crash. Weslan started swearing, his words slurred.

Drunk. I sniffed and I rolled over to face the wall, fuming silently. Even if he didn't spill our secret intentionally, he was out of control. You couldn't trust someone like that with anything. Too late. Zel had already told him. We would just have to wait and see.

~

The next morning, Zel woke me with a gentle shake that I pretended didn't scare me as much as it did. I sat up in bed, and she pressed a small cloth bundle into my hand.

"What's this?"

"A little something for the market," she said. "I did some harvesting in the garden. Some of the herbs were ready sooner than I expected. That should bring you more than enough to buy fuel until the next rations day."

I held the bag gingerly to avoid crushing the precious herbs inside. "Thank you so much, Zel. I don't know what we would do without you."

Zel pulled me into her arms and held me close. "I told you that everything is going to be fine. You just need to trust me."

I wrapped a thin cardigan over my old work dress and rushed out the door to the market, even though the sun had yet to rise. I wanted to get there and back in time to cook a real breakfast, something to make up for yesterday's sad fare.

The vendors who had been waiting months for Zel's next harvest were happy to exchange marks for Zel's herbs. I took the marks to the other side of the market and purchased more cinderslick, grinning when I had enough left over to purchase a dozen eggs and a pound of smoked bacon.

I clutched the precious packages to my chest as I hurried out of the market. Today was going to be a good day. I sped down a narrow alley. It was hidden from the rising sun, dark and cold, and no luminous street lamps lit the way.

Halfway through the alley, a noise behind me startled me. I whirled around, nearly dropping the packages, to see if anyone had followed me. A man stepped from the shadows. Was it … him? The man of blood? Was he real?

"Hello there, Miss Ella," a gruff voice said softly.

A shiver went down my spine. Inspector Cyrus. Not the man from my nightmares, but not a good man to run into all the same. We were the only two people in the alleyway. There was no way he would believe I hadn't heard him.

I dropped into a small curtsey. "Hello, sir. Good to see you. I was just heading home with our market supplies."

"You're here early this morning," he said, edging closer to me.

"Yes. We were out of a few things and I just had to run in to pick them up." I was blathering like an idiot. "I'll be going now. Have to get started on breakfast."

I turned to go, and my stomach sank when he gripped my upper arm. "Hold on now. We have a matter to discuss."

I looked up at him, pretending innocence.

His bloodshot eyes looked straight into mine. "Not sure if you realize this, but your stepmother is late in paying her merchant tax this year. As a child, you may not realize how important taxes are to the running of the city. But if she doesn't pay the tax this year, you'll find yourselves without a bakery very soon."

I feigned ignorance. "Oh, I hadn't realized. I'm sure it's just a misunderstanding. I'll just run home and tell my stepmother immediately."

I tried to pull out of his grip, but he tightened his grip. "You know, I've been wondering something. Maybe you can help me." His voice dropped to a lower register. "I never see your stepmother around. She came to a few of the required meetings for the Merchant Quarter, but it's been years since I've seen her at one. Is she some sort of recluse?"

It took all my self-control to keep from cringing. I didn't know what to say. It was not a good sign that he had been paying enough attention to notice. Most people thought she was lazy, sitting around at home and making me run the errands and handle the bakery. I averted my eyes and made a noncommittal noise.

"I've heard the stories, of course," he said, stroking my arm with his thumb while maintaining his grip on my arm. "I know she doesn't treat you well. And I worry about you."

What a rat. I'd just bet he did.

The corners of his mouth curled upward in an oily smile. "But I wonder if there may be more going on than a simple cruel stepmother."

"What stories, sir? Zel is a wonderful stepmother. We are all very happy." My stomach began to twist and tumble.

What would he do if I lost last night's dinner right here on his shoes?

"I think there's something else going on," he said, eyes glinting. "Something you don't want the Quarter Guard and the trackers to know about. And if you don't pay your tax, I'll have no choice but to tell them to investigate your bakery."

I tried to keep my face blank, but his smile broadened. He knew he was on to something.

"Don't worry, Miss Ella. There's another option." He towered over me as he pressed his body up against mine. I began to shake. When he slid his other hand down to my hip, my mind went blank with fear. "You offer me something now, and I'll look the other way for a while until you get your taxes in. I'll forget about contacting the trackers ... for now. You and your family can live in peace. What do you say? Have we got a deal?"

Chapter 6

I couldn't tear my eyes from Inspector Cyrus's gloating expression. My heart pounded at a furious pace, and my breath came in desperate gasps. I was at his mercy here in this dark alley. Just like when the Blight—

No! Not this time. I had to get away.

In one quick motion, I shot my knee up to his crotch, and he doubled over, cursing as he loosened his grip on my arm. I yanked my arm from his grasp and ran. He sputtered and cursed me as I rounded the corner and sprinted toward home.

I flung open the door of the bakery, slammed it behind me, locked it, and rushed into the kitchen. Zel was there. I dropped my bundles on the counter and flung myself into her arms.

"Zel!" My voice broke, and then all I could do was sob.

"What's happened? Please, talk to me!"

I told her what Inspector Cyrus had said about the taxes.

Zel stared off into space for a moment, a cold, blank look on her normally warm face. Then she flinched and her smile returned. "It's fine," she said. "Everything will work out."

"You don't understand." I looked over my shoulder at the door. Would he come in after me? "He threatened me too."

"He did what?" Zel's expression went from calm to utterly furious in an instant. She balled her fists. "What did he do?"

I told her about the way he had held me still and about his proposition.

"What happened next?" An eerie, icy calm coated her voice.

For the first time in years, I remembered that Zel was dangerous, terribly so. I took a deep breath and tried to calm down, for her sake, if not my own. "I ran away." Something scuffed behind me, and I spun around. Weslan stood in the corner of the kitchen, his lips pressed together in a thin line. Had he been there the whole time?

"Did the inspector follow you?" Zel asked.

Weslan glanced at the shop door.

"I don't know," I said. They probably thought I could be arrested. Technically, I had disobeyed a government official when I fled. I'd even assaulted him. It would be my word against his if he decided to arrest me. I wrapped my arms around myself to ward off a sudden chill. I had never felt so helpless. Two weeks ago, I had been a top student at the Royal Academy with a promising future in government. Now, here I was, little more than a kitchen girl. Nobody would take my side against even a low-ranking, sleazy official like Cyrus.

Anger ripped through me then, replacing the fear with hatred. "I didn't hear any footsteps behind me. I suppose if he were planning to come here, I would have been arrested by now."

Zel and Weslan exchanged looks, but I couldn't tell what they were thinking. Then Zel looked down at her dress and smoothed her hands over it. "I'll go to him," she said, once again with that icy, terrifying calm in her voice. "I'll speak to him, and he'll see that we have nothing to hide."

"What? No, Zel! You can't leave here. What if he's already contacted trackers?"

She shook her head resolutely. "He hasn't. It's too early, and I know men like him. He's lazy. He only cornered you because he thought you were easy prey. Because everyone thinks you're easy prey. Because of the rumors we've intentionally circulated about your status in this home." Zel looked at me. "Those rumors used to protect us, and I'm grateful for all the sacrifices you've made to keep us safe. But if those rumors are endangering you, we must put them to rest. We must make it clear that no one may threaten you and get away with it. It's the only way."

I bit my lip. What if a tracker happened to come across Zel while she was out? Or what if they came across her trail a few days later? "What if you're caught?"

No one but the trackers themselves knew for sure how it worked, but I'd heard rumors that some of the best trackers could still pick up a mage's trace days or even a full week later, and that they would know immediately what kind of mage she was.

Trackers were only slightly absorbent mages. They should have been nearly useless, but instead, the Mage Academy trained them to hone their minute absorbent power to the slightest sensitivity and used them to police other mages. And if they found Zel's trace again, her trail would lead them straight to the bakery, where she'd been hiding for the past thirteen years.

Zel interrupted my spiraling thoughts. "If I'm caught, they'll know that I have the Touch, and we will deal with whatever results."

I jumped at her plain statement. We'd been hiding it for so long, the clear words pricked at my ears in the quiet kitchen. I couldn't help looking at Weslan, who appeared grave-faced but not at all surprised.

Zel took one step backward, away from me and toward the door. "I'm grateful for all that you've given up for us, to hide us, to protect us. Your father would be proud of you.

You will always be as dear to me as my own daughters." She reached up and flicked her long braid over her shoulder, then smoothed her skirt. "But now you need to let me protect you." With that, she left the kitchen and slipped out of the bakery's front door.

~

"Zel will be fine, Ella," Weslan said.

"How do you know? And why do you care, anyway?" Without meaning to, I touched the scar on my face, but when I realized what I was doing, I grabbed the package of bacon and a skillet off the rack above the stove. At least if I was busy cooking, I wouldn't have to look his way.

"I'm just telling you not to worry."

I shrugged one shoulder. "I'm not worried."

"Well, that's good, then." Was he smiling? A chair scraped behind me, and it creaked as he settled into it.

Go away. But I didn't say the words aloud. "If you're going to stay, find something useful to do." I sounded shrill, but his silence unnerved me. "What are you waiting for?"

"Maybe I like the view."

Unbelievable! Did he dare to mock my discomfort? My fingers itched to stick the meat fork right in his mighty arrogance and watch him deflate. Instead, I kept my back to him.

"What did Zel mean about your father and her daughters? Aren't they your half sisters?"

Despite myself, I answered the question. "They are my stepsisters … sort of. Zel was pregnant with them when she moved in. We are not related by blood. And the truth is, Zel was never actually together with my father. The plague took him not long after she sought shelter with us, and it was easier just to pretend she was my stepmother."

The meat sizzled, and its aroma sent me back to my childhood. I was five years old when Zel came to us. She was the most powerful absorbent mage alive, carrying a negative imbalance of magic so strong it was simply called the Touch. With the slightest brush of her little finger, she could drain the life of a grown man before he had a chance to scream. She was only nineteen years old when she found refuge in our bakery, yet she was already a murderer, an assassin, and a fugitive. But to me, she was just Zel.

I remembered snippets of that time, vivid even after the passage of thirteen years. My father rubbing his fingers over his eyes and crumpling a note in his hand. The sound of my slippers padding on the stairs as I ran upstairs to hide. And the young woman slipping inside, covered in dust and clothed in rags, her face gaunt and her belly oddly swollen.

I peeked from the top of the stairs as she stood inside the bakery door, speaking in hushed tones with my father. She looked strange to me and terribly poor. No one in Asylia ever looked like that, I was certain, but Zel had come from Draicia via the Badlands.

She spent the first night on a pallet in the kitchen, keeping warm beside the oven. And in the morning, my father put her to work in the bakery. She was weak and tired and couldn't do much more than put the loaves of bread in the oven and take them out. But he was kind and gentle with her. He made sure she ate enough and found her clean clothes from my mother's old wardrobe.

When I first saw Zel, scrubbed clean and wearing a soft blue dress of my mother's, I cried with joy. I ran to her and hugged her tight, pressing my face into the side of her pregnant belly. Zel thought I believed she was my mother, returned to me from the grave. But I somehow knew Zel would be my new mother.

Three months later the plague arrived in a contaminated shipment of imports from the West and the city walls were sealed to prevent its spread, opening for nothing but the daily export of bodies. My father was one of the plague's first victims.

I curled up in Zel's bed, making room for her belly, which seemed to have stretched impossibly large. "Are you my mother now?" I asked her. I was having trouble understanding what it meant that my father had gone away forever.

"No," she said. "But I can be your stepmother."

I kept quiet, annoyed at her refusal, turning ideas over in my young mind. "But I'll love you like a mother," I finally said.

She stayed silent for a long time before she murmured the quiet words that sealed our fate. "That's fine, Ella. I'll … I'll love you too."

The bacon finished cooking, and I speared the pieces onto a plate. Weslan scraped his chair back, and walked past me to lift more plates from the shelf. He caught me watching, but he didn't ask any more questions.

~

We had finished cooking breakfast when Zel entered the room. "It's done," she said.

A chill went over me at her calm voice. I wondered if I was catching a glimpse of the old Zel. What did she mean, it was done?

"I spoke to him, that's all," she said with a sad smile, as though guessing my thoughts. "I informed him that we would be happy to offer an additional fee because of any inconvenience our late payment has caused. I promised we'd pay after the selection ball. We should have more orders that week, and if not, that gives us enough time to sell a few more things and put the funds together."

The tension went out of my shoulders at her words, and I sighed.

"But," Zel said, looking hard at me, "I don't want you going to that market again. Don't even walk on the street near the inspector's office. Do you hear me, Ella? Weslan goes to the market from now on in your place. Cyrus may still see you as the vulnerable one in our family. I don't want to scare you, but …"

Zel put some flatware on a tray and frowned. "Sometimes, I think all our lies and illusions have done you a great disservice, El. You've made the most of it, and I'm proud of you for that. But it's not right for you to act like a second-class citizen in this household when we both know that you're not." Her voice was firm, even hard, and I felt like a child being chastised.

I shifted uncomfortably and looked around, trying to figure out what she wanted me to say in response. "I know you love me, but remember that I was willing to do this. I was willing from the start, and I still am. It was no great burden for me. You know I don't care about what other people think of me."

Much.

"I want to make sure that we think things through before you take any unnecessary risks."

The whole family depended on me to deal with the outside world. Not even the twins could leave the bakery safely. Bri and Alba had both developed mage powers at a young age. Alba had a strong expellant ability that might one day make her a healer, and Bri had just enough absorbent capacity to become a tracker herself. But if any tracker were to cross paths with them in the city, they'd wonder why the girls weren't at the Mage Academy or living in a Procus patron family's compound. And if they knew there were two unregistered mage girls roaming Asylia, of course they'd want to find their mother. Then the Asylian government would turn Zel into a weapon, as she'd been forced to become one in Draicia. We could never let that happen.

Zel nodded. "Of course, Ella. You've always been the thoughtful one." She smiled at me gently and patted me on the shoulder. "You think about whatever you want to think about," she said, her mouth twisting into a grin, and I narrowed my eyes at her. "But the facts haven't changed. You need to trust me when I tell you that everything is going to be fine."

She filled her tray with half of the breakfast we'd cooked and left the kitchen to take it upstairs.

I sat down at the table. Weslan joined me, and we ate our own breakfasts in silence. When we'd finished eating, neither of us got up. We both fiddled with our dishes, and then finally, staring down at the table, I spoke. "I can't take this," I said. "I can't have Zel taking risks like that for me. That's not the way this is supposed to work. She's been through so much. The twins have suffered so much." I scowled at the table and then looked up at Weslan. "It's not right."

Weslan shrugged one shoulder and drummed his fingers on the table restlessly. "It's pretty simple, Ella. You need to stay away from this Cyrus fellow, that's all. Shouldn't be too hard, right?"

Leave it to Weslan to make light of the whole mess. "I know. But where are we going to get the money to pay him? What if Prince Estevan's ball doesn't boost orders as much as Zel thinks it will?" I fingered the knots in the wood table and the rough splinters that were beginning to come loose. This table had anchored our family's kitchen for generations. I needed to care for it better. I blew out a breath. "Well, I'll figure something out."

Weslan raised an eyebrow questioningly.

"The money, I mean. I'll find a way. So my original plan to get a government job didn't work out. It doesn't matter." I jumped to my feet. "I'll do whatever it takes to get that money. I'll pay off the taxes and whatever else Cyrus needs to get him to leave us alone. That's the only way." I shoved my hands into the tattered pockets of my work dress. "One way or another, I will find that money, and we will get through this."

Weslan eyed me strangely for a moment, as though he were thinking something he wasn't saying. "I believe that's what Zel's been trying to tell you." A half smile ghosted across his face.

For a moment, I forgot all about the wretched feeling of Cyrus grabbing my arm. All I could see was Weslan's smile, and the strong cut of his jaw, and the way his golden hair fell across his brow, begging to be brushed away by my fingers. He met my eyes and didn't look away. Was it my imagination, or was he just as fascinated by me as I was by him?

He cleared his throat, and I busied myself collecting our dishes. "Well, I guess we'd better get started on chores."

He stood and stretched, and we went about our day.

Why did I like his attention so much? And why did I want him to keep looking?

It was pointless to entertain such thoughts. Mages married other mages. They looked down on lowly commoners like me. And no doubt it was better that way. What common girl wanted to bear children who could grow up to be government slaves?

Later, in my quiet, dimly lit room before bed, I discovered the scraps of red paper resting beside my pillow.

Chapter 7

I picked the scraps of paper up and shifted them in my hand, confused. Had Alba or Bri been playing in here without my knowledge? But why? There was a snap, and the red paper scraps shimmered and turned black. They dug into my palm with cruel pinches like a swarm of hungry beetles. I screamed and scraped them off my palm, but they disappeared into thin air before they hit the floor.

My door swung open, and Weslan stared down at me, looking concerned. "Ella? Are you well?"

I searched wildly. There were no hints of red, no dark beetle-like scraps anywhere in my room. What had happened? No matter how much I gasped for air, I couldn't get enough.

"Ella?" Weslan's voice was soft. He approached me slowly, his hands in the air as though to prove that he meant me no harm. "Was it another nightmare?"

It took several moments for his words to sink in. "No, not another …" I shook my head and trailed off. Or was it? Had I dozed in my bed before turning off the luminous and dreamed the painful paper bites?

I held up my palm and stared at it. Perhaps I could see the faintest of red marks, but were they truly there? Or did I only see them because I was looking for them?

Weslan wore a look of pity on his face.

My heart clenched. "I'm fine." The words came out harshly, and he took a quick step back. I cleared my throat. "I'm fine," I said again, a bit softer. "You were right. Just a nightmare."

He stepped out of my room, face shuttered, and closed the door without another word.

~

"Alba, what's going on? Don't you want breakfast?" I climbed the stairs to their living quarters, balancing a tray in one hand and lugging a pitcher of water with the other.

The door at the top of the stairs opened, and Alba smiled. She'd been quick to forgive me after my nastiness to her about the ribbon. I didn't deserve her good humor, but I was grateful for it. "Yes! Sorry, El. Mama's been up on the roof all morning, and Bri and I got so caught up we forgot to eat." She giggled. "Not normal, huh? No wonder you were worried."

I smiled as I handed her the tray. "Well, eat up now. Growing girls and all that."

She stepped backward into the large, well-lit room they shared with Zel. The room that served as their home, schoolhouse, and prison was very tidy. I supposed it helped that they had so few possessions.

Bri waved to me from where she sat, cross-legged and serious, on her bed, the tattered curtain that hung around her space for privacy shoved to the side. She always acted far older than her almost-thirteen years. She was tall like Zel, with blonde hair and golden skin, but an air of restlessness hung about her most of the time. Confinement in the cramped living quarters above the bakery seemed to chafe on her more than on anyone else.

It took a moment to realize the voices I was hearing came from inside the room instead of the street outside. I tensed. "What's that? Who's in here?"

Alba looked at me from the table where she was getting into the small bowl of brambleberries. "Oh, that? It's the fabulator crystal Weslan gave us! Isn't it amazing?"

I stared at her as she popped another brambleberry in her mouth. Fabulator crystals had been the latest mania among my old Procus classmates. They weren't expensive, but they were very rare—only a few were created in each batch, and the Procus ladies almost never sold them. What need did a Procus lady have for more money? Suspicion and worry warred within me. "Where did he get it?"

"You didn't know? His mother is the mage who created them. The Falconus family is her patron. He got these ones for free!" She flopped into a chair at the table, and I realized there were two small crystals sitting beside the breakfast tray. "Watch this." Alba pulled the crystals apart.

Immediately, the actors' melodramatic voices went silent. "And then ..." She pushed them back together, and the voices resumed, arguing about someone named Lucien and his undying love. "The first crystal holds the magic, and the second holds the instructions from the mage. It saves magic, so it doesn't run out too quickly. I think." She shrugged and then propped herself up on an elbow to listen.

I drew up a chair, and Bri joined us at the table, digging into the plate of honeybread and cream that I'd brought with the berries. We sat quietly, listening to the voices and music that filled the room from the two small crystals.

"How can you give up now?" cried a woman's tearful voice.

"Oh, Valencia ... I would stay if I could, I swear it," came a deep male voice's reply.

"But what about ... your daughter?" The accompanying music reached a crescendo, and I held back a snort of laughter.

"My ... my daughter?"

As silly as the whole thing was, I couldn't deny that the story drew me in. Before I knew it, the brambleberries and honeybread were gone, and Alba was swiping her fingers through the last few bites of cream. Then the daughter's childish voice rang out in a soft final song, and I leaned closer to the crystals to listen.

Asylia, the City of Hope,
You never sleep but always dream.
I know you love those who love you,
No matter how hard you may seem.
Though darkness comes, we will never fear;
You stand firm through all our tears.

The crystal's music faded to silence, and I wiped an unexpected tear from my cheek.

Alba did the same. "Lovely, isn't it?" said Alba. "I still cry every time we hear it."

I nodded, feeling off-kilter and confused as I ducked out of the room and went back to work in the kitchen. If Weslan had shared something this nice with the girls, that had to mean something good, right?

But I'd always hated that nickname for Asylia. *City of Hope.* Ludicrous. As if this city had ever done anything for anyone but a Procus. As if there were any reason for any of us to hope.

Weslan and I fell into an uneasy rhythm over the next few days. We weren't happy—neither of us were. How could we be?

He'd fallen from a life of luxury into a life of servitude at the bakery. But he seemed to be doing his best with the chores.

I'd been hard on him at first, and even now, I had to fight the urge to critique his attempts to learn my work or take out my bitterness on him.

He, in turn, would make the occasional nasty, sarcastic comment which would send me into a state of simmering anger that took every effort to keep from bubbling over. But I tried to be kind, and he worked hard. We operated in a shaky truce each day.

Not that it was easy, by any means. Before the attack, I had rolled out of bed eagerly in the middle of the night to start the dough rising and get to work with my studies. Now, I lay in bed until the last possible moment, not rising until I heard Weslan moving around in the kitchen. The motivation and energy I used to have in such abundance had dried up completely.

But the constant fear was worse than the constant despair. I was scared all the time—scared to go out, scared to stay in, and scared of everyone.

Zel, the twins, and Weslan pretended not to notice when I jumped at loud noises and humiliated myself. I had trouble sleeping, and when I did fall asleep, the man with the face of blood terrified me in nightmare after nightmare. I was tired all day and found it difficult to get work done, so it was a good thing Weslan was there to help. I don't know what we would've done without him. He proved to be trustworthy, and I couldn't deny my gratitude, although admitting the fact to him would be something else entirely.

Weslan went out at night from time to time. But he always got his work done, so I didn't say anything. I didn't want to think about what he did when he left. But late one night, I was alone in the kitchen, prepping a mixture of walnuts and dried frostberries to use in the morning's baking when Weslan stumbled through the kitchen door.

I gave him a hesitant smile. "Hello."

But instead of smiling back, he curled his lip. "I should've expected you'd still be up working. Do you never get tired of playing the martyr?"

I wiped my hands on my apron nervously. I was supposed to be kind, right? "I'm not sure what you want me to say," I said after an awkward moment of silence. "I'm doing my best here. This isn't easy for me either. But I'm trying."

"You think I'm not trying?"

"No, of course not. You're twisting my—"

"I guess I never do enough to merit the perfect Ella's good opinion, do I? I wonder how many loaves of bread I need to bake before I'm finally good enough. Do tell." He leaned against the counter and crossed his arms.

I put my hands on my hips. "I don't know what you're talking about, but you know what? I'm done with this. I don't like the way you're speaking to me." My voice rose, but I didn't care. I was sick of his bad attitude popping up when I least expected it, keeping me constantly on edge. "You have no right to talk to me this way."

"Oh, that's right. Because you're my employer. A little kitchen girl, bossing a mage around all day long. Bet that feels good, doesn't it? Is it any wonder that each day here is like torture for me?"

My heart pounded in my ears. "Well, if that's how it is, why do you stay? It's not like we're forcing you to stay here." Each word threw fuel on my hot temper. "In fact, I wish you would go back to your mage friends and leave us alone. They would probably love to have their fellow leech back where he belongs."

His eyes flashed. "Maybe I will," he growled.

"Then go! I certainly don't need you!" And in a burst of anger, I picked up his jacket from where he had tossed it on the floor upon entering and threw it at him.

It hit him in the face, and he reared back and ripped it off with a roar of anger.

I took a quick step backward, bumping into the counter behind me. Weslan glared at me, his chest heaving, his face twisted in a furious scowl.

Abject fear flooded my chest until I could barely breathe. Would he attack me? *Not again. Not again. Not again* …

Zel's cold voice chilled the air: "Weslan." Just one word, but a promise of infinite danger filled it.

All the fight went out of him. He deflated like she had poked him with a pin and popped his tension with a single jab. He clutched his jacket to his chest, and his shoulders slumped.

Zel strode to place herself between us, covering me like a human shield.

I stared at her strong, unmoving back, trying desperately to slow my hysterical, too-rapid breaths.

No one spoke. No one needed to. Weslan left the bakery, shutting the door quietly on his way out.

~

For three days, we neither saw nor heard from him. I didn't realize how much I had come to rely on his steady—if bad-tempered—help. All the downstairs chores and bakery work fell to me, and I fell into bed at the end of each day.

Nightmares plagued my nights, and terrifying imaginings ruined my days. As tired as I was, sleep always escaped me. My eyes drooped during the day and burned painfully by evening. A girl could only miss so much sleep before the exhaustion took its pound of flesh.

Flashes of red appeared and disappeared multiple times each day to torment me. A soft red scarf left forgotten on the bakery counter wrapped itself around my neck like a vice. Later, it was nowhere to be found. A handful of red marbles on our front stoop flew into my face like hail stones and disappeared the moment a neighbor looked over. I was losing my mind. There was no doubt.

I stood in the kitchen on the fourth night, chopping vegetables in a bleary-eyed daze. Someone coughed behind me, and I swung around. I gripped the knife tightly, dread creeping up my spine.

Weslan stood in the kitchen doorway, his face marred by smudges of dirt and heavy, dark creases under his eyes. His hands hung awkwardly at his sides, as though he didn't know what to do with them. He almost didn't look like himself without his signature arrogance.

"Where have you been?" My voice was scratchy, and I realized I probably didn't look much better than he did.

He opened his mouth to speak, but words seemed to fail him. The kitchen door stayed open behind him. "I found a few places to sleep. And I ... well, I didn't think I'd be welcome here anymore."

I fingered the small knife in my hand. It felt paltry and small, but I gripped it anyway. "Are you still a threat to us?"

His face seemed to cave in on itself. "No," he rasped. "Never. Ella, I ... never. Please, believe me. I-I'd been drinking far too much. It's no excuse, but you must believe me—I would never have hurt you. Never. And I can never forgive myself for scaring you like that."

"Then why are you here?"

He ran a hand over his hair which was several shades darker from the grease and dirt in the past three days. "I-I wanted to apologize. And I wanted to show you that I am truly sorry."

I watched him silently. He seemed sorry, but was it an act? How could I be sure?

I clenched my jaw. We couldn't keep living this way. I didn't know how much longer I could continue to run the bakery and support Zel and the twins on my own in my current state. We needed help. We needed someone we could trust with Zel's secret, and Weslan was the only one who knew. But trusting Weslan again could be just as dangerous. This was impossible.

I opened my mouth to say something—anything—but indecision closed my throat. I looked down at the knife in my hand. We were trapped, as always.

Either I kept pushing myself to the brink of exhaustion and madness, with no idea how much more I could take, or I accepted help, never knowing if it would blow up in our faces. For some reason in that instant, I thought of my father's old friend, Gregor. He'd been the first spice merchant in the city to sell imported ingredients after the gates were unsealed, when the city trackers had learned how to inspect imports for traces of the plague.

Everyone had hated Gregor for taking that risk. But his shop had been the first on our lane to recover from the plague, and he supplied half the merchants in the quarter now. What was worse? To risk everything for the future? Or to have no future at all?

I placed the knife on the cutting board and faced Weslan. "Should we sit down? I'm so tired, I'm asleep on my feet."

He nodded hesitantly, pulled out a chair for me, and took the chair across the table. He tapped his fingers restlessly and ran them across the table's rough surface in a nervous gesture. "I am so sorry." His voice cracked, and he coughed again. "I am so very, very sorry. I didn't mean to scare you or threaten you." He shook his head vehemently. "I've never done anything like that before. It's not right, and I can't just let it go."

His expression was bleak, as though the light had gone right out of him, as though the layers of arrogance and charisma had been stripped away, revealing the real Weslan underneath.

I clasped my hands in my lap. "What do you mean, you can't let it go?"

"I want to …" He stumbled over his words. "I want to share something with you. I want you to have a way to know, for certain, that you can trust me from now on."

What did that mean, exactly?

"How much do you know about mages?"

"Not that much," I confessed. "Only the basics. Absorbent versus expellant, that sort of thing. And some of the history." I hesitated. "That you … they … the Kireth were a race of mages who invaded from the North. And they used to rule over everyone, enslaving us, treating the Fenra like animals. But seven hundred years ago, the founding families of Asylia revolted against the invaders and forced the most powerful mages to help them create the first walled city, then trapped them there. And other Fenra people followed suit, establishing the other walled cities of Theros."

The words sounded awkward on my tongue. It was one thing to learn about the evil mages of Kireth in history class, but it was quite another to recount the story in the presence of one.

He nodded, his face serious. "It's true that before the walled cities were founded, the mages of Kireth ran wild and used their powers for cruelty and gain, simply because they could. But do you know how the original Procus families gained the upper hand?"

"By banding together?" No one had ever covered that in history class. It had always been so distant, so obvious. A seven-hundred-year old twist of history that had been inevitable, no longer worth questioning. Moral of the story? Don't trust mages, and don't treat Fenra people like animals. They'll get you back eventually.

He took a deep breath and blew it out. "There was one Kireth mage who was even greedier and more violent than all the rest. They called him Death's Master, because he had the Touch, like Zel. He didn't only want to subjugate humans. He wanted to subjugate other mages, too, and create an empire across the whole continent. The Master was a powerful absorbent mage, but more than that, he was clever and ruthless.

"Through cruel experiments, he discovered a way to derive the magical core of a mage's spirit. I think it came from an ancient ceremony of some kind. Once he had found that core and derived its essence—its True Name— he could control it."

"Control it? Control ... other mages?"

"Yes. The founding Procus families were a group of Fenra men and women who heard about this mage, about the empire he was building for himself. They were crafty enough to realize what he had been too greedy and shortsighted to consider—that if all that was needed was to find out a mage's True Name, what was to stop a Fenra human from using the True Name to control a mage?"

A chill went down my spine at his words, and the incongruous pieces of our history began to click into place.

"They used certain unsavory methods—nothing worse than what the mages had been doing to them for three centuries, of course—and they found out the names of a few powerful mages who were not under the control of the Master. They forced these mages to overthrow the Master and take control of his subjects, relaying their True Names to their human controllers.

"By the time they conquered him, the founding families knew the True Names of scores of mages. They decided to consolidate control. They set up a walled encampment and forced the mages they controlled inside. The humans made the mages use their powers to serve the encampment, to create things humans had long labored for like shelter, healing, clean water, food, and safety."

I had written these points on my ill-fated final exam. The founding families were our city's heroes, the ones who had changed everything for the Fenra people. The mages, working for the humans, had built our first civilized settlements, and those had become the walled cities we lived in today. "I've never heard of this True Name." Morbid curiosity made me ask, "Do they still use it?" How fantastical, like something that belonged in one of the fabulator crystals that Alba and Bri loved so much. Fantastic but terrible too.

Weslan swallowed. "Yes," he said tightly, "they do."

"Do they ... the government ... control you?" I whispered. Our conversation had gone from strange to terrifying. My tiredness evaporated on a wave of fear.

"They do."

I tore my gaze away from his strained expression. My hands clutched the table's edge. He was under government control! He knew everything about our family, every law we had broken, all the secrets we had been hiding for years—

"No, no, no!" He interrupted my whirling thoughts. "You don't need to worry about your family, Ella. Really, you don't. The government doesn't want me anymore. They don't think of me as any sort of asset, anyway." He rubbed his palms on his trousers. "I was more trouble than my two-bit talent was worth. That's not why I'm telling you this. But first, you need to know something else."

I wrapped my arms around myself and huddled forward in my chair. What else was he going to shock me with today? I didn't know how much more I could take.

He cleared his throat and looked over my shoulder for a moment. "Back when I was at the Mage Academy, I wasn't a great student."

What could I say to that?

His words tumbled out in a rush. "I mean, I did some bad things. A lot of bad things. I just wanted to fool around and have fun. I didn't care about developing my talent or getting a good government job. I knew I would find a patronage like everyone else in my family, and thanks to my family, I had offers by the time I graduated."

So he had taken a Procus patron after all. I nodded to show I was listening.

"When I moved into my patron's compound, I was still young. Immature. I shouldn't have been there. I didn't deserve to be there, but I thought I deserved that much and more. I kept up my old tricks—playing pranks, acting dumb, trying to be funny, trying to get this one girl's attention." He looked disgusted with himself.

I couldn't help but interrupt. "But surely all young mages are the same at that age. And the young Procus lords too. It's not just you."

He stared at the wall and continued as though I hadn't spoken. "I finally got her attention. She was the granddaughter of my patron. I felt like it gave me some form of power over her family, but really, they had complete power over me.

"Then one day, we got caught. They told her grandfather, my patron, and he went into a rage. I had tried his patience too many times. The pranks were one thing, but laying my worthless mage hands"—he avoided meeting my eyes—"on his precious granddaughter was the last straw. He had me cast out of the Mage Division and blacklisted from any other Procus patron. He said my minor talent wasn't worth the trouble I caused, and that was enough for the Mage Division authorities.

"My mother risked everything to see me before I was kicked out. She told me that the Golden Loaf was known for taking in the … unwanted … and she hinted that other cast-off mages had found shelter here before. She didn't know that your father and mother had passed. So I came to Zel and begged for shelter. She took a chance on me, and then—"

His voice cracked again, and he ran a hand through his hair. "I threw it back in her face. I scared you, and you were my last chance. You are my only chance for a fresh start before I really do lose everything. I can't go back there, but not just because they won't let me."

Weslan leaned forward and met my eyes. "I don't want to be that mage anymore. I want to change. And I don't know how that's going to happen, but somehow, I think I need to be here at the bakery. I see how hard you all work for so little, how you're so afraid all the time—don't deny it, I know that you are—and it kills me. I don't know how to change, but if I can help you—if I can forget myself for a little while and be here, help the bakery survive, and help you pay the tax—maybe I'll figure it out."

Weslan had been breathtakingly handsome the day Zel introduced us in the entryway of the bakery. He was still handsome but in a leaner, sharper way. He looked … raw. And for a moment, even marred by the dust and exhaustion of the past few days, he looked simply irresistible. It terrified me. Again, what was worse? To risk everything for the future? Or to have no future at all?

I forced myself to look away, knowing I'd stared at him far longer than was appropriate. "I … thank you for telling me." I couldn't help looking his way again. "I'm sorry for all the times I've said nasty things to you because you're a mage.

It can't have made it any easier for you to make a fresh start, and I regret it now."

He nodded, but his hands tapped a tattoo on the table. Was there something more he wanted to say? If possible, he seemed more nervous than when we had first started talking. "It's fine, Ella." His lips tilted up. "Most of the time you were right, anyway. But ... I explained about True Names because I want to do something. For you. I want you to know you can trust me, to never fear being threatened by me again."

I fought off a yawn. "What are you talking about?"

"I want to give you my True Name."

My mouth dropped open. "Why? It's fine, Weslan. As long as you stop drinking so much and you keep Zel's secret and you ... you help me, you can stay here. I need you to stay here." It wasn't until the words were out of my mouth that I realized they were true. Apparently, if I had to choose between staying safe and having a future, I'd choose the future, and that was that.

He shook his head. "You shouldn't forgive me so quickly. You don't know what an idiot I've been in the past. I-I can't explain it. I just know this is something that I need to do for you. That I want to do for you. I hate seeing you constantly afraid, jumping at loud noises and looking over your shoulder. I hate hearing you cry out in your sleep at night."

I pressed my lips together. I hadn't realized he would be able to hear me from where he slept in the kitchen.

He continued. "I don't want to ever again be someone else you have to fear. And this is my way to make sure that you will never, ever have to fear me."

"I don't know what to say." I scrubbed my tired eyes. "I accept, if you're serious about this. Whatever it takes for you to stay."

"Good." Then he spoke a word that sounded at once distant and achingly familiar, and it sank deep into my very bones. And though the language was one I didn't speak and

I couldn't have written the word out if I'd tried, somehow, I knew that word.

I spoke it aloud, wondrously, relishing the soft tones on my tongue.

He stiffened at the sound and stared at me, eyes wide, and the slightest hint of regret flashed across his face.

"Oh, Ella, Weslan ... what have you done?" Zel stood inside the doorway, staring at us in horror.

Chapter 8

Zel had sent us to bed the night before with nothing but an icy glare and a warning, but today, she'd dragged me from my bed as soon as the sun was up and begun to lecture me. "After everything, Ella! I can't believe that you ..." Zel pressed her hands against her eyes. We were seated at the old wooden table in her living quarters while the girls hid out on the rooftop and Weslan worked in the kitchen. His lecture was no doubt coming next.

"I'm sorry, but I don't—"

"What were you thinking?" She dropped her hands and glared at me. "A bond like that? With Weslan, of all people? In Draicia, she—they controlled me with my True Name. They forced me to do horrible things, evil things. No one should have such control over another person!"

I shrank back in my seat. Zel had never told us how her captors in Draicia had controlled her. I only knew that she'd been forced to use her power against her will. "I didn't know, Zel. But this is completely different—"

"It's no different. In fact, it's worse. They tortured me with the threat of killing my parents until I gave up my True Name, only to murder them before my eyes anyway. But you had a choice!"

The room spun around me. I'd never known ... If I'd known ...

"The True Name is old magic from the Ancient Ones, and even the old Kireth people knew not to use it. What makes you think you and Weslan know any better?"

I pressed my hands together in my lap. What could I possibly say to make it right?

"The Ancients used it for marriage ceremonies to tie two mages together for life. For life, Ella! But even they realized that it wasn't right for husband and wife to control each other. And now you've gone and ... I just ... Oh, Ella." Her shoulders slumped, and finally, she looked me in the eye. "Do you realize that for a commoner, holding the True Name of a mage is a treasonous offense?"

My lungs squeezed together. I took a gasping breath. "What?"

"If anyone ever finds out, they'll execute you. Only a Procus or another mage in the structure of hierarchy here may hold a mage's True Name. It's rigidly controlled. Think about it. Every mage, even the weakest, can be wielded as a weapon, one which non-mages are helpless to defend against. If they know you can control Weslan, they can't allow you to live and put the system at risk. It's that simple. And the True Name bond lasts for a lifetime. There's no taking it back now. The only way out is death."

"I didn't know." I leaned forward against the table. "You have to believe me. And I'm sure Weslan didn't realize either. He only wanted to assure me that I would be safe with him."

Zel sighed. "I wish ... Never mind. What's done is done. But you must promise me that you will never use his name. Don't do to him what they did to me."

I nodded rapidly. "Of course! I won't. I swear. Never. I would never do that."

She stared at me, a sad look coming over her face. "I know."

~

I went to the kitchen to begin preparations for the noon meal, and Alba passed me on the way. "You know what tomorrow is," she sang giddily.

I was still smarting from Zel's lecture, but I couldn't help but smile at Alba's excitement. "Tomorrow? What's tomorrow?" I asked, feigning ignorance just to torment her. It was the twins' thirteenth birthday, of course. As if I hadn't been preparing for months now. We didn't have much, but when it was someone's birthday, we always had to do something special to celebrate.

My inner smirk must have shown on my face because she grinned at me. "You know!" she shouted. She twirled around on the landing, spinning her skirt as she laughed. "I can't wait for tomorrow," she sang, sounding exactly like Valencia, the dramatic woman from the fabulator crystals.

I shook my head, laughing despite myself, and descended the steps.

Later that day, Weslan joined me in the kitchen. He looked shaken after his meeting with Zel, and I wondered what exactly she had told him. When I asked, he shrugged it off, so I didn't press.

Throughout the day, a gentle pull drew me to him. Was that the work of his True Name? We worked in silence in the kitchen, cleaning and preparing doughs for the next day, and I couldn't shake a strange new awareness of his presence. Even when I went to my room or upstairs to visit with the twins, I never felt truly alone. I could still feel our connection. It was strange, but oddly comforting at the same time.

Weslan seemed to feel just the opposite. As the day went on, he grew increasingly tense. I regretted our decision, too, but there was nothing we could do now. I was willing to let it go. Why wasn't he? Then it hit me—he was waiting for me to speak his Name again.

"I won't do it, you know." I wrung out a rag and hung it up to dry on the rack beside the sink. "I'll never use your True Name. I promised Zel. And I'll promise you too. I'll never do it."

Weslan paused, his fist still buried in a mound of soft, floury dough.

His hunched shoulders broke my heart. What *had* we been thinking? I couldn't help myself. I reached up to his shoulder and gave it a gentle squeeze. "Never. I'll never use it."

Finally, he met my eyes. "Thank you." His voice was rough. "You don't know how much that means to me."

I tore my gaze away and dropped my hand. I had a fierce desire to step closer and wrap my arms around him, so I took two steps away from him for good measure and forced myself to get back to cleaning. I watched him from the corner of my eye, and gradually, he relaxed.

After we finished cleaning up after dinner and everyone else had gone to bed, I asked him, "Are you ready?"

He folded his arms across his chest. "For what?"

"Time to bake a birthday cake for the twins." I grinned, feeling happy for the first time in weeks. "I've got all the ingredients."

I'd been setting aside small amounts for months. The days when we could easily put together a cake with what we had on hand were long gone. Ever since the rationing started, we hadn't been able to make a lot of the foods my mother used to make. We had been surviving on rations and squirreling away little bits of nicer foods for years now. It was hard to believe that we had ever done anything different.

Weslan watched me get the ingredients for the cake out of my hiding places and put them on the counter.

I began to mix the ingredients and directed Weslan to butter the cake pan and prepare the oven.

Then he stopped. "We may have a problem. How long do you need the oven to run?"

I bit my lip. Not again. "About an hour."

"Well, if you think we can cook it low and slow …"

"No, that won't work. The cake must be baked at the right temperature, or it won't turn out. That's the only thing that matters." My temper began to simmer again. I knew the girls were looking forward to their birthday treat.

"We only have enough cinderslick for about a quarter hour at high temperature," Weslan said.

I stared at the batter inside my mixing bowl. My precious ingredients would go to waste. "It won't finish baking that quickly."

Weslan held up his hands helplessly. "There's no money for another bottle this time. Maybe Zel could—"

"No! Don't tell her. I don't want her to worry about this on top of everything else. And I don't want the twins to think their birthday is a burden. They'll feel bad and insist they don't want a cake, when I know they do." I sighed. "We have to figure something out ourselves."

I racked my brain for a solution. Maybe we could sell some seldom-used pots and pans to a pawn shop and buy them if we made enough money in time.

But what would we do if we needed those pans in the meantime? Besides, shouldn't we be putting every bit toward our merchant tax?

I groaned aloud. After everything that had gone wrong lately, not to mention our mistake last night that made Zel so furious, couldn't something go right? Was that so much to ask?

"Wait." I grabbed Weslan's arm and released it just as hastily. "What kind of mage are you?"

His expression switched from surprise to amusement. His laugh sounded self-conscious. "Appearance. I'm a weak expellant mage, so I specialized in appearance manipulation."

"Helping Procus ladies get ready for balls?" I asked, half-joking.

He nodded, looking embarrassed.

Well, that was awkward. I imagined all the beautiful Procus ladies he had probably helped dress, and I couldn't help looking down at my scruffy, secondhand dress. But none of that mattered. All that mattered was if Weslan could use his magic to help me.

"If you can affect a person's appearance, that means your magic changes her clothes, right?"

"Of course," he said. "No problem."

"Well, could you affect an object that isn't clothing?"

"Sure." He leaned against the wall. "I mean, I worked on things like jewelry and hats and gloves all the time."

He didn't seem to know where I was going with this, but he was playing along.

I tapped the oven. "Do you think you could affect something like this?"

His gaze traveled from the oven to my face. "I could make it look like it's made of pure gold or velvet brocade, but I'm guessing that's not what you mean …" He fell silent.

He had to know what I meant.

Long moments passed while he thought it over. "I might be able to add some heat to the oven. I'm not a mover mage. I don't have the training or the power, but a mover could do something like this, easy. I could probably do it for a short time. The question is, what would happen? Magic can be dangerous, Ella. I spent years training to affect things like clothing and shoes and everyday items. But an oven …" His eyes narrowed. "It would take heat at just the right temperature for the right length of time. The same way cinderslick does when you add it in the right amount. Mostly."

A little thrill of victory went through me. He was considering my request. "Well, we'll never know unless we try. And maybe it would make it better."

"Maybe." He furrowed his brow. "But the thing is, mages don't do this. I've never heard of a mage as weak as me using expellant magic to affect a household object like this."

"But what about the mages who work in government service? Don't they use their magic to do things like make large supplies of clean water or healing salve or victus?"

"Yes, they do, but they're creator mages. They're incredibly powerful, and they're trained to work their magic directly on the raw material. Not on the tools. There must be a reason why, right?"

He seemed to be changing his mind, so I scrambled for an argument. "But what if there is no reason why? What if they're too scared to try? What if they like the way things are because it means everyone depends on the mages every time they want some clean water? If they somehow created a mage-craft that anyone—not just mages—could use to purify water, we wouldn't need the mages anymore."

"Well, I don't know about not needing mages anymore," Weslan said broodingly, "But you may be on to something."

I waited for a few moments. "What are you thinking?"

"Just trying to remember. Wondering if I can think of any other reason why mages don't usually do things like this. I've always been taught to only affect objects for direct use. But my magic isn't strong enough to make food the way the government mages do. I couldn't make this cake out of nothing but flour, the way the creators turn clay into victus. But if I could make the oven hot enough to bake the cake …" he tapped the oven thoughtfully. "Fine. I'm in. I want to try."

"Do you think it's dangerous?"

He laughed, and the laughter transformed his face. "Yes, I think it's dangerous. But if it works, we won't need cinderslick to make bread anymore."

For a moment, I was transfixed by the change in his expression. I shook off my fascination. *Focus, Ella.* I rubbed my hands together. "Which means we could sell our rations and put the extra money aside to pay the tax. And … oh, there's so much that we could do if we didn't have to use cinderslick!"

"Hold on. One thing at a time. Let's see if this even works."

I poured the cake ingredients into the buttered pans. Weslan put his hands on either side of the oven while I made sure the cake batter was evenly spread. He seemed to be practicing. When he yanked his hands away and shook them off, I thought it had to be working pretty well.

Finally, I lifted the cake pans, and he opened the oven door. I placed the cake in the oven with some trepidation. If this didn't work, there would be no cake tomorrow. If this didn't work, all the ingredients we could ill afford and the expensive roseberry essence I'd been hoarding for months would be wasted. So we had to try. I closed the oven door and nodded to Weslan.

He placed his hands on either side of the oven again. "Tell me again, how hot do you want the oven?"

I bit my lip and consulted my mother's recipe for the umpteenth time. This was a terrible idea, wasn't it? "It should be at a medium-high temperature. The same as around five drops of cinderslick. And it should bake for about an hour at that heat." Then a thought struck me. "Wait, does that mean you'd have to stand here with your hands by the oven for an hour? Won't you be burned?" As usual, we hadn't thought this through enough. It seemed to be a pattern with us.

He shook his head without hesitating. "No, I think I can just add enough magic for the oven to maintain the same temperature for about an hour, and then it will start to fade off. I'm not just adding magic—I'm giving it simple instructions, too, to control its behavior." He placed his hands on the sides of the oven and closed his eyes for a minute. Suddenly, he yanked them off and plunged them into the sink which he'd filled with cold water beforehand.

Had he been burned? What had we been thinking?

A moment later, he shook the water off his hands, wiped them on his pants, and grinned. "One cinderslick-free cake, coming up."

Excitement whipped through me. I couldn't wait to see if it worked. We spent the next hour cleaning the kitchen as the delicious fragrance of butter, sugar, and roseberry permeated the bakery.

After an hour had passed, I wrapped my hands in towels and took the cake pans out of the oven. Each layer was a beautiful golden-brown color. And the smell? Amazing. I couldn't stop inhaling the pure scent of roseberry and butter, reveling in the absence of burnt cinderslick. I waited a few minutes and turned the cakes out onto racks.

When they'd cooled, I placed the first layer on my mother's crystal cake stand. It was a heavy piece from a different time, back when the larder was always full and delicious spices from the West crowded the kitchen shelves. I poured a soft pink icing mixture over the cake, one layer at a time, and then placed a small white flower from Zel's garden right on top, in the center.

Weslan and I stood back and admired it in silence for a moment. It was beautiful. For some reason, it made me want to cry.

~

The next evening after dinner, we surprised the twins with the cake and a song. They were overjoyed. Even though I baked a cake for them every year, they were always inordinately pleased and surprised. This year, their joy was like a vice, squeezing my chest. I wanted them to have so much more than a cake—a better life, a life of freedom. I didn't want them to be stuck in this bakery forever, constantly fearing for their lives. I didn't want them to look forward all year to a little cake made by squirreling away ingredients we couldn't really afford.

As Zel and the twins gathered around the table to cut the cake, despair nearly overwhelmed me. All the excitement I had felt last night withered away, and I had to get away from the group.

I went into my room, closed the door, and splashed cold water on my face. The anger and fear that had simmered in me since the attack raced through me at a furious pace, and I sat on my bed, taking deep breaths in a fruitless attempt to calm down.

I was sick of being at our limit, of always being about to break. I was tired of seeing the twins' innocent faces marred by hunger, fear, and sorrow. Someday, Alba's sweet, hopeful face would be emptied of its hope. What would she do when she longed to go and live a real life, but couldn't? And Bri was so strong, fierce, and full of energy. How could we keep her in this bakery much longer?

I pulled the hairpins from my loose bun and twisted it back into place, jabbing the pins in with more force than necessary as I fought to get my racing thoughts under control. Wasn't I supposed to trust Zel? If I was worried, Zel had to be worried too. She always insisted everything would work out at the right time and in the right way. I supposed if Zel could escape capture and evade trackers for thirteen years, anything could happen.

I returned to the kitchen. Everyone was enjoying the cake, smiling and laughing with each other. The sight thawed my cold heart and brought back some of the joy from last night, but it wasn't the same. What was wrong with me? Why couldn't I be happy like everyone else?

Weslan wrapped one strong arm around my shoulder. "Great job with the cake. It's delicious."

I tried to relax my shoulders, but they hunched up nervously.

"I mean, seriously, it's really good," he said around a mouthful of cake. "You could sell this."

I snorted. "Why would anyone want to buy a cake from someone like me? And besides, we can barely afford ingredients to make cakes for ourselves." We weren't the only ones struggling to get by in this awful city. Only wealthy Procus families had done well since the plague.

"I mean it. You could sell this. It's better than a lot of the food that I've had at Procus banquets, and that's saying something."

I narrowed my eyes at him, not quite sure whether to believe him. "We bake bread. Our customers couldn't afford something like a cake. And why would they want one, anyway?"

He laughed incredulously. "Trust me. Anyone with a living, beating heart would want a bite of this."

I shook my head.

He waved his fork in front of my face, and the mixture of cake and frosting nearly fell to the ground before he popped it in his mouth. "You're a really good cook. I think you could do something with this." He released me. "But hey, don't listen to me. I'm just a mage, right? What do I know?" He left me, and reached to get another piece.

I shivered, cold without his warm arm over my shoulders. I couldn't deny the satisfaction of watching Bri and Alba take seconds and then thirds of their birthday cake. Not much had gone well lately. For once, I'd done something good. That had to count for something.

Alba swiped the last crumb of cake before her mother shepherded her upstairs, and I went back to my bedroom and shut the door.

The night was dark and cloudy, so I turned the luminous dial and puttered about the room in the dimly glowing light. I'd changed into my nightgown when something moved on the floor. I jumped.

Was it a mouse? A spider? I bent over and looked closer, careful to keep my feet as far from the creature as possible. A scrap of red ribbon lay coiled on the floor. Was that the ribbon Alba had borrowed and lost?

Then it wriggled like a snake, scooting rapidly toward me across the floor. I let out a screech and leapt onto my bed.

Was it a red snake?

But I'd only seen a ribbon moments ago.

It reached the bed and, to my horror, the ribbon snake raised its front tip as though it were a head, looking at me with invisible eyes, ready to strike at me with invisible teeth. I screamed again.

"Ella?" My door swung open, and the ribbon snake disappeared before my eyes.

I dragged my gaze from the spot where the ribbon had vanished and stared at Weslan. I quickly shut my eyes, for he was dressed only in his trousers, his hair rumpled and wet with water. What could I say? I'd been attacked by a ribbon? And it conveniently disappeared the moment you entered? I opened my eyes and looked at him again, doing my best to keep my eyes away from the muscular torso that I should not, absolutely should not, be noticing.

Before I could speak, he rolled his eyes and stepped back. "Let me guess—you're fine." The faintest hint of bitterness tinged his words, making the air taste sour. And with that, he snapped the door shut.

I kept the luminous on all night. I didn't try to sleep. There was no point. I couldn't stop seeing that ribbon, wriggling unnaturally along the floor, raising its tip as though it could see me. I scanned the floor again and again, but it didn't reappear. Sometime around the third hour after midnight, Weslan's words repeated in my head. "You're an incredible cook. You could sell this."

You could sell this. You could sell this.

Had exhaustion sent my brain into an irrational state? Had fear and desperation kicked my good judgment out of its authoritative seat? What if there was a way we could make extra money to pay the tax, help with the bakery's expenses, and save enough money to move Zel and her daughters somewhere safe? Somewhere out of Asylia?

The harebrained plan took root like a weed in the garden, and for the next few hours before dawn, I nearly forgot about the snake. If my plan worked, it could change everything.

Chapter 9

"Wake up. We have to get started."

Weslan grunted, stretched, and opened one eye to stare at me. "Started with what?"

"I have an idea, but we have to do it now, before everything else."

He yawned. "Before breakfast? What are you talking about?"

"We're going to use the ingredients we would've cooked for breakfast." I shook my head. "I don't have time to explain. I have an idea, but you have to trust me."

"I do," he said, surprising me with his ready agreement. "What do I need to do?"

"Just wait for a minute, and then I want you to do the oven again."

I used the last of our butter, sugar, flour, and eggs to make the same cake batter we had made the previous day for the twins' birthday cake, but this time, rather than making it into three separate layers, I poured it into a tray of small molds that once, long ago, my mother had used for making candy.

I nodded to Weslan. "Same heat as last time, but I think we'll need to bake it less. Maybe ten minutes?"

He looked bemused, but once I'd put the trays in the oven, he placed his hands on the oven to heat it. He yanked them off a few seconds later and shook them. We waited with bated breath.

Ten agonizing minutes later, I pulled the tiny cakes out of the oven. They were a beautiful golden-brown color, like small drops of sunlight, each one only half the size of my palm. They smelled like a perfect mixture of butter and roseberry essence.

As we waited for them to cool, I mixed the ingredients for the roseberry frosting, trying to beat them as fast as I remembered my mother doing. The other night, I'd only managed a thin, drippy pink frosting that had poured over the cake like thick milk. My mother had whipped her frosting several minutes until it was thick and airy. I stirred until my arm ached. How had she ever done this?

Weslan watched me, and when he offered to take a turn, I happily gave him the bowl. He beat it quicker than I had, his strong arms tense as he gripped the whisk and bowl. But then he stopped and looked at me. "Can I try something different?"

I eyed him. What did we have to lose? "Go for it."

He stood the whisk in the middle of the bowl, touching it with the tips of his fingers at the handle's end. He frowned in concentration, and the whisk spun like crazy, all by itself.

I gasped in amazement.

Then he winced and pulled his hand back, and the whisk fell to the side of the bowl. His fingers were bright red, as though they'd been burned.

"Friction," he said ruefully. He plucked a towel off the table, wrapped it around the end of the whisk, and placed it back in the bowl which he gripped with one hand. Once again, after a moment of quiet concentration, the whisk whirred around the bowl at a speed no human hand could ever achieve.

Bits of frosting flew around the kitchen, but I didn't care. Before my very eyes, the frosting mixture thickened and grew into a billowy mass of pink frosting so soft and airy it looked like it could float right out of the bowl.

Weslan stopped the spinning, pulled the whisk from the frosting with a flourish, and waved his hand over the bowl. A cloud of golden sparkles hovered over the frosting for a moment and then disappeared, leaving the frosting a shimmering mixture of sparkly pale pink and gold. He winked at me. "Is this good enough?"

I smiled up at him, struck for a moment by the change in his demeanor. I wanted to find whoever had said the words "two-bit talent" and knock them over the head. I grabbed one of the tiny cakes from the candy mold, dipped it into the frosting bowl, and popped it right into Weslan's mouth. The surprised look on his face was priceless, and I laughed before realizing how incredibly forward I'd been. I pretended not to notice. "What do you think?"

He raised an eyebrow. I wasn't sure if he bought my cool act, but he smiled as he chewed. "It's amazing," he said around a mouthful, and a shiver of excitement went down my spine.

We frosted the rest of the little cakes and placed them on a tray. I took a deep breath. This was it. I left Weslan inside to clean up the mess and headed outside with our tray of sweets. The dawn rush of students running to school and neighbors heading to the market had begun, and a steady stream of traffic made its way down our lane.

I stood outside the bakery door and cleared my throat. This was going to be awkward. Could I copy the vendors at the marketplace? I opened my mouth and shouted, "Sweet treats! Cakes! Get cakes for just a quarter mark each!"

A shocking number of people diverted away from the road and headed straight toward me. I sold out within fifteen minutes, and my apron pocket bulged with marks until I thought it might burst at the seams. The moment the last little cake sold, I waved good-bye to the crowd and slipped back inside to lean against the door. Had that truly happened?

Weslan, putting the finishing touches on a sparkling clean counter, looked strangely tired when I entered the kitchen. There were bags under his eyes that hadn't been there before.

But then I remembered the marks. "Weslan, take a look at this." I pulled the marks from my pocket and dumped them on the table before us. "I sold out."

He stared at me. "But ... that's ... it's only been a few minutes!"

I grinned. "I know. It worked."

The next thing I knew, I was in his arms, and he was squeezing me tight and spinning me around the room. Then he put me down and grinned. "You did it, Ella."

"What are you talking about? You did it. This would never have worked without you."

He ducked his head and shrugged, a flush mantling his cheeks. "Should I go get some food to make for breakfast? Since we seem to have cooked and sold everything in the kitchen?"

I scooped up several marks from the table, handed them to him, and shoved the rest into a money pouch.

Half an hour later, he returned with a bundle of fresh groceries that had my mouth watering. We made a hot breakfast of eggs, bacon, and frosted spiceberry rolls, with plenty left over for Zel and the girls. Weslan took a tray up for them, and I stood alone in the kitchen, grinning like a fool. We'd done it. We'd truly done it.

We were cleaning up after breakfast when Zel entered the kitchen. I turned to her, smiling broadly. "You're never going to believe this."

Zel smoothed her hair. "Morning, dear. Believe what?"

I set the money pouch in front of her.

She approached cautiously and I nearly laughed aloud at her hesitance as she peeked inside. She didn't touch it. "What is this? Where did you get this?"

"You know how, last night, Weslan said my cake was so good that we could sell it?"

She nodded, looking wary. "It was good. You're a talented cook."

"Well, this morning, I made another cake. Actually, I made a whole bunch of small cakes with Weslan's help. And then I sold them in the street before anyone was even down for breakfast. All the students and workers on their way out of the quarter snatched them up. I sold out before a half hour had passed! Can you believe it?"

"They bought them all?" Her voice sounded dangerous.

Why did she sound so unhappy? "Yes. I charged low prices, so I guess it was an easy sell. But we made more than enough money to cover the cost of the ingredients, and Weslan used some of the profit to buy more ingredients for breakfast today. And the best part is—"

"Hold on. You sold them in front of the bakery?" Zel shook her head as though in disbelief. "What were you thinking?"

"What are you talking about? I thought you would be happy! We finally made money."

"I told you not to worry about it, Ella! I had it covered." This was the first time I had ever seen Zel looking quite so flustered.

Usually cool, calm, and confident, she turned red, anger and worry marring her beautiful face. She lifted the pouch in the air. "Money is fine, sure. But not at the risk of giving away our safety here. You could've led any tracker to our door with the kind of attention you must've drawn." She thumped the bag of marks down and stormed from the room.

~

I avoided Zel for the rest of the day, but at dinner that night on the roof, I tried again. "Zel, I have an idea for a way for us to make more money without attracting attention to the bakery. Trust me, I care about protecting you and the bakery too. Haven't I proven that over the years?"

Zel's silence was broken only by the distant sound of laughter from the tavern down the street and the twins' forks clanking against their plates. The days had grown hotter and the kitchen was too warm by evening, so we'd taken to eating dinner on the roof. The dark, cloudy night was lit by the small luminous lamp on the table, which provided enough light for me to see the frustration on Zel's face. Had she honestly thought I would drop the matter?

She crossed her arms and glanced from me to Weslan. They exchanged a look I couldn't interpret, and then she looked back at me. Finally, she spoke. "So what's your idea?" Her voice dripped with skepticism.

"What if we set up a market stall in a different quarter? One where people don't know us? That way, no matter what we do, it won't draw any attention to the bakery."

"What market? Ferus Lane Market is the only one nearby."

I took a deep breath. This was my chance. "I know you're not going to like this, but please, consider it. I heard from Gregor just yesterday. They're reopening the market on Theros Street."

Bri gasped, and Zel frowned. "They would never—"

"They are. I suppose they decided that it's time to move on." Weslan looked confused, so I elaborated. "Theros Street Market was the site of the Crimson Blight's first major attack two years ago. A lot of people died, and they never reopened it after the attack. But if they're reopening it now, it must mean that it's safe now, right?"

Weslan rolled his shoulders, an odd look coming over his face. Would he want to back out now?

Zel shook her head. "I don't know. And even if it were safe, I don't think we can afford it. You'd spend any profits from your baking just paying the rent on the stall, and you'd have even less time to take care of the bakery. You know I want you to have a chance to do something outside of the bakery. But is now really the right time to take a risk like this?"

"But that's just it," I said. "The rates are low because they're trying to get people back into the market. This could be the perfect time for us to pick up a lease." Zel was silent, and I seized the chance to press my case. "We can figure something out. I just feel like this is something that I need to do. I'm smart, right?"

Zel looked surprised at the subject change, but smiled softly. "Yes, of course. I've always said you're smart."

Weslan and the twins stayed quiet, watching us talk.

"Well, I thought I was. I thought I had a future. But it turns out that I don't." I hadn't meant for the words to sound so bitter. "Can't you let me use my mind for something else? I tested my idea this morning, and it worked! This could be a way for us to make money and to pay off Cyrus before he takes things any further. We could hire help for the bakery. We could eat real food every day, not only once in a while. Everything I was going to do with a government job, I could do with this. But you have to let me try."

Zel shook her head. "It's not that I don't think you're smart or that I don't believe in you. It's not that I don't want you to use your mind and try to build a real future. Of course, I do. I love you. You have to believe that."

"I do, but—"

"Listen, it's just not safe. Even if you weren't being targeted by Cyrus, what if the Blight comes back and hits the same market again because they don't want it reopening?"

Alba's fork clattered as she dropped it on her plate, and Weslan shifted in his seat as though suddenly uncomfortable. Could Zel be right?

I hated to admit it, but that sounded like exactly the kind of thing the Blight would do. "That may be true. But we can't live in fear forever, right? Like you said, nothing is safe in the city anymore. I was attacked at my own school, in a classroom of all places. Cyrus threatened me at our own neighborhood market. Those are the two places I should've been safest besides the bakery."

The man with the face of blood flashed before my eyes again and a strange wave of dizziness overtook me for a moment. I shook it off. "At some point, we must try something new, right? Because what we've been doing isn't working. Cyrus is proof enough of that. And maybe they'll have better security, since it's just reopening. I'm sure everyone will have the same questions about safety that we do."

"I think Ella's right," Weslan said, interjecting for the first time. A flutter of excitement warmed me at his words. He was with me after all.

"If this is the first time it's opened since the original attack," he said, "I bet security will be better than that at any other market in the area. They won't want it to happen again."

Zel glared at him, but the look on Zel's face said she knew she was losing. An air of resignation settled around her.

I pressed forward. "The fact remains—the only way to stop Cyrus is to make more money. Now, we can wait until the ball to see if we get more orders. But it didn't happen before the last ball. I remember that clearly enough." I stood and started clearing the dishes. "I think my idea gives us a good chance. We'll have to sell less from the bakery to focus on the market stand, and yes, I know that's risky. But everything we do is risky, isn't it? And I think that this plan has the best chance of success."

"Fine." Zel leaned back in her chair.

I took a deep breath and exhaled slowly. She'd agreed. She might not like my plan, but she'd go along with it. The moment didn't quite feel like victory, but at least it wasn't defeat.

Alba and Bri looked at me like I'd grown another head. I'd never opposed Zel so strongly before, but I wanted to do this. I *needed* to do this. As much as Zel wanted to protect me, she couldn't leave the house without the chance of getting caught by trackers, so there was only so much she could do.

Weslan lifted the tray of dirty dishes, and left the roof. I followed close behind.

Every night, the nightmare man haunted my dreams and half of my waking moments too. But if I could do this, I'd be taking control again, proving to myself that my nightmares hadn't won. I wouldn't live in fear forever, and I wouldn't let it stop me from protecting my family or from seeking out a real future. I had to try.

With Weslan working with me, we had a chance to do something that we never would've been able to do before. In fact, I didn't know any other merchants who worked with a mage in their shop. Perhaps mages helped in the kitchen in some Procus households, but I didn't think so. The Procus families were far more likely to have mages use their powers on objects directly. Why wouldn't they?

Procus families had basically unlimited access to fuel and resources. They didn't need tools or replacements for cheap, rationed cinderslick like we did. They had all the high quality cinderslick they could ever want. But this was something new. We could do something different. And deep down, under the fear and exhaustion and worry, I was absolutely thrilled about the prospect.

The next evening, however, my excitement turned to frustration.

"Come on, tell me. What else do we need?"

I slumped at the table while Weslan paced in front of me, waving a notepad and pencil in the air. What had I been thinking? There was no way we could afford this.

"Well, each batch takes a pound of butter, a half-pound of flour, a quarter-pound of sugar. Oh, and winterdrops. That's what makes the cake smell so good. For different flavors like roseberry or lemonburst, we'll need different essences. Those can be expensive."

He paused from his furious scribbling and chewed the end of the pencil. "Let's see ... butter goes for three marks per pound. Flour goes for one mark per pound. I can't believe I know that now, by the way." He looked at me with an expression of mock-despair on his face.

I rolled my eyes.

He grinned. "Kidding, kidding …" He continued scribbling and muttering to himself, but then he stopped.

I lifted my head from where I had rested it on my elbow. "What?"

He ran his hand through his hair. "I don't think we can do this after all."

Chapter 10

Weslan tapped the pad of paper with his pencil. "Essences and spices. We have money for all the basic ingredients, but there's no way we can purchase the special flavorings too."

Darkness had fallen, and Zel and the twins were upstairs, getting ready for bed. The silence in the bakery added to the tension in the kitchen. I rubbed my forehead. "Spices. Spices." How could we afford spices *and* the rental for a market stall?

We needed help. There was only one possible solution.

After Weslan and I finished adding up all that we would need for the new bakery stand, I made my way down the street to Gregor's shop. I knocked on the door, sweating even in the cooler, evening air. Even from outside, the rich scent of spices, sugar, and wheat emanated from his shop.

Gregor opened the door a crack and then hurried me in with a broad smile. He locked the door behind me. "Ella!" His jovial mood was at odds with his behavior. "What can I get you?"

I remembered the day Gregor's wife, Calista, was taken by the plague. She was one of the first to die on our little lane. Before she took ill, Gregor and Calista were always at our bakery, sharing meals and gossip, talking late into the night with my father about mages and equality and other speculations too deep for a child to understand. Gregor and Calista were petite, wiry, and dark-skinned. Their dark brown hair was dusted with strands of white. Older than my parents, they were always full of energy. Joy radiated from them, enveloping everyone they met.

Back then, Gregor brought me little trinkets from the other cities, gifts from his trading contacts. When the plague came from the West, we had to burn everything from there, by royal decree, to destroy the imported goods that had carried the plague into the city. No one could take any chances. I threw the trinkets into the raging bonfire in the middle of the street, too scared and overwhelmed to cry. The fire that night smelled of burnt spiceberries and winterdrops—the scent of Gregor's imported inventory going up in flames.

In the first few days of the plague, Gregor lost his wife, his riches, and his livelihood. We were all he had left. Not long afterward, my father died, and the same was true for me.

I looked around his shop, wondering why it felt different. It was much darker than usual. "What's that on your windows?"

Gregor shrugged. "Some men from the tavern got a little rowdy the other night. They're all broken, but it's fine. I had these boards handy already."

The shutters closed on the other side, so I hadn't noticed. "Gregor ..."

He shook his head. "Don't worry, Ella. They'll lose interest eventually and find someone else to pick on. For now, who needs bright front windows in this hot weather? I've got the back door open for a breeze. This way, my place stays cool." I smiled at him, unable to resist his kind face for a moment, and then I felt the smile drop from my face.

"What's wrong, Ella dear? They giving you a hard time at the bakery too? Need any help patching things up?"

"Actually …" I told him about our idea for the bakery stand at Theros Street Market. "But we don't have the capital to buy the ingredients and get started."

Gregor beamed and clapped his hands together. "Say no more, Ella girl!" He rubbed his palms together. "How's this? I'll give you the ingredients for now, and you can pay me back once you've started to turn a profit."

My mouth dropped open. I'd been hoping for a small discount. "Gregor, no! That's far too—"

"It's exactly what you deserve, and you know it. If you hadn't take a chance on me when the trade routes reopened, I'd have no ingredients to sell today." He slapped a hand on the counter beside him. "You give me your list, and I'll see to it by tomorrow night. And no more arguing. Understood?"

"Y-yes," I said haltingly, swallowing against the lump in my throat.

"Ah, none of that," he said, wrapping one warm arm around my shoulders. "I believe in you, Ella. Always have. Let me do right by you."

~

"Don't argue now," Weslan said, "but I have an idea for how we can draw a crowd of customers at the market." He'd been in a good mood ever since I got back from Gregor's with the news.

"Fine, what's your idea?" The thought of a large crowd pressing around us made me uncomfortable. But the chance to get Inspector Cyrus off our backs was worth a bit of discomfort, right? It wasn't as though I was used to living in comfort.

He shook his head. "I can't tell you."

"What? What are you talking about?"

"I can't tell you, because if you knew, you'd never let me do it."

I gritted my teeth. "You have to tell me. We're in this together."

"I know, but there are some things that we need to do that you're not going to like. Plus, it'll work a lot better if you don't know ahead of time. Just trust me."

"Fine." I glowered at him. "Just tell me one thing. Is it illegal?"

"I don't think so, although we don't have a great track record where that's concerned."

I had to laugh. "Is it going to hurt?"

"No! 'Course not. What do you take me for? Listen, Ella"—he put his hands on my shoulders and looked into my eyes—"Do you trust me?"

I nearly stopped breathing. I would've agreed to anything at that point, but the honest answer was yes. Somehow, after everything, I had indeed come to trust him. I nodded. "Whatever you want to do, I'm in."

After making plans to wake earlier than usual the next morning to bake our small cakes for the market, we called it a night. I spent the nighttime hours chasing after the nightmare man and seeing scraps of red every time I opened my eyes. By the time morning came, I was only too happy to give up on sleep and get out of bed.

Weslan grinned as I entered the kitchen. "Today's the day." He looked fresh and energetic, clothed in floury slacks and a white button-down with the sleeves rolled up.

I dragged my tired gaze away from the corded muscles in his arms. "It sure is." I couldn't hold back a smile. The Theros Street Market opened today, and we were finally launching our bakery stall.

We baked and frosted the cakes, and Weslan hummed cheerfully the whole time. When we stood back to look at the finished cakes, I nearly wept.

The small golden cakes sat in neat rows, covering the entire surface of the kitchen table. Each cake dripped with billowy, light gold winterdrop frosting that sparkled with golden light that Weslan had added with a flourish as the finishing touch.

I wanted to eat one for breakfast, but they were almost too pretty to eat. Besides, eating the cakes would be like eating money. The very thought gave me a stomachache.

We loaded them carefully onto covered plates and carried them into the alley where we stacked them on the hand cart we'd borrowed from Gregor.

Weslan stepped back and dusted his hands. "I need you to do one thing. And remember that you trust me."

I raised my eyebrows.

"Go upstairs," he said, "and ask Zel if you can borrow a long black dress and some black slippers."

"What?" I gaped at him.

"A long black dress and slippers." Humor glinted in his eyes.

"I heard you the first time." I batted him on the arm. "I mean, what's wrong with this?" I gestured to my worn work dress and immediately regretted the question as I looked down at the threadbare skirt.

"Just trust me."

"Her clothes won't fit me. I'm going to look ridiculous and—"

"Just trust me? You promised."

I resisted the urge to roll my eyes. He was taking this so seriously. Then again, he hadn't had much to be excited about lately. Perhaps I should go along with it, just to encourage him.

Zel smiled knowingly when I made my request, and then she handed over a long dress and a pair of slippers. They didn't fit me in the slightest. Sure enough, I looked ridiculous in them. I wasn't even sure how I would make it to the market without tripping over myself.

When I came downstairs, Weslan nodded resolutely. "Perfect. Let's go."

Theros Street Market was in the Common Quarter, crammed in to an alley between a secondary academy and a tall apartment building. We made our way to the back entrance, looking around with wide eyes as we walked to our rented stand.

The market buzzed with noise even this early in the morning as vendors chatted with their neighbors and called greetings to friends from across the market. Dawn's light colored the sky a gentle, pale blue. Fresh white canopies covered each stall. We'd no doubt be grateful for them when the summer sun reached its peak later that day.

When we reached our stall, we transferred our trays to the rough wooden counter that came with our market stand. But I looked around dubiously. We were way back toward the end of the alley, where rents had been cheapest. Our nearest neighbor was a watch repairman, and beside him, an elderly lady set out dusty, frayed wigs. "All the other food merchants are at the front," I said.

A bell rang, interrupting my spiraling thoughts. The market was open for business.

A trickle of students, clerks, and other early-rising shoppers entered the market. As I had suspected, none of them even glanced toward our end of the market. What had we been thinking? This was the cheapest stall for a reason. After all our work and Gregor's investment, my idea would come to nothing. How would I ever pay Gregor back?

Weslan grabbed me by the hand. "Come this way." He pulled me around the booth and pushed me to stand right in front of it. "Stay there. And whatever you do, don't move, don't argue, and don't scowl like that."

"Like what?"

"You know exactly what I mean."

I rolled my eyes but tried to achieve a kinder expression. Weslan stood beside me, facing the crowds that now clustered near the market entrance.

He ignored my questioning look. Suddenly, he shouted, "Let me tell you a tragic story! The story of the beautiful maiden called Cinderella."

My skin tingled all over, and my face grew hot. I couldn't believe my ears. What was he thinking? This city hated me! The last thing we should do was call attention to me!

I reached out to grab his arm and somehow stop him from speaking, but he pushed my hand down and gave me a sidelong look. "Remember your promise?" He whispered. "Trust me."

A few people looked our way, but they did not approach. This was so awkward.

Weslan raised his voice even louder. "Let me tell you the story of Cinderella, the poor orphan girl who lost her father in the plague at a young age and was treated as a kitchen servant by her stepmother for years."

A few people gave me sympathetic smiles, and I fought the urge to glower at them.

Weslan made things worse. "Poor Cinderella. All she ever dreamed of was escaping to a better life. Through sheer hard work and determination, she got a coveted scholarship to the Royal Academy. Early every morning she woke up to cook and clean for her stepmother, and late into the night she studied her books. She excelled in her schoolwork and surpassed the privileged Procus students at her school."

I cringed. Did he not know about all the people who hated me for winning that scholarship instead of staying in my assigned place in the Merchant Quarter? For openly purchasing imported ingredients after the plague instead of pretending to use Asylian goods like everyone else?

A few people in the crowd drew closer, curious expressions on their faces.

My chest tightened. What would happen when the crowd turned on us?

Weslan continued his tale. "As I said, all poor Cinderella ever wanted was to escape to a better life. But what did she get for her dreams? The cruel monster known as the Crimson Blight attacked her at her own school, leaving her scarred and nearly dead." He gestured to my face, and a few people gasped. Others nodded their heads knowingly.

I clenched my fist to stop from covering my scars. I supposed a lot of people knew about the attack on my school.

"First, the Crimson Blight attacked her school, destroying her chance to graduate and scarring her face. Then, the government healers refused to heal her scars because she couldn't pay."

A few people booed at his words, and the crowd drew closer. Weslan straightened his shoulders, and I watched, fascinated despite my misgivings, as he stepped even further into the role of charismatic storyteller. "We won't speak of the heartless education ministry bureaucrats who denied her graduation certificate, or the admissions officers who refused her entry into a new school even though she had been a model student and was with within days of graduation."

The crowd stirred angrily.

"Poor, ill-treated Cinderella was trapped. Trapped in the kitchen, forced to sleep in front of the oven to stay warm at night, forced to spend her days smelling of cinderslick and her nights sleeping on the hard kitchen floor. Forced to wear her stepmother's discarded hand-me-down rags, long dresses that didn't even fit."

The audience took in my ugly black dress with evident pity.

I didn't look that bad, did I? More people joined the crowd.

"And yet, beneath Cinderella's humble, tragic exterior ..."

I cringed. Tragic exterior? I didn't like the way this was going at all.

"Beneath her tragic exterior, there is a hidden beauty and intelligence that no one could guess."

No one could guess?

He had been right not to tell me he was going to do this. But I'd be vindicated when the crowd soured on us as they always did. This city hated me.

"Then one day, Cinderella made the acquaintance of a mage with the power to change everything." He gestured comically at himself and took a dramatic bow, drawing giggles from the girls in the crowd. Their attention shifted from me to Weslan—the handsome, broad-shouldered, confident Kireth mage who clearly didn't belong next to me.

I braced myself against the burning desire to pick up this obnoxious black skirt and run from the market.

"Cinderella decided that she was done hiding, done being trapped. She would no longer hide her beauty or her intelligence behind her scars and scruffy rags. She would reveal them to the world. Beginning right here. At this market. Right now."

The crowd shifted as one, moving even closer to us.

I kept my eyes straight ahead, and tried not to make eye contact with anyone. I was going to kill Weslan. Then a warm cloud of shimmering, golden sparkles swirled around me.

Chapter 11

The sparkles vanished, and the crowd gasped.

The plain black cloth of my dress had been transformed into an extravagant pale blue ballgown. Voluminous skirts stretched out around me like a sparkling silk waterfall, and I fingered the fabric with one white-gloved hand, stunned by the way the dress shone and shimmered. Tiny crystals were embedded throughout the fabric, so small you could barely see the individual crystals, making the dress appear to glow in the early morning light. Long, white gloves covered my hands and arms to well above my elbows. I reached up to feel my hair. I'd have given anything for a mirror. My hair had been twisted into a high bun with some sort of headpiece on top of my head.

I forgot the crowd for a moment as I stared at Weslan. I had no idea he was so powerful, so talented. What had the Mage Division been thinking when they kicked him out?

He stared back at me with a matching look of awe upon his face. His gaze darted up and down my body, and when he met my eyes again, his face was lit with unmistakable longing.

I opened my mouth to speak, but he only cleared his throat, bowed to the crowd, and gestured toward the table with our covered cake trays.

The crowd gave a shout of delight and surged forward.

I twisted around carefully, afraid to move too quickly in the extravagant gown, just in time to see another cloud of shimmering gold dissipate over the table. The covers on the trays became as transparent as glass, revealing our gold-frosted winterdrop cakes beneath. The crowd let out another shout, and I froze, unsure of what to do as the people pressed in around me.

Weslan removed the cover from the first plate and handed it to me.

I took it numbly, and turned back to the crowd. "One quarter mark each," I croaked.

Like a whirlwind, people yanked the little cakes off the plate and shoved their marks into the money purse that Weslan held up beside me.

I held the plate as curious faces appeared before me and snatched up the cakes, giving me brilliant, crumb-filled smiles after they popped them into their mouths.

~

We sold out in less than an hour. No one here seemed to care who I was. Perhaps the people in the Common Quarter were kinder than those in the Merchant Quarter. Or perhaps the presence of a handsome mage and dozens of magically frosted cakes put everyone on their best behavior.

Whenever someone stared at my glorious pale blue gown or looked me up and down with a smile, I felt like a princess. But inevitably, I would see the pity and mockery in another person's eyes, and I would transform from a princess to an imposter. A joke. Even if they had no idea who Cinderella was—even if they'd never heard of me or our bakery—they must think I was the city's biggest fool, standing here in a Procus lady's dress like a child playing dress-up.

When the last treat sold, the stream of customers left our little back corner of the market, and we were alone.

"Oh, Weslan," I said hesitantly, "Don't you need to do something about this?" I gestured at my dress.

"Oh. Right." He glanced at me with bloodshot eyes and waved a tired hand in my direction. The blue dress disappeared, leaving the worn black dress in its place. It was like being doused with a bucket of cold water.

I glanced at Weslan as I put the last tray in the cart, expecting him to be jubilant with his success, but his face was haggard and downcast. Huge bags had appeared under his eyes, and his shoulders drooped. He didn't seem to have enough energy to pack up the trays.

"Do you want me to help?"

"No," he said gruffly. "I've got this."

I rubbed my upper arms. What was his problem?

We walked back to the bakery in silence, and what should've been a walk of joy and victory was tense with frustration and awkwardness. Weslan was strangely exhausted, but he wouldn't let me help.

I was hurt and humiliated, sweating, and uncomfortable in that horrible black dress. As soon as the cart was unloaded, I mumbled an excuse about returning Zel's dress and raced upstairs to her room, leaving Weslan in the kitchen. The normally comforting smells of winterdrop soap and old books welcomed me like a warm embrace, but instead of calming me, the familiar scents heightened my frustration. This home wasn't an oasis anymore. It was a prison—one I'd never escape, thanks to the Blight.

I found the work dress I'd left on Zel's bed that morning and changed into it. Zel came down from the roof, then, and I tried to keep my face neutral.

The moment she saw me, she crossed the room, her eyebrows furrowed. "What happened? Did something happen at the market?"

"It was great," I said, trying to smile. "Sold out of everything a little while ago. They loved everything that we made, and we … we drew a huge crowd."

"Oh, no." Zel's voice was hard. "Did they harm you?"

I nearly laughed when I saw her fists clench. Was she going to go out and threaten everyone who mocked me now? "No. The crowd was fine. It was …"

She leaned back. "It was the dress, wasn't it? The mages in Draicia worked the same way. As long as they had some plain black fabric to work with, they could create the most beautiful dresses. I figured Weslan was going to do something at your stand to draw in customers."

I twisted the tattered hem of my work dress, now more tattered than ever. "He did. But … I … I don't really know what to say. It was so humiliating. It felt like he made a spectacle of me, of my life. He made it all more painful. And the dress! He gave me a taste of what I'll never have and showed the whole world just how pathetic I am." I scowled at the floor. "No matter how much money we make, I'll never be more than the kitchen girl." My voice broke on the last word.

I'd always hoped for so much more, but everything had been taken for me. For the first time, it occurred to me that not even money could bring me the status that I would've had if I had graduated from the Royal Academy and found a government job.

Was that what I had wanted all along?

I'd told myself the Royal Academy scholarship was simply part of my plan to support Zel and the twins, but what if it was more about me?

Zel patted my hand. "I understand what you're saying, but I think you need to take a step back."

I frowned at her. Why did she always have to take his side?

She didn't give an inch. "What Weslan did was more than just put a pretty dress on you."

I pulled away and sat at her dressing table, which was neat and bare except for an old comb and three crooked hairpins. I avoided my own image in the mirror and kept my eyes on the worn table instead. She came and stood beside me. "How did the crowd respond? Did they like it?"

"It was a spectacle. Of course, they liked it. These are the same people who gather around fomecoach accidents for entertainment."

"I have a feeling it was more than that. The common people in Asylia have almost no experience with magic. You didn't ... other than using mage-crafted rations to provide for us or taking the occasional harrowing ride on the trolley."

I smiled despite myself and met her eyes in the mirror. "That thing is a death trap."

Zel smiled back. "It is. You gave common people a chance to experience a beautiful taste of magic themselves—at their very own market. That's so much more than a simple treat. You gave them a chance to touch magic, to enjoy it for themselves, not for survival but for luxury. When Weslan used his magic on you, maybe it was just part of the experience. It wasn't about you. He did it to let them experience magic in a new way."

I remembered our customers' wide smiles and the way they'd admired my shimmering skirt. I hated to agree with Zel's statement. "But it hurt," I said hoarsely. "I'm not saying it's about me—"

I cut my protest short and grimaced. I *had* been thinking only of myself.

"I just ... I'm still so mad." The stream of words let loose, and I couldn't have stopped the torrent if I had tried. "I'm so angry, Zel. I was so close to a real future, and it all got taken away for no reason. And I just ... I'm furious, all the time, and I can't stop it. And I hate being reminded of everything that I lost. I mean, I already know what I've lost. Trust me, I know. I don't need the reminders," I finished under my breath.

And then another thought occurred to me. "Besides, won't Weslan get in trouble for using his powers in public? There's a reason they don't let mages roam free, right?"

I looked at Zel when she didn't speak. Of course, no one knew what I was feeling better than Zel herself. She had lost everything too. From the day her Touch had been discovered, she'd never known a moment of true peace or safety. And she never would.

She gave my shoulder a gentle squeeze before sitting on the side of her bed nearby. "First, don't worry about Weslan. If the government thought his powers were a threat to the city order, they never would have let him go. He told you everything, didn't he? He caused a lot of trouble, but he didn't break any laws. They couldn't keep him, but they couldn't imprison him either. I doubt the Asylian government will care if he shows off a bit for a few commoners in a tiny market in the Common Quarter.

"And second, I want you to try something. Find one thing that you can enjoy in this. You may not like being the center of attention, and you may not like being reminded of what you've lost. But if you can find one thing to enjoy and focus on that one thing, you'll survive this."

What could I find to enjoy about being a spectacle?

"Sweetheart, thanks to your courage, we have a chance to pay the taxes and get out of this impossible situation. Do you see what an incredible miracle that is? I used to think I was all alone in the world. That I couldn't trust anyone to look out for me. And then I met you and your father. You've worked tirelessly to help me and the twins and sacrificed so much for us. You've inspired me. You'll never know how much."

I bit my lip. I had never expected that.

Zel continued her speech. "And seeing you use your intelligence and try your hand at something new, something I'm not sure has ever been done before, even when you feel like you've lost your future ... It's a beautiful thing. An inspiring thing. And it's nothing to be ashamed of or embarrassed about. So can you do that? Can you find one thing to enjoy in this?"

"Besides the money?" I asked, but I could feel the corner of my mouth creeping up in a half smile.

Zel laughed. "Besides the money."

"I'll try."

~

Moments later, I found Weslan seated at the kitchen table. I opened my mouth to speak, but I held back my words when I got a close look at him. His head rested on his hands, and his eyelids drooped so much they were nearly shut. I'd never seen him so exhausted. I approached him hesitantly, remembering his terse demeanor on the way home. "Weslan, what's wrong?"

"I'm fine," he said, not bothering to lift his head from his hands. "I'm just hungry."

"Do you want me to cook you something?" We hadn't eaten yet.

He shook his head. "I'm just going to eat some of that victus in a minute." The canister of victus was sitting out with the lid off beside a pitcher of water.

"But we have enough money now—"

"I'm fine. That money is for the tax. I don't want to waste it on fresh food when I have victus to eat."

"I suppose …" I trailed off. It wasn't as though he were asking my permission. It hurt when he brushed me off so harshly, but he didn't seem to notice. I puttered around in the kitchen, eyeing him for any clue as to what was going on.

Eventually, he got up and mixed up a bowl of victus and water. He shoveled it down, and then we dragged ourselves through the motions of cleaning the kitchen and preparing the next day's work.

I tried several times to tell him to go rest, but every time I broached the subject, he shook his head and ignored me.

Finally, I gave up. I did as much of his part of the work as he would let me. Spending the morning at the market had put us far behind in the rest of our work.

I finished drying the last dish and put it away. I was about to ask Weslan about the plan for tomorrow, but there he was, asleep on his pallet in front of the hearth. Somehow, he had slept through the noise of me putting the dishes away. He looked practically dead, but I leaned close enough to see his chest rising and falling in tiny motions. He slept through dinner too.

At last, I shut off the luminous dial in the kitchen and went to bed early as well. I supposed we were both tired. That had to be it, right?

~

"So was it more like this one or this one?"

Alba and I sprawled on her narrow bed, poring over the fashion pages of the *Herald*. I pointed to the feathery one. "This one. But with a better shape. Light pink and not so fluffy."

"Wow." Alba stroked the dress on the page and fell silent. Each day, after we came home from the market and had a chance to clean up, she dragged me upstairs to pepper me with questions about the dress. My chest ached each time because she never said what I knew she was thinking— she would give anything to be at the market with me. If there had been a chance that she could go and not get caught, I would have happily traded places with her.

As the days passed, Weslan shortened the story and added less embellishment. But I still had to remind myself not to clench my fists and scowl at him.

Each morning, the crowd devoured the story and the cakes, admiring my magical transformation with gaping mouths and shouts of delight. A few brave children, particularly the girls, crept close enough to stroke my dresses.

Such glorious dresses! In the week since our stall had opened, Weslan had conjured a stunning array of designs—a sparkling, golden gown that flowed around me like a bell, a yellow dress so light and airy it could have been made from butterflower petals, and today's dress—my favorite so far—a pink, feathery creation that should have been utterly frivolous. Instead, it was perfect, swirling about my hips as though I'd been born to wear it.

Weslan's creations were extravagant and luxurious, but they were also soft and beautiful. I didn't find them obnoxious or silly the way I usually viewed Procus fashions. His work was different, somehow. Better. More beautiful and more comfortable all at once. The gowns were like nothing I'd ever seen before. None of the Procus ladies who paraded around in their fomecoaches ever wore anything as gorgeous as my dresses. Weslan had real talent. No doubt, Mage Division wouldn't have let him go so easily if they'd known he was so good. Yet another thing to worry about.

I'd promised Zel I'd try to find one thing in this whole mess that I could enjoy. It turned out that I loved Cinderella's magical dresses.

Our stand was a runaway success all week. New people came to Theros Street Market for the first time because they'd heard about our cakes, and we had to buy new ingredients from Gregor each day. By the time our first week at the market was over, we had nearly enough marks to pay off our merchant tax.

But Weslan was grouchy and irritable, and it seemed to me that the only time he was happy and animated was when he was giving his morning performance.

Every afternoon, he struggled through his chores, exhausted and silent, but he wouldn't accept help. Downright pitiful. He was also ravenously hungry, but he wouldn't let me cook anything for him using our profits. He insisted on eating cold victus, bowls and bowls of it. It was free and didn't use up our rations cards, so it didn't matter how much he ate. But I knew the victus tasted horrible.

Alba and I flipped through several more pages of the *Herald* and I answered her questions as best I could, forcing myself to be patient. Her hunger for the outside world made my head hurt. If only she knew what an ugly city we lived in. But the *Herald* itself was one of the few bright spots.

The *Herald*'s ancient printing press was built from imported parts after we discovered the Western cities across the desert plains, before our mages learned how to replicate Western inventions. The old press was all noise and grease, while the mage-crafts were clean and silent, powered by invisible magic. Since the *Herald* didn't need any mages or Procus money to operate, it had been the only newspaper to keep printing even during the plague. Some days, they'd printed nothing but long lists of names—the names of the dead, the names of the families that survived them.

Five years ago, they'd printed that ill-advised story on me, "Ariella Stone: First Commoner to Win Royal Academy Scholarship." I grimaced at the memory. If I'd known it would make me the most despised thirteen-year-old in the city, I never would have gone along with the interview. The old woman who had interviewed me had kindly, wrinkled eyes and callused, ink-marked fingers. She probably hadn't expected that her beloved Asylia would hate an ambitious common girl quite so much.

Finally, I patted Alba on the back and dragged myself off the bed. "I've got to go prep for tomorrow," I said, stretching. "Have a good night."

I marched downstairs with one mission in mind—I had to confront Weslan, surliness or not. I took my chance while we washed the dishes. He kept fumbling with the pans and utensils, but when he nearly dropped one of our plates, I'd had it. "Enough." I grabbed the plate from his hands and plunked it on the counter. "Sit down before you fall down."

He plopped down at the kitchen table without a word of protest. Maybe he really had been about to fall. His eyes were bleary and bloodshot even though he had been sleeping at least ten hours a night the past week.

"What is going on? Have you been drinking? Is it ... aurae? You can tell me anything, Weslan. I won't get mad. I just need to know what's happening. I want to help." I plopped down in the seat across from him and watched his face for any sort of reaction.

He shook his head and attempted a smile. "It's not like that. It's nothing so terrible or dramatic."

I smiled back in what I hoped was an encouraging manner. "What's going on?"

"Really, it's not a big deal at all. It's just ..." He seemed reluctant to continue.

"It's what? Just tell me already!"

"I've never used my magic so much in my life. Every morning, I do the oven and the frosting, and later, I do that whole trick to draw crowds and ..." He didn't finish the thought.

"You make me pretty?" I grinned, hoping to get a real smile out of him.

He shook his head, his eyes glinting with humor for a moment. "Oh, you're already pretty."

I ducked my head. Must be the exhaustion speaking.

"Here's the thing," he said. "In my school days, I did everything I could to avoid working. I used my magic for pranks and did the bare minimum to pass my classes. That means I was only using my magic once a day or even every couple of days. When I started working for my patron, my only job was to dress the patron's granddaughter. I only did one thing at a time—the bodice, the skirt, the shoes, the hair. Simple. Easy. She just wanted to look good, and she didn't care how long it took or whether I did it with any flair or drama."

He shrugged. "But I wanted to attract a crowd for you, and I wanted to give the crowds a chance to experience the magic for themselves."

So Zel had been right. How had he known to try something like that? I never would have thought of something like that, not in a million years.

"So I tried to do it all at once. I'd never done that before. I didn't even know if I could that first day."

My eyes widened. "You didn't know? What if something had gone wrong?"

He grinned. "Don't worry. It would've worked out. The important thing is, I did it. I've been doing things all week that I never thought I had the power to do. And I think I'm so tired and hungry all the time because my power is growing."

I'd never suspected a mage's power could grow. At school, we were taught that all mages had a fixed absorbent or expellant capacity that determined their classification, like a bucket of a certain size that could empty or fill but never more than its inherent volume.

"I think it's like a muscle," Weslan said. "The more I use it—well, the heavier I lift with it, so to speak—the stronger it gets. But my body needs to refuel. I need lots of sleep and food, apparently. I'm sure it will get better once I reach my actual, innate expellant capacity. It turns out that I don't know what that capacity is." He rubbed his knee. "It's pretty embarrassing."

"No! Don't be embarrassed. I think you're amazing, Weslan."

He raised an eyebrow.

I forged ahead, hoping he wouldn't dwell on my slip-up. "I mean, I think what you're able to do is amazing. I didn't even know you could increase your magic ability."

"I can't," he said. "At least, I've never heard of this happening before. They certainly didn't teach us to strengthen our magic ability this way at school." He frowned at the table, running his hands along the wood grain for a moment. "In fact, I wonder what the Mage Division would do if they knew I was getting stronger. The only reason they blacklisted me was because they thought I was more trouble than my talent was worth. But if I can do more …"

It made sense. It also made me nervous. If they found out that Weslan was stronger than they'd thought, they probably wouldn't hesitate to press him back into service again. And what would they do if they ever discovered he'd shared his True Name with me?

"Don't look like that. I'm sure it will be fine."

I was pretty sure it would not be fine.

"Really, this is a good thing. I've always wanted to be a stronger mage. I'm finally getting what I wanted, and I'm paying the price now. But I doubt anyone will ever find out."

Chapter 12

But Weslan's magic kept growing. My dresses grew increasingly extravagant, and the cakes grew more dazzling. The daily work of baking and frosting accelerated. Weslan's confidence returned, and he wore a smile most of the day, flirting and laughing with girls at the market, shining with light and confidence. He was too bright to stay in our dark, ugly corner of Asylia for long.

Yet here we were, broiling in the hot morning sun, selling cakes to Asylia's lowliest, most despised citizens.

I wanted to be happy for him. I did. He was very talented, and it wasn't fair that he'd been blacklisted for doing something that no doubt many mages had done. But every time he smiled or squared his wide shoulders, I was reminded that he didn't belong with us. He shouldn't be here, laboring all day with a scarred, angry commoner like me. From the way he occasionally watched me, a strange look on his face, I had to wonder if he felt the same way.

He was so powerful and skilled. Did it chafe him to waste his powers serving lowly commoners? Did he long to be recognized by his own kind, to be welcomed home by his friends and family the way he should be?

I finished selling a cake to a young man in a school uniform. Someone screamed, raising the hairs on the back of my neck. I craned my neck to see what was happening. Why was everyone running in different directions?

Men in black clothing and red masks poured into the market. My nightmare held my legs in an invisible grip. My blood pounded in my ears like a drum. The Blight was here. At the market. I couldn't think. I couldn't scream.

Then I was on my belly, my face pressed into the rough ground, and Weslan's weight pressed into my back as he covered my head with his arms. "Don't move," he whispered.

His weight crushed the air from my lungs, but I didn't move. I was too scared to move.

He held me close forever, the longest moments of my life. I tried to focus on his warm breath by my ear, the safe feeling of his heavy weight on my back, and the feel of his heartbeat as his chest pressed against me. We were both alive … for now. I held on to that feeling.

"Don't move," he whispered again.

I hadn't planned on it. What had happened to everyone? Why couldn't I hear anyone screaming?

A pair of boots entered my line of sight and crunched closer. "Do you see them?" A man's voice. The Blight. They would see us any second now.

"No," said another man. "They must've split. There's a second exit back here."

Crash! Glass shattered above our heads. Something sharp hit my cheek, and I held back a yelp of pain. If they hadn't see us yet, I wasn't going to be the one to give our position away. It sounded like one of our display stands had been destroyed.

More glass shattered. The polished black boots stopped three inches from my nose. They were right next to us. How did they not see us? Then the boots crunched away from us.

The market was eerily quiet for a moment, as though holding its breath. Weslan didn't move and neither did I. Had they truly left?

And then the Quarter Guards' loud whistles split the air, and then screams and sobs filled my ears. The people around us were begging for help and healing. Weslan released me, and we stood up together.

"What just happened?"

Weslan didn't answer, so I looked his way. Oh, no. He was covered in blood and looked gray in the face, more exhausted than I had ever seen him. His eyes were shut, and he swayed on his feet. "Weslan." I searched his body for wounds. "What happened? What's wrong?"

He opened his eyes a crack. His words slurred together. "I think they were after us. Me. They don't ... they don't like what we're doing."

Had this disaster been our fault? Had the Crimson Blight attacked Theros Street Market for the second time, all because of us? My stomach turned sour. I pressed my eyes closed for a moment and waited for the wave of nausea to lessen. "What happened to you?"

"Just glass. I'm fine." He held his arm and showed me where shards of glass from our table displays had hit his arm. The bleeding had already stopped.

"Then why do you look so awful?"

He put a hand on my shoulder to brace himself. "Used too much magic. I made it ... hide us ... so they couldn't see us." His voice was a whisper.

I'd never heard of such a thing. "You can do that?"

"Apparently." We stared at each other wordlessly, both of us covered in small shards of glass and spatters of blood.

I didn't know what to say. He had saved my life, utterly and completely. There were no words that could ever be enough. I wrapped my arms around him, drawing as close as I physically could, and buried my face in his shoulder. I couldn't get close enough. His warm skin felt so alive, so precious. I savored the rise and fall of his chest as I held him, my throat so tight I couldn't speak.

He was still for a moment, and then his hands moved to my back to return my embrace. He bent his body over me and held me like a drowning man.

I never wanted to move. "Thank you," I whispered. There was nothing more to say.

His grip tightened. When I stepped away after a few moments, his hands lingered on my back, as though he wasn't quite ready to let me go.

I looked around the market, clearing my throat. "I should help. And you should sit down and rest."

He nodded and let me help him to a nearby bench.

I picked my way closer to the street's entrance where the remaining people had congregated. I was terrified of what I might find, but unlike after the attack on my school, I was awake and able to help. If Weslan was right, the attack was our fault. I pressed my hands to my stomach at the thought. I had to do what I could to help.

Half of the vendors were gone, and I realized they must've run for the exits as soon as the Blight's men had stormed in. Other people had crouched behind their stands, and only now did they seem to be coming out of their hiding places.

Several bodies sprawled on the ground at the entrance. The first person I reached was still alive, thankfully. I yelled and waved the healers over, and they came running.

Then I saw another body, off to the side. Long, auburn hair curled around the girl's face, and something about her looked chillingly familiar. I stopped in my tracks. I knew her.

The auburn-haired girl had just visited our stand. I had given her an absent smile and a lemonburst cake with sparkling yellow frosting. It lay in gold and yellow pieces beside her limp hand. In fact, I was certain she'd been to our stand almost every day since we'd opened.

I heard a high keening noise. My chest hurt, and it took several moments to realize the noise was coming from me. And the next thing I knew, I was sitting on the ground several feet away from her, rocking back and forth. Someone's strong arms wrapped around me.

Weslan had dragged himself over to me. I couldn't get enough air as I gasped, "That poor girl. All because of us. All because of me. The Crimson Blight came because of me."

We'd practically painted a target on this market and on anyone who bought goods from us.

I looked up into Weslan's bloodshot eyes. "What have we done?"

Chapter 13

Thankfully, someone had run straight to the Quarter Guard, and the area was crawling with guards and healers. One of them saw to Weslan's arm, eventually, and when there was no one left who needed help, we went back to our stall. We packed our gear, cleaned our area, and returned home in exhausted, miserable silence.

When we reached the bakery at last, it was twilight. We stopped at the back door as Zel slipped out of it. When she saw us, she froze. Then she leapt forward and grabbed me, pulling me into her arms. She rocked me back and forth, silent at first. "I was just coming to find you," she said, her voice breaking.

"What? That would have been a disaster." What was she thinking?

"I heard from Gregor. About the market. No one knew what had happened. All I knew was that a lot of people had escaped, but you didn't come home. I was coming to find you." She bit her lip. "I'm so glad you're well."

I shivered. If Zel had come to the market, the trackers would've found her immediately.

We unloaded the cart, and Weslan collapsed at the kitchen table.

I mixed a large bowl of victus and set it in front of him. I couldn't stop myself from placing a soft hand on his shoulder. For some reason, I needed to touch him and be near him again.

He leaned subtly into my hand and looked up at me, his gaze heavy with something I couldn't read.

I would never forget the feeling of his warm weight covering me while the sound of boots crunched around us. "Eat this," I said. "Then go sleep in my room. I'll handle the bakery myself while you sleep."

He didn't even argue, which told me how exhausted he really was. He scarfed down the victus in a few minutes and hauled himself into my little closet room. We didn't hear from him again until late the next morning, when he stumbled out of my room to devour yet another bowl of victus. Then he went back to my room and collapsed on the bed.

I closed the door quietly and hoped the sleep would help him. What happened to a mage who used too much magic? What if he couldn't recover from this?

~

Zel came in later that morning while I was alone in the kitchen. The worried look hadn't faded from her eyes. She was always the picture of calm serenity, but in the past few weeks, she had begun to fray.

Or maybe I was seeing things the way they truly were now. Nagging doubts poked at my mind. How much longer could we continue to survive like this, hiding the twins and Zel in the bakery? It was an impossible miracle that we'd survived for the last thirteen years.

She glanced at the closed door to my room. "I went to see Inspector Cyrus," she said quietly. "I paid our tax, plus the late fee I promised when I first went to see him. He took the money, but he wanted to know where we had gotten it. I didn't want him to think we had anything more to hide, so

I told him about your stall at the market." She chewed on her lower lip. "That was the night before the attack at the market. What if he … somehow … told someone about you?"

The sick feeling came back to my stomach, but then I shook my head. "Don't worry, Zel. It's not as if it was a secret. We've been doing everything we can to promote the stall and bring in more customers. He would have heard about it eventually, if not from you."

Her worry lines didn't fade, but she nodded. "I suppose."

"Do you think he'll leave us alone now?"

She was silent for a long moment as she decided how to reply. "No. I don't know. Oh, Ella, I wish I could say yes. But when I told him about your stall at the market, I saw the look in his eyes. He looked … hungry. I don't think we've seen the last of him by any means."

The kitchen was baking hot in the midday sun, but a strange cold chilled me to the bone. If Cyrus wouldn't let this go, we would never be safe. All the money in the world wouldn't stop him from trying to blackmail us. But what could we do? We needed a way out, but try as I might, I couldn't seem to find one.

~

I couldn't shake the trapped, claustrophobic feeling that came over me after Zel's admission. Weslan was up and about later that afternoon, fit enough to help me with the bakery, but even the sight of his familiar face did nothing to remove the feeling that I'd been locked inside a cage.

Finally, I couldn't take it anymore. I put down the flour I was measuring with a powdery thump and wiped my hands on my apron, ignoring Weslan's curious look. "I'll be right back." I slipped out of the kitchen door, not bothering to wait for his response.

I hurried down the street, ignoring the children shouting and playing in the late afternoon summer sun. Then I darted into Gregor's narrow entryway half a block down the street from our bakery and knocked.

He opened the door and pulled me inside, folding me into a tight hug. "Oh, Ella girl. I heard. I'm so glad you're safe."

I melted into his hug for a moment, taking comfort in the familiar smell of spiceberries that clung to his clothes. Then I pulled away. "Gregor, I just ..." Now that I was here, I was embarrassed. It was hard to get the words out. "I can't do this anymore."

"You mean you can't keep going to the market?" He frowned.

"Not just that. Everything. It's as though everywhere we turn, there's someone else who's threatening us or waiting to take everything from us. And I just ... I can't." I pressed my lips together as a solitary tear escaped and rolled down my cheek. I dashed it away and looked around at Gregor's neatly organized shelves of spices, flour, and sugar as a distraction. Finally, I turned back to him. He was watching me with a thoughtful look on his face.

Just say it, Ella.

"If we need to ... get out of Asylia ... without ... without anyone knowing, would that be possible? Is that something you could do?"

He raised an eyebrow, and I rushed on. "I know you have contacts in the other cities, and with traders, since most of your shop's inventory comes from the other cities. So. I just thought, maybe, you would know someone ... someone who could ... help."

He sighed heavily. "What makes you think somewhere else would be better than here?"

Because it had to be. "I just think some of the other cities might not have so many trackers and guards interfering with our lives. And I would like that." I didn't know what else I could say without giving Zel away. "To be able to live on our own, without interference for once."

He nodded slowly, and I hoped desperately that he would accept my vague reasoning.

"I understand that, I think," he said. "And I might know a few people who could help. But the other cities are no better off than we are. Draicia's the worst, but the others aren't much better. I do think that there's a demand for good bakeries like yours, especially what you and Weslan were doing at the market. You could make a living somewhere else, perhaps." He crossed his arms. "But if you want my advice, you'll do what you can to make it here first. This is your home. If the good people give up and leave, the Blight wins."

~

I left Gregor doing an inventory of his latest imports and went back to Weslan, who was almost done mixing the dough for the evening. We finished the work in silence. I thought he would question my absence, but he must have guessed I needed some space tonight.

I had not the slightest inkling of what to do. Gregor thought he could get us out of Asylia and settled into a different city. That made me feel better. But his admonishment about not abandoning the city weighed heavily on me.

If people at the market had died because Weslan and I had attracted the ire of the Crimson Blight, then would we be helping or hurting Asylia by leaving? Would giving up our bakery stand protect more people, or would it mean lives had been lost for no reason? And why had the Blight come after us in the first place? How could we be held responsible for the decisions of madmen?

There was a knock at the locked front door to the bakery, and I jumped. Weslan glanced at me and then went to the door, wiping his hands on his apron as he went. "Who's there?" he said softly.

"Marus, from Theros Street Market," came the muffled reply.

"Open it," I said. "Let's see what he wants." My voice shook despite the confident words. Had he realized the attack was essentially our fault? Would he be here looking for retribution?

Master Marus slipped in the door, and Weslan shut and locked it behind him. In the week that we'd been at the market, Master Marus had been jovial and friendly, always making the rounds and personally introducing himself as the market owner to all the new vendors. His rotund belly, laugh lines, and black hair peppered with gray had become a familiar sight to us all. And now he looked … broken.

"What can we do for you, Master Marus?" I asked, stepping around the counter as he came inside.

"I had to talk to you, Ella." He glanced at Weslan. "You, too, Weslan."

I swallowed down against the sick feeling in my stomach. "Come in and have a seat, then."

We entered the kitchen, and I poured Master Marus a cup of black coffee while he sat heavily at the kitchen table. Weslan sat across from him, and I sat gingerly beside Weslan, anxiety warring with guilt and twisting my stomach into knots.

"The trackers who came today believe there is little doubt that the Crimson Blight attacked our market again yesterday," Master Marus said gruffly. "Though they did not use suffio, as they usually do. This time, they used knives to attack people at random, whoever happened to be closest to the market entrance." He spread his hands. "We knew they might come back. Of course, we knew it. And we had private guards and a tracker on loan from the Quarter Guards. We took many other measures in case of an attack. But it wasn't enough to—" He choked and tears welled in his reddened eyes.

I could barely hold back my own. "I'm so—" I began.

"Wait, Ella. I-I've something to say." Master Marus took a deep breath. "I know they came for you. I've heard multiple witnesses say their apparent leader made a beeline for your stand once they were in the market. And they couldn't find you anywhere."

Beside me, Weslan tensed.

"I don't know why they came after you," Master Marus continued, staring down at the table between us. "But I ... well, I've got an idea."

I stared at him. Could Master Marus possibly know why we had been targeted? We were somehow to blame for the attack, but why?

He shifted in his seat. "No one knows who the Crimson Blight is. But I've noticed the kinds of places they target. Commoners. Trolleys. Markets. Factories. Slums. The Royal Academy is one of the only places they ever attacked where Procus families were hurt, and no one was killed in that attack. I think they've got some kind of grudge against us commoners."

I opened my mouth to speak, but he held up one finger. "I know, I know, the Guard says they've got no hint of motive or identity of these guys. Maybe these are the ramblings of an old man whose lost more than one man should in his lifetime. But I think they caught wind of what you two were doing at our market, and they didn't like it. They didn't want the common people to have a little bit of fun, a bit of magic in their lives beyond the basic rations the government says we can have. So they decided to stomp all over us because they could." He clenched his fists, and met my eyes for the first time.

It took all my courage to meet his intense gaze.

"That's why you've got to come back, Ella. Weslan. You can't let them win."

Surely, he couldn't mean—

"I'm reopening the market as soon as it's cleaned up, with double the number of guards and daily sweeps by the Royal Trackers. I have word that Prince Estevan himself is determined to keep our market open. And I'd be honored—humbled—if you came back to the market the day it opens."

I glanced at Weslan. The pain on his face mirrored my own. "Master Marus," I said slowly, "we are honored to have you visit us and to hear your request. But how can you want us back when you know they were there because of us? People—" My voice broke. "People died."

Master Marus reached across the table and covered my trembling hand with his large, callused one. "And that's why you must return, Ella. The Crimson Blight hit us because they thought we'd give up. But we'll show them we won't ever give up, not ever. They've been running around this city for years—killing, wounding, and destroying—thinking they can rule us by fear. But they can't." He squeezed my hand and looked fiercely into my eyes. "And together, we'll show them how wrong they are."

We saw him out a few minutes later with a promise to consider his request but no guarantee. I could barely think straight after the stress and terror of the last two days, and Weslan was in no better shape after his near coma. I could truthfully admit to Master Marus that we were in no state to decide this today.

I bade Weslan goodnight, and Weslan settled back on his pallet. I let myself into my room, shut the door behind me, and leaned against it, eyeing the rumpled bedcovers. It would be strange to spend the night in a bed Weslan had just vacated. No doubt I should change the sheets first, but I was too tired to do it tonight.

I changed into my nightclothes, brushed my hair out, and settled onto my bed with a novel in my hands. It was an old favorite, and one that both Bri and Alba constantly snuck in to borrow. I flipped it open to the place I'd read last, and a small scrap of paper slipped out and fell into my lap.

I stared down at it, breathless. Had I marked my place with a scrap of paper last time? I didn't, normally, but perhaps Alba had borrowed it and marked it for me.

I picked up the paper in trembling hands and flipped it over, and then I pressed one hand against my mouth to silence the scream threatening to erupt. There, on the small scrap of paper, someone had scrawled *STAY HOME, CINDERELLA* in red, bold block letters.

Chapter 14

"They won't let it happen again. Master Marus was certain of it. Think about it—he's invested everything he has in this market. Prince Estevan himself wants the market to stay open. It will be as safe as they can possibly make it." Weslan sounded a lot more certain than I felt as he told Zel about our meeting with Master Marus.

We sat around the breakfast table on the roof after the twins had gone to listen to their fabulator crystal.

As much as I complained about Asylia's problems, I had to admire the people who continued about their business in the face of danger. I wanted to be one of them, but ...

"But how can you be sure it's safe?" Zel spoke my thoughts aloud.

Weslan frowned as he considered her question. "We could always see if we can find another market space somewhere else."

I shook my head. "We won't find another space as cheap as this one, and now, we need all the profit we can get." I thought for a moment, eyes fixed on the rusty old table before me. I felt their eyes on me as I bit my lip. Was it worth the risk? And what if we were putting everyone else on Theros Street at risk by being there?

Based on the note I'd received last night, the Crimson Blight didn't want us going back. But the thought of staying home simply because the Crimson Blight wanted me to made my skin crawl. Who were they to think they could intimidate me in my own home?

Then again, what if the note was another imagining, like all the strange things I'd seen in the past few weeks? When I'd turned the paper over, it had been blank, as though the message had never been there at all. Perhaps my cowardly subconscious was coming up with reasons not to go back to the market.

Weslan spoke up. "If they have better security, this market might be safer than the other ones now."

Zel pressed her lips together, clearly frustrated, and then she began to question Weslan again about the security measures Master Marus had promised.

I ignored their argument, my head spinning with the worries and doubts that had plagued me for days. I'd lain awake for hours last night, clutching the crumpled blank paper in my hand. All I wanted to do was take Gregor up on his offer and get our family out of Asylia. I couldn't live like this anymore.

Did that make me a coward? Was it cowardice to run if your family was in danger? At some point, didn't we have to put the twins' safety first? And what about Zel—hadn't she been through enough?

And what about Asylia? What about all our customers? I cringed as I remembered the grubby, childish hands fingering the sparkling folds of my skirt and the kind faces of our customers beaming at me with frosting on their lips. Then I thought of the girl's limp hand, the crumbled pieces of cake ground into the gravel beside her, and my stomach twisted like it was being wrung out like a rag.

I'd spent five years at the Royal Academy preparing to be a public servant, and now I was ready to abandon the city completely. What good had this miserable city ever done for me? For the girl who had died? For anyone?

I couldn't shake the feeling that I was the wrong person to be making a life or death decision for the people at the market. I hadn't even told Zel and Weslan about the message I'd received—or at least, the message I thought I'd received—last night. Somehow, voicing the words aloud would make the fear too real, as though I might never come out from beneath the terror again. It would only smother me more, stripping away whatever bits of courage I still had until I was a shivering, nervous shell of the girl I had once been.

"Let's try." The sound of my own raspy voice silenced the argument, and I shut my eyes, hardly able to believe what I'd said. Was I losing my mind? But even as I regretted the words, I knew they were the right ones.

I cleared my throat and opened my eyes, forcing myself to meet Zel's gaze. "We can't give up, not without knowing that we've given it our all first. We should go back and try again. If it doesn't work out or there's another attack, fine. We can leave and try something else." *Somewhere else.* "But if we give up now, when others are willing to try …" I didn't finish. I looked at Zel, willing her to understand.

"But what if it's—" Zel's voice broke.

"Regardless, I protected her once, and I can do it again," Weslan said firmly. He shifted his gaze to me, and his expression changed slightly, as though he'd answered a silent question in his head.

I tore my gaze away, feeling unaccountably flustered, but the look of sheer determination on his face stayed with me.

Zel looked between the two of us, frowning. Finally, she nodded. "I don't like it, and I won't pretend otherwise. But I understand."

~

"I'm ready for you," I said, after an embarrassingly long yawn. I'd hardly slept for the second night in a row, and it was hard to be up and about before dawn to prepare for the market's reopening.

"Done," said Weslan, sounding suspiciously smug.

I whirled around. The hundreds of small cakes I'd frosted, which littered the kitchen counters and table, were shining with magic. Weslan had transformed their plain white frosting into a glittering violet to complement the tangy, summery brambleberry flavor we'd chosen for today's cakes. "Already?" Normally, it took Weslan several minutes to add his special touch to so many cakes.

He smirked at me, and I had to roll my eyes. No single person deserved to have so much confidence. It just wasn't fair.

We arrived at Theros Street Market before the opening bell, and set up our cakes in the new display trays we'd borrowed from Gregor. I hoped these wouldn't meet the same fate as our own.

I stood in front of the table, shivering in the light summer rain, and I waited for the bell in silence as Weslan hovered over the cakes, adjusting the arrangement here and there. He seemed lost in thought, something that rarely happened, and I ached to ask him what he was thinking. But though I'd felt closer to him since he had saved my life, I had a hard time acting on the closeness.

What if he didn't feel the same way? What if he thought of me as his employer or as his fresh start, as he'd called it?

Besides, most mages would think me below him. I was a useless commoner, without the powers of a mage or the wealth of a Procus. Perhaps he once had thought so too. Did he still feel that way? I couldn't risk humiliating myself.

I busied myself with observing the rest of the market. Most of the original vendors were there, an impressive showing that spoke to their loyalty to Master Marus. And to their courage. Only a few stalls sat empty. I looked away rather than torment myself by wondering whether their owners had been killed by the Blight or had simply given up.

The sky was too gray and rainy to tell what time it was. But then the opening bell rang, a loud, defiant peal that echoed down the street and set my nerves on edge. To my surprise, streams of determined-looking shoppers poured through the entrance. My heart pounded.

Weslan stood close to me, a spare inch of space between his arm and mine, as we watched the crowds surge toward the back of the market. Toward us.

When the first group was about six feet away, he stepped in front of me, his body forming a solid shield between me and the crowd. And then he began to call out the tragic story of Cinderella, injecting more emotion into his voice than ever before.

It wasn't long before the crowd was eating out of his hand. They booed the Crimson Blight with such force, I took a quick step back. And when he recited the part about my inner beauty, they hollered and cheered.

I felt a genuine smile creep onto my face, the giddy, happy butterflies in my chest at odds with the shaking hands I hid in my skirt. When Weslan stepped away from me, my heart pounded even harder. Please, don't let the Crimson Blight come back again. That was all I could think as I looked out at the brave, cheering crowd.

Weslan waved his hand and a cloud of warm, glittering magic enveloped me once again. It disappeared, and I looked down, speechless as I admired the new dress. The gown was better than anything he'd ever made. The lush, sparkling skirt was a pale, pure violet with a train longer than a Procus lady's wedding gown. The material pooled like water on the ground around my feet. The delicate bodice was covered in shimmering lace, falling off my shoulders in a way that was almost, but not quite, indecent, and hugging my waist in a lacy grip before flowing down around my legs.

The crowd gasped, and a joyful cry went up around the entire market. I looked around, confused, and suppressed a shout of surprise myself. Decorations of shining gold and glittering violet covered the entire market, and gold canopies sheltered each vendor's stall, going all the way up to the market entrance.

Then a sound that was part sigh, part laugh went up from the crowd as a flurry of violet and gold flower petals floated down from the sky around them. Weslan had transformed the very rain drops as they fell. Children ran among the adults, catching the petals in their hands, and a few young ladies spread their arms wide and twirled in the magical shower of petals.

When the shower ended, the crowd surged forward, snatched up our frosted brambleberry cakes, and stuffed quarter marks into Weslan's money purse.

I handed each cake out with a genuine smile, thanking each customer with as much sincerity as I could press into the two simple words. We didn't deserve their loyalty. That much was certain. And yet, here it was. I could no more abandon them than I could abandon Zel or the twins.

~

For what must have been the tenth time that day, I wished for a mirror.

I'd been getting admiring glances from the young men at the market, and I desperately wanted to see what the gorgeous violet dress looked like on me. But the crowd of customers kept us busy, and I barely had time to catch my breath.

Occasionally, between customers, I sent a sidelong glance at Weslan. He would sometimes catch my eye and give me a knowing smile, looking obnoxiously proud of himself. That drove me even crazier than the desire to see a mirror.

A new thought crossed my mind. Obviously, he'd become more powerful since the attack on the market. Using his magic to hide us from the attackers must have been the equivalent of several weeks' worth of bakery work which explained why he'd slept so long and why he'd gained so much power. There was no way he could have decorated the entire market in the space of a breath a week ago, much less when he first used his magic to work the oven in the bakery.

But if he was growing more powerful, how long would he be content to remain at the bakery? He'd told me he wanted a fresh start and that he thought he needed to be with us to make it. But he could have his fresh start any day now if the government discovered his growing powers, rescinded his expulsion, and pressed him back into service.

A raw ache took over my throat at the thought of losing him. Because I didn't want his help at the bakery. I wanted him. That was always my problem, wasn't it? Reaching too far. Wanting something I could never have. You'd think I would have learned my lesson by now.

I tried to focus on the line of customers and the feeling of triumph that had warmed me throughout the day. We were doing it. We weren't giving in to fear. That was what mattered, right? We were standing firm and—

Two grave-faced men shouldered our newest customer out of the way, cutting off my train of thought. One wore the official Quarter Guard uniform. The other, a younger man with dark hair and pale skin, had the gold armband and black uniform of a tracker.

"Ariella Stone?" said the guard, one hand on the baton at his side.

"Yes?" My voice sounded small.

"Are you the owner of this stand?"

"Yes." Had they found out about our True Name bond? Or worse, about Zel? I began to sweat.

"We're here because we received an anonymous tip that you have been using magic for unapproved purposes."

"Unapproved? I didn't know—"

The guard continued as though I hadn't spoken. "You'll be required to submit to a formal audit investigation. Or if that's a problem," he said with a sneer, "you're welcome to protest this investigation from the dungeon."

Weslan and I glanced at each other uneasily. We had no choice. "Of course," I said, trying to sound certain. "Whatever you need."

We answered question after question as the tracker pawed through our remaining cakes, examining them every which way as though looking for clues. All Weslan had done was change the color of the frosting. And, well, a few other things. How complicated could it be?

Unless … could he pick up traces of Zel? She had never touched our cakes. We'd been careful—extremely careful. Surely, even the best tracker wouldn't be able to catch her trace.

And then, to my horror, the tracker walked over and began to pat down my dress. I stepped away reflexively, and Weslan glared at him. But the impassive tracker showed not the slightest expression.

"Comply, or you're headed to the dungeon," the guard said menacingly, and the tracker resumed his exploration of my dress. I held my gaze straight ahead, trying not to think of his hands as they left an invisible path on every inch of the violet dress I had loved so much. I heard a small noise, like a grunt of surprise, and glanced down at the tracker.

He said nothing else, and his face remained a mask of cold disinterest.

Finally, after an hour of intense questioning, the officer handed me a sheet of paper. "You're being charged with improper use of magic, Miss Stone." I scanned the piece of paper in my hand.

Unapproved use of magic to provide heat. 400 marks.

Unapproved use of magic to make food without being tested for safety or quality. 400 marks.

Unlicensed sale of goods comprised of over one-tenth mage-crafted substances. 400 marks.

"But this will ruin us!" I forgot myself and cried out angrily. Both men looked at me, the tracker with the slightest hint of satisfaction on his face, and the guard with utter disgust. "How can you expect us to pay this much?"

"Well, there's a simple solution," the guard said dryly. "Stop breaking the law."

"But if we close our bakery, we'll have nothing. We need this money!"

"Again," the guard said, his tone reeking of condescension, "Stop breaking the law and you won't have a problem. This fee is due at the end of the week. If you persist in breaking the law, you'll pay this fee every week. If you're lucky. If you're unlucky, you'll both spend the rest of your days in the dungeon."

The tracker looked hard at Weslan and spoke for the first time, his voice gravelly and low. "Be careful who you associate with, *Wes*."

Weslan stiffened beside me. Did they know each other?

"I would've thought you'd been taught not to use your magic for such low purposes."

Chapter 15

"Who was that tracker?" I couldn't help asking once they'd left.

Weslan's cheeks were flushed and his shoulders tense. He gripped the edge of the stall, and for a moment I thought he might flip it on its side. Then he let go. "Just an idiot from the Mage Academy." He stacked the empty trays with a series of clatters. "A year ahead of me. I didn't like him then, and I don't like him now."

Neither did I.

Master Marus approached us as we finished packing up our ruined cakes. He must have been waiting for the guard and tracker to leave. "What did they want?"

I handed him the slip of paper. "Unapproved use of magic. Apparently, it's expensive."

Master Marus swore, his cheeks turning red. "Of all the—"

There was a crash as Weslan slammed one of our display stands into the hand cart a little too hard. "Sorry," he mumbled.

I didn't reply. I felt like smashing things too.

We'd have to work every day for the next week to make enough money to pay the fine, and then, if the officer followed through with his threat, they'd hit us with another fine for another week of unauthorized operation of the bakery. We were ruined.

Master Marus threw the paper down on our stand and gave me a hearty pat on the back. "Cheer up, Ella. You can't give up yet."

I glared at him. Surely, he couldn't accuse me of giving up if the city government itself was trying to drive me out of business.

He winked, his earlier frustration seemingly forgotten. "The prince may not have a good reputation, but I've heard that he's a reformer. Trying to help merchants and such."

Behind me, Weslan scoffed. "A reformer? He's a beast, Master Marus. If you knew half the things he did when his father was alive …"

Master Marus shook his head. "He's changed. Or at least, he's changing. He got wind of what happened at our market and sent us our own tracker. Would a beast do that?"

Weslan only grunted in response.

"I've heard the like from other merchants too. It may be that things are changing, Ella. The next petition day is coming up in two days. If you make a formal petition, maybe he'll forgive all those fines. After all, the people love your bakery. You're making great cakes, and you draw repeat customers to a market that many people have been afraid to visit even once. You're a boon to us. The city needs you both. Don't give up yet."

I raised my eyebrows. I'd never considered trying to petition Prince Estevan. I didn't know anyone who had ever been to the monthly petition day. Getting the attention of any Procus family—especially the royal family—was never a good idea in Asylia. But all I told Master Marus was, "We'll think about it." On our way home, I asked Weslan, "Do you really think we should do it?"

"I think *you* should do it," Weslan said gruffly. "Not me."

My heart turned over in my chest. Was he planning on leaving us? "But … aren't we in this together?"

He shrugged one shoulder as he hauled the hand cart down the street. "I'm like a leper over there, Ella. They kicked me out, remember? If I come with you and anyone recognizes me, there's no way they'll let you see the prince, much less grant your petition."

I was silent for a moment. "But you're the reason people love the bakery stand so much. If it was just me, why would they care?"

He shook his head, keeping his eyes on the road in front of us.

I ached to do something to grab him, to get his attention, but as always, fear held me back.

"The whole thing was your idea," he said at last. "You've got the brains for this, Ella. I make it sparkle, but without you, it would never exist in the first place. As much as I don't want you going anywhere near the prince, I don't think we have much of a choice. These fines will keep us under until he either changes the regulations or gives us a pass on the regulations. Or we give up and they lock us up because we can't pay the fine."

I knew he wasn't being completely serious, but the words still sent a shiver down my spine. How would Zel and the twins survive if I were in the dungeon? Or working off a sentence in the farms and mines outside Asylia?

Zel wouldn't last two weeks before a tracker caught her trail, and who knew what would happen after that?

"I'll try it," I said. "It's hard to imagine that things could get any worse."

Weslan gave me a half smile. "There's the spirit," he said ruefully.

I couldn't help but laugh. But of course, things could always get worse. If anyone knew that, it was us.

~

Two days later, Weslan and Zel came to the kitchen to see me off before dawn.

"It's best for you to show up as you really are," Weslan said, walking around me with a critical eye. "No magic. Might make you less sympathetic."

The soft pink morning dress was threadbare but clean, an old-fashioned relic from my mother's old wardrobe that Zel had hemmed to fit my smaller frame. It was the best I had, but after a week of wearing glittering ball gowns fit for the Procus set, I felt vulnerable and underdressed even in one of my mother's best dresses. At least I didn't smell like cinderslick anymore.

I tucked the sheath of notes into the skirt's pocket so my sweaty hand wouldn't cause the ink to run any more than it already had. "I guess I should be going, then."

"Remember, don't leave out the important parts of the story." Weslan stopped his inspection to stand before me with his arms crossed over his broad chest.

"I know, I know …" He wanted me to tell Prince Estevan how I'd been orphaned in the plague and how I had survived a Crimson Blight attack on my school. Play on the sympathy of the prince and his court the way Weslan did at the market. "I'll try. That's all I can promise."

Nerves danced and jumped in my stomach. I couldn't bear to eat any breakfast, so I said a quiet good-bye to Weslan and Zel before dawn and headed via trolley to the Royal Precinct at the center of the city. I walked down the clean footpath, appraising the government buildings around me with new eyes. Now that I knew I'd never enter one, they looked unyielding and proud.

Why must there be a divide between the descendants of the city's founding families and those of the commoners that had found refuge in Asylia alongside them? Seven hundred years later, couldn't we set aside our history and just … live?

I shook my head. Treasonous thoughts.

The palace grounds were massive. It took me ten minutes of walking to get from the corner of the palace to the front entrance where Master Marus had assured me I could enter for petition day. I had only to follow the ragged stream of commoners ahead of me to know that he was right.

Stark stone grounds shone on the other side of the high iron fence as I walked. There were no lush gardens here, no gilded detailing on the fence posts. And the palace itself, set back half a block's distance from the fence, was several stories high and made of cold, gray stones.

The Procus family compounds in the adjacent Procus Quarter were opulent and luxurious, estates meant for pleasure and excess. But I knew from my history lessons that the palace itself had been built for defense. It was one of the first large buildings ever constructed by the mages who'd been forced into serving the founding families. But why hadn't the later kings ever called mages in to renovate the palace? The lower levels didn't even have windows. What kind of prince willingly lived in a fortress like this?

I followed the commoners through the front gates and joined the end of a line that extended to a set of wide, tall doors at the front of the palace. The crowd's loud chatter echoed off the stone grounds and walls, and I looked over my shoulder and frowned. I'd only arrived, and already the line was extending out past the gate and around the corner. What were all these people doing here? Did they truly all intend to petition the prince?

The sun rose over the city, and the dark blue sky brightened to a bright, pale blue as I waited. I tapped the bony, rag-covered shoulder of the woman in front of me. "Why isn't the line moving?"

She looked back at me and rolled her eyes. "You think the crown prince of Asylia wakes up before dawn to meet with a bunch of commoners?"

I pressed my lips together. What had I been thinking? We'd probably be here all day. Too bad I'd skipped breakfast.

Hours later, the sun high in the sky, the line moved forward at a snail's pace. By noon, I had only made it a few feet forward, just inside the shade of the palace doorway, and I was so hungry I felt lightheaded. Should I leave and find a bite to eat? But if I gave up my place in line now, I would never make it back in line, and I would have to wait another month for the next petition day when there would be the same problems all over again. This was it. This was my chance. I kept repeating the words, trying to keep my mind off my growling stomach.

The hours passed with agonizing slowness as the late afternoon sun heated the palace, and I was soon drenched in sweat. I fanned myself with my notes, giving up on keeping the ink from smearing. The palace entryway where I'd been waiting for hours was neat and sparse with nothing but simple tapestries on the walls. They probably didn't want any of us to enjoy the luxury of sitting down. We were commoners. Luxury was for the Procus families.

Finally, I made it to the door of the throne room and craned my neck to peer inside. The line snaked around this room in folds until it ended in front of a man I'd only ever seen in etchings in the *Herald*. Crown Prince Estevan. He sat on a modest, carved throne with a writing desk, of all things, in front of him. He bent his head over the desk and scribbled rapid notes, never once raising his head.

His hair was dark, his skin darker than mine, but he had the tall, broad build that hinted at Kireth blood too. It was rare for anyone to be true Fenra anymore, but still, it struck me that even the royal family had obvious Kireth blood running in their veins. So why did everyone have to make a big deal about it?

I'd never understand this city. The prince wore a crisp, dark suit. He had a deep purple cloth band around his heavily muscled upper arm instead of wearing a crown on his head. What kind of prince didn't wear a crown?

His late father, who'd died ten years ago, had always worn a crown in public appearances, hadn't he? But I'd never set eyes on the king, so what did I really know? An assortment of men in dark suits surrounded the prince, some taking their own notes, some lounging and talking as though they hadn't a care in the world.

The gaunt woman in front of me shoved me back into my place with an annoyed grunt, so that was all I could see. I busied myself smoothing my skirt and running over my petition in my mind, moving my lips to the words in silence.

Another hour passed, and I made it inside the door to the throne room. I eyed Prince Estevan as he bent his head over the desk and wrote. He was much larger than I had originally estimated. I had a feeling that if the prince were standing, he would be far taller and broader than Weslan, and Weslan was the tallest person I knew. Definitely, Kireth blood. But the cold, blank look on the prince's face was a stark contrast to Weslan's characteristic warmth and humor.

As I watched, I realized he hadn't once looked up at the commoners giving their petitions before him. He only wrote and wrote, an intent look on his well-sculpted face. Some man, perhaps a steward, dismissed each commoner with a few words the moment their petition was done. The steward didn't even glance at Prince Estevan for his comment or approval.

What was happening here? Was the prince taking notes on their requests, or was he ignoring them altogether?

I kept my eyes on the next commoner to speak. I was too far away to hear his voice, but he turned away, downcast, after the steward spoke to him, and the next person stepped before the prince. Had this been happening all day?

The scene repeated itself as the afternoon dragged on into evening, and then, when I was only three places from the front of the line, a bell rang.

Prince Estevan stood abruptly and strode from the room without a word. The steward gave the crowd a hasty gesture. Everyone around me bowed to the prince's departing back.

I sank low to the ground in a curtsy, keeping my eyes lowered, and tried to smother the growing fury within me. I'd waited all day, and they were turning me away now? Was this some kind of cruel joke?

Chapter 16

I looked around the throne room, but no one even muttered or groaned. The rest of the commoners turned in silence and shuffled toward the door.

So that was why nearly everyone had come prepared with victus for lunch, blankets to sit on, and even the occasional small stool. This must be how every petition day went. These people came back every month, trying to get their chance to petition a prince who would ignore them.

What was the point of this ridiculous scene? What good would it do anyone? In the time I'd spent waiting in line in the throne room, I hadn't seen a single petitioner receive a favorable response from the steward, and I certainly hadn't seen the prince take notice of anyone.

I crumpled my sweat-stained notes back into my pocket and followed the rest of the crowd out of the palace, my feet aching and my legs weak from hunger. I didn't understand. They'd persevered, knowing their efforts would achieve nothing. Why? Why would they be willing to—

For the first time, it hit me. The people weren't here because they believed in Prince Estevan. They were here because they were desperate. And that meant I was one of them. I, too, knew that painful, burning hunger that drove me to attempt the impossible again and again because I had no other choice. Because no matter how bad things got, hope could never fully die.

~

"I wasn't sure you'd come back at all." Weslan sat at the table in front of me as I practically inhaled the last bite of my cold victus and orange blossom honey. "I thought—" He clenched his fists as they rested on the table. "I worried … I don't know what I was thinking, letting you go there alone. No one in the royal family can be trusted, Ella. It's the first lesson mages learn."

"I'm fine," I said around my gritty bite of victus. "I don't understand why Master Marus told me to go. The prince didn't answer a single petition. He wasn't even listening."

Weslan was quiet for a moment. "Maybe Master Marus wanted you to see it."

Goosebumps rose on my arms despite the kitchen's heat. Could Master Marus have known how much it would affect me? I couldn't deny that something had shifted in me since I'd left the palace. I couldn't quite put my finger on it, but I felt … different.

Those desperate faces haunted me. All those people were willing to spend the day trying for a request that would never be granted. And they returned each month rather than give up. Hadn't they been through worse than me? At least I had my education, even if I didn't get the graduation certificate. And I had Weslan. Between the two of us, we'd discovered the potential to build a truly profitable shop that didn't depend on any government rations. How many of those people, even if their petitions were granted, would be able to do that without a mage by their side?

"I have a confession," I said softly. Weslan glanced up from the table. "I've been talking to Gregor about getting out of here. Getting a place in one of the other walled cities. Maybe even in the Badlands, if it's safer. All of us." He frowned at me, and a strange tightness threatened to close my throat. "We can't keep living like this. Zel and the girls are trapped in the bakery, and the Inspector will keep asking for money. We all know he's not going to let it be."

Weslan nodded his head curtly. "You're right about that," he said, glowering down at the table. "Rats like that never leave things alone. It's not in their nature. Once they've discovered a weakness, they can't help but exploit it."

"But seeing everyone at the palace today, I don't know. It doesn't feel right to leave. Even though it would be better for our family to leave ... well, I wonder if there's something that we could do. Not just for our family, but for everyone. For the city."

I fell silent, struck by the audacity of my words. Why was I thinking like this? I needed to take care of Zel and the girls, not stir things up even more. But I knew I couldn't be satisfied with escape. That was no kind of life.

"You know what would really change things?" Weslan focused on the table, tracing the knots in the wood with his fingers. "The mages. Right now, we can only use our powers for government service, or if we're lucky, we can secure Procus family patronage. Create a few dresses, a few works of art. But what if the mages were free to work for any merchant or to start a shop and work with whomever they chose? You and I, we fell into this because neither of us had any other choice." He glanced up at me. "And don't get me wrong—I'm glad that we did. For so many reasons."

My heart sped up. There was something in his eyes that made it impossible to look away.

He held my fascinated gaze. "But if mages were free, free to choose who we wanted to work for, free to use our powers as we chose, there could be other shops like ours."

I shook my head. "Why would any mage choose to work with a commoner? I heard what that tracker said the other day. Besides, your life is miserable now, Weslan. Don't deny it. You went from living like a prince to working long hours, eating cold bowls of victus, and serving commoners in one of the smallest markets in the city. Would any other mage be willing to do that?"

He looked down at the table, playing with the splintered wood for a moment, a wistful expression on his face. "I think so. My life was easy before, but it was empty. I had no hope. At worst, I could be a tool for the government. At best, I could be a pet for the Procus families. I had no real hope for control over my life or my powers. It was … stifling. You've got to believe me, Ella. I've never done mage-crafts so well as in the past few weeks. Out of all the gowns I've created in the past, none of them come anywhere close to the ones I've been making for you."

Warmth lit my chest, and I couldn't help but smile. "I'm a fortunate girl."

He laughed. "I'm being serious. This has been good for me. I never want to go back to the way things were before. I love using my powers to do something different, and I enjoy profiting from them on my own terms. I want this life. And if I want it, maybe there are other mages who would want it too. But we'll never know, will we?"

He was smiling as he spoke, but his tone held a tinge of pain.

It was true. I'd lived my whole life in my own sort of bondage—to poverty, to secrecy. I'd worked tirelessly to gain some stability for our family, and I'd failed. But Weslan had never known that possibility. He'd never known freedom. He'd never gotten the chance to try, even if it meant failure. At least, he hadn't until he was cast out and lost everything.

What would Asylia be like if commoners and mages had the freedom to work together? If mages could use their power for something other than government services for commoners and extravagant luxuries for Procus patrons?

Maybe some mages would become rich and build shops more profitable than the richest merchants. More mages would grow strong through heavy work like Weslan had. That was the problem. No one wanted mages to get stronger or more powerful than they already were. After a moment of quiet, I voiced my concern.

Weslan agreed, his voice subdued. "So it will never happen," he said, staring down at the table. "I know. Just a thought."

We said goodnight, and I lay in bed, fidgeting and restless despite the long day. Something about this didn't feel right. Our business had broken laws, but it had also made people happy. We'd had the chance to build a real life, to thrive instead of merely survive. Why was that so wrong?

We couldn't live our whole lives in slavery to fear. We already lived in fear of the Crimson Blight every day. I thought of all the vendors and customers who'd come back to Theros Street Market the day it reopened. If they could be brave in the face of danger, couldn't we?

~

I shoved the two crystals together, and Valencia's clear, melodious voice rang out in the kitchen, singing something about Lucien and his amazing hair.

"What are you doing?" Weslan frowned at me.

"Look at this." I pulled the crystals apart, and Valencia's voice went silent.

"I know what those are," said Weslan. "I'm the one who brought them, remember?"

"I mean look at the crystals! Alba said that one holds the magic and the other holds the instructions, right? Well, what if you did the same thing for the oven? Find a … well, a rock, or something, and add the magic to it. Then you'd need to add the instructions to the oven. When you put the rock on top of the oven …" I waved my hand in a goofy imitation of his magic act at the market.

Weslan laughed. "My mother is one of the strongest creator mages in the city. And she spends weeks on each batch of fabulator crystals. There's no way I could do something like that."

I raised an eyebrow. "Didn't you decorate the entire market in a matter of seconds the other day? Besides, how will you know unless you try?"

He ran a hand through his hair, stared at the oven, and then crossed his arms. "I don't know. Where'd you get this idea, anyway?"

"I was just thinking last night after we talked. Even if mages were free, not many merchants could afford to pay a mage an income big enough to tempt them away from their Procus patrons or government stipends. But what if the merchants didn't need a mage? What if they only needed mage-craft tools like the oven? Like these crystals?"

I told Zel and Weslan the rest of my plan after dinner that evening, after having sent the twins downstairs. There was no use worrying the girls unless we had to.

As I'd expected, Zel was skeptical. But instead of pressing me, she leaned back in her chair. "Fine." She sighed. "I don't know what else to say, El. Just promise me you'll be careful."

I leaned forward and gripped her hands. "I will! Of course, I will. And … well, if this works and they change the regulations on mages, maybe you and the girls could be free too."

Zel's face showed none of Weslan's excitement. If anything, she looked oddly resigned. "Perhaps."

My enthusiasm waned slightly, but then Weslan spoke up. "Whatever happens, at least we can say that we tried, right? I don't … I won't …" Weslan stopped speaking as Zel sent him an ice-cold gaze.

There was an uncomfortable pause, as though the two of them were having a silent conversation, and then Zel shoved her chair back and stood. She balled her fists on her hips. "It's on you, then, Ella." But she was looking at Weslan. "I won't stop you. But know this is on you."

I kept quiet as Zel left the rooftop. Weslan gave me a rueful smile. "We're in this together. Don't worry. I'm not going anywhere."

His words warmed me more than I ever would have believed possible.

We took the next day off from the market. Instead, we visited the other shops on our street, making conversation with the owners, feeling them out for support. We were about to do something I had never heard of anyone doing before. It was risky and most definitely illegal. We stayed cautious, never asking anyone outright for their support, and then went home to make a list of the people who might be open to my plan. Of all the merchants on our street, three seemed like a good possibility—Gregor, of course, Master Lagos, the brewer, and Master Anton, the carpenter.

I wanted to add more, but Weslan insisted that the fewer people who knew what we were doing, the safer we would be. I knew he was right. I wanted numbers on our side, but we had to be careful in case it didn't work out. We contacted our chosen three, and then Weslan and I got to work, covering the kitchen table with notes, lists, and sketches.

Late that night, after everyone had gone to bed, a knock rattled the back door of the kitchen. Weslan raised an eyebrow at me. "Here's your moment."

We answered the door together and ushered each visitor into the kitchen as he arrived.

I set mugs of hot coffee and a plate of honeybread in front of them, and then Weslan and I joined them at the table. The three men glanced between the two us, looking bemused.

For a moment, my nerves sizzled uncontrollably, and I wasn't sure if I could do it. What if they laughed in my face? Or worse, what if they reported me?

Weslan must have guessed what I was thinking because he reached under the table and squeezed my leg for a moment before letting go. The quick contact startled me, but when I looked at him, he just smiled and gave me an encouraging nod.

"Gentlemen," I spoke as confidently as I could, trying to ignore the slight shake in my voice. "We have invited you here tonight because we have an … idea. As you may have heard, we've had some success at Theros Street Market."

The men nodded. Master Lagos, the brewer, folded his hands over his large belly. "I heard something about you raking in the marks over there."

"It's true." I squared my shoulders and plunged ahead. "Thanks to Weslan's power and my own experience and skill, we managed to launch a bakery stand in the market the day it reopened. The stand brings in a great deal of profit." I took a deep breath. "In fact, within the first week of operation, we saw a return of over one hundred times the initial investment of twenty marks. Our cakes sell for four to five times more than what we pay for the ingredients."

You could have heard a pin drop. Then the carpenter, a reedy, dark-haired man with pale skin, scoffed in clear disbelief. "I don't know anyone who has profits like those. What are you doing, cooking with sawdust?"

I looked at him steadily and tried to hold his gaze. "Nothing like that," I said. "In fact, we've done the opposite, and our cakes taste all the better for it. We're no longer cooking with cinderslick."

They stared at me, and then Master Lagos placed his fist on the table. "Then how are you—"

The carpenter, Master Anton, broke in. "Are you using wood fuel?"

At the same time, Gregor asked, "What are you thinking, Ella?"

"We're not using wood fuel. We would never do that and risk endangering the whole city. No, we're using something better than fuel, because it doesn't run out quite so easily, and it doesn't have the same quality issues that the government rations tend to have." I reached across the table and grabbed Weslan's hand. "We're using Weslan."

Weslan gave a theatrical bow from his seat.

"Weslan is a mage who is working for our bakery."

The brewer frowned at Weslan. "Why aren't you working for a patron or for the government?"

I shook my head dismissively, silently willing Master Lagos to drop the topic. "That's not the point here. The important thing is he now works at the bakery, and he's been using his magic to help our shop. For example, he only touches the oven once, and it bakes at the right temperature for the right time without using cinderslick. The end result is a cake without the slightest scent or taste beyond the flavoring we use. People love the taste of our cakes so much at least in part because we don't use any cinderslick to make them.

The men gave Weslan appraising looks. Gregor glanced between me and Weslan, and I wondered what he was thinking.

They grumbled among themselves for a few minutes, and then Master Lagos spoke up. "That's all fine and dandy for you," he said, "But none of us have a mage like Weslan in our house. I'm not sure how you got so lucky, but we don't all have sweet pretty faces like you." My face grew hot, and Weslan glared at him. "So what does any of this have to do with us? Or did you call us here to brag?"

"The truth is, what Weslan is doing for our bakery could be done in other ways for other shops, and yes, if you had a mage working in your shop and you made use of their powers effectively, you would probably see the same profits that we see today. But you don't have any mages who can work in your shop, and you never will, because mages are not free to choose. They're forced to work for the government their whole lives, and their only alternative is to take a Procus as patron."

They eyed me skeptically, so I pushed as much confidence into my voice as I could. "We believe the solution to our problems, and all of your problems, is for mages to become … well, essentially, free. For mages to have the opportunity and the choice to seek employment among common merchants. They should be free to use their powers for profit and not just for government services and

Procus luxuries." I held my breath and squeezed my hands together in my lap. Had I gone too far?

The brewer's eyes narrowed. "What you're saying sounds dangerously close to treason, young lady. Give me one good reason why we shouldn't report you."

This was it. I lifted my chin and met his gaze. "Because it isn't treason, and you know it. And we're not really rebelling. As many of you know, I've been training to work in the government for the past five years. While that ... dream ... was cut off, the fact remains that I have been trained. I know how the Asylian government works. I know if there's anyone who has a shot at convincing the government to change this policy, it's me."

I wanted to cringe as the arrogant words passed my lips. I'd never said anything so boastful before. But I needed them to help us, and to do that, I had to convince them to put their faith in me.

"Here's what we're going to do. We're going to give the Asylian government the information they need to change the regulations on mages. Government bureaucrats need numbers for every decision. They must depend on hard facts, not emotions or pity, for every decision. If we can convince them that letting mages work with common merchants will be good for the city, they'll listen. What we need to do is prove it will be good for everyone. Once we can put together the facts and make a proposal, I will personally take it to the government to ensure that they listen and give our proposal a chance."

Weslan gave me a sidelong glance. I still hadn't told him this part of the plan.

"How are you going to do that, young lady?" said the brewer, still looking suspicious.

"All you need to know is that I will. I'll hand our proposal to the prince himself if I must. But one way or another, the government must know how important this could be for the city. It could change everything, for everyone."

Gregor spoke up for the first time since arriving. His tone was gentle, but his face was serious. "I still don't understand that part, Ella. Those are pretty words. A nice dream, for certain. But there aren't enough mages in the city for each merchant to employ one, not since the plague, and each shop makes just a little money. There's no way a mage would be willing to come down to our level. Why would they live like us when they could live with a Procus family or have a stable allowance from the government?"

"That's all true," I said. "But not every shop needs its own mage. There are so many ways that we could …" I stopped myself and took a deep breath. "If we never give the mages the opportunity in the first place, then you can be sure it will never happen." I looked at each man in turn. I had to convince them I was serious. "Back in the old days before the plague, when trade with the West first started, Asylians first started using things like the printing press and indoor plumbing. Those new inventions changed the city, didn't they? They gave Asylia a chance to grow and develop more like the West instead of being left behind, trapped and stifled behind our walls."

I rapped the table with my knuckles to emphasize my point. "But since the plague, no one invents anymore. No one has the extra time or money, and we have no more contact with the West. All we do is depend on the rations for anything we need to survive. If mages were free to work with merchants, all it would take is one or two who were willing to try to make their own inventions. If they did something in a different way, it might ignite more ideas with other people, the way it did in the past." I looked from man to man, silently willing them to understand. "We don't have to live like this. Things could be different, but we have to try."

Weslan gave me a small smile, but the rest stared at me skeptically.

Gregor crossed his arms, frowning at me. "You've said that it's not treason, because you're putting together a government proposal and you want to work within the government to make this policy change. It makes sense to me," he said. "But I don't know if it's going to make sense to them. How do you know they won't arrest you the moment you hand over the proposal?"

I smoothed the folds of my skirt under the table and forced myself to sit up straight. "I don't. But like I said, if we never try anything, then we can be sure that nothing will ever change."

Mr. Lagos leaned back in his chair. "And what exactly is going into this proposal?"

"That's why we need your help. We want to prove that using magic in a common merchant's shop would have the same returns for another type of shop as it did for ours. Because unless we prove it, it will only ever be a nice dream, as Gregor said. Here's what we are hoping you will do. For the next three days, write down all the main measurements in your shop—the ingredients or materials you use, how much they cost, how many marks you bring in for each item you sell, how many hours you work, how many employees you have, and how many hours they work. Everything— every last number that you can measure—write it down and give it to us."

The carpenter blew out a snorting laugh. "It would take us as much time to write all that down as it takes us to actually do our work."

"But we're not just asking for a favor, sir. We're giving you something in return. At the end of those three days, Weslan is going to make your shop a custom mage-craft tool that will make your shop more profitable, the same way he did for our oven. For free. Then you'll simply do everything again for three days, record your numbers, and give them to us."

One by one, they leaned forward in their chairs. They were all interested, including the brewer, the biggest skeptic.

"So will the mage-craft tool still work after three days?" Master Lagos asked Weslan.

"No. We cannot guarantee exactly how long it will last. That depends on the specifics of the tool, which we don't know yet. But at least three days at full strength are guaranteed. Remember, this is an experiment. We need numbers to present to the government, so things can truly change for the long term."

Their faces fell a bit, and I felt bad.

"Still," said Gregor, "I'd sure love to try something like that." Slowly, the other men nodded their agreement.

I smiled. I couldn't help it. "Magic changes everything. Take it from me."

~

For the next three days, Weslan and I operated the bakery stand in defiance of the government regulations. Besides, it wasn't as though we had much choice. We needed the money to pay off the fines, and I didn't see how else we were going to get it.

What surprised me was the joy I felt when we ended each day at the market. Even knowing that every penny of our profits would have to go toward the last week's fines and the new ones that would hit at the end of the week, I loved the bakery. I loved working with Weslan, baking beautiful cakes every day, and putting them into the hands of smiling customers. It was strangely gratifying, though it was far from what I'd always dreamed of doing, and it wasn't about the money. I was enjoying myself immensely, though my family would not see the slightest bit of profit from my labor.

After three days, we got the numbers from our partners and spent the evening brainstorming ways to create the tools that they would need. For the brewer, we decided on a magic stone for him to add to the stove beneath his copper cauldron to heat the malt and water without the use of cinderslick. For the carpenter, we settled on a sanding cloth that, when held with a magic metal clamp, vibrated and sanded all on its own the way our whisk whipped the frosting. For Gregor, we chose a cooling cabinet to preserve his most perishable ingredients, keeping them fragrant during the hot summer weather.

We worked late into the night. Weslan added magic to each of their tools, and I tested them on the sample materials they had given us. The next morning, we delivered their tools, and three days later, they turned in their new figures. We reviewed them in the evening, after cleaning up the bakery, and we were shocked by the results. Every shop had seen efficiency and profitability improvements. Master Anton had reported better profits than we had at our own bakery stand.

Weslan was tired from all the extra work and lay down on his pallet in the kitchen when the sun set. But I didn't sleep. I tossed and turned in my bed, head spinning with all the possibilities that lay before us. If I could create a convincing proposal, one that could persuade Prince Estevan to change the regulations, Asylia would never be the same again.

I shifted again in my bed. I couldn't get comfortable tonight. Was there something wrong with my sheets? Finally, I got up and patted my mattress down, trying to find whatever kept poking me in the back. A small, red scrap of rough fabric was tucked into my sheets, and I had lain right down on it. My hand shook as I turned the luminous dial and picked up the fabric, holding it to the light. A pattern of black thread was woven into the center of the red square. *THAT WAS UNWISE, CINDERELLA*

Boom! Something exploded outside. Boom! Boom! Someone in the street began to scream.

Chapter 17

I threw a robe over my nightgown and ran through the kitchen toward the front door, nearly crashing into Weslan as he raced in the same direction.

We rushed into the street which was filled with our hysterical neighbors.

A whistle rang out and the Quarter Guard arrived. Healers raced toward the end of the street where several injured people had collapsed on the ground. A sick feeling formed in the pit of my stomach. The three shops with the worst damage were the three that had been using Weslan's mage-craft tools.

We raced down the street, and then I slammed to a stop in front of a gaping hole where Gregor's shop used to be. A message scrawled in red paint marred the rubble-strewn street in front of his shop.

KNOW YOUR PLACE

"Gregor!" He staggered through the rubble of his shop and fell onto the cobblestones. I landed on my knees at his side to check his body for wounds. His face was dark from soot, his gray hair strangely dark and wet. "Gregor? What's wrong? What happened?"

His wrinkled eyes cracked open, and a small noise like a sigh and a groan exited his mouth.

"Gregor! Healers, get over here!" The dark, wet substance coating my hands was his blood. My stomach twisted painfully. "Gregor, say something!"

"El—" he started to say, and then he broke off and smiled softly, his face relaxing before my eyes.

"Don't give up," I sobbed, my voice high and hysterical, unrecognizable to my own ears. "Please, you promised. You said ... you said you'd always be there for me!"

But even as I spoke, the light went out of his eyes. His chest rose once, fell, and didn't rise again.

No, no, no, no ... not Gregor. Not like this. Not because of me. "Please ..." Tears coursed down my cheeks, and I pressed my face to Gregor's chest, unable to speak.

Then a rough hand gripped the back of my nightgown and lifted me from my knees. A man with a protruding stomach and wild, greasy hair spun me around and thrust a finger in my face. "You," he spat out.

It took me a moment to recognize the brewer, Master Lagos. I'd never seen him so angry in my life.

"This is all your fault."

I stared at him, numb with shock, only dimly aware of Weslan's attempts to edge between me and the enraged man. The brewer hauled me close to his purple face and hissed, "You will never speak to me or my family again. I want nothing to do with you and your stricken proposal."

The hate and fear in his eyes shook me as much as if he had shouted. I tried to speak, but my throat was bone dry, and I reflexively put up my hands to try and break his grip on my robe. Weslan shoved his shoulder between me and the brewer, and Master Lagos loosened his grip at last.

I stepped out of arm's reach, gasping for breath.

"We had no idea that something like this would happen," Weslan said.

"No idea? No idea?" Master Lagos shook his head, his face twisted into an ugly mask. "This is what happens when you step out of line in this city. You should've known. I should've known. And I want no part in it any longer."

~

Zel pounced on us the moment we were safely inside the kitchen. "Are you hurt?" She grabbed me by the shoulders, unknowingly pressing the painful bruises left by Master Lagos's cruel grip. "What happened out there?"

The twins peered anxiously around the entrance to the stairwell with owlish eyes. There was no sugar coating the horrible news. "Gregor's store was attacked by the Blight. He's dead." I gulped back a sob. "Gregor's dead. Several other people were hurt."

Zel took charge, sending the twins to bed and Weslan to his pallet before guiding me into my room. Tenderly, she helped me wash the blood from my hands and slipped me into my oldest nightgown. As if I were five years old again, she held me as I sobbed. When I'd calmed, she tucked me into bed and left the luminous burning low.

The tears came in even more waves after Zel left. Just when I thought there could be no more tears left, I had to dry my face on my sleeve again. Abandoning any attempt at sleep, I sat up in my bed and turned the scrap of red cloth over in my hands.

When my father was near death, he'd called me to his bedside. Zel had come with me, holding me by the shoulders so I would stand at a distance and not risk coming too close.

"Take care of Gregor," he'd rasped, his face gray but still softened by a gentle smile. "We're all he has left. Take care of him, Ella girl. Promise me."

I'd promised in a wavering voice, still confused about what was happening to my father, to everyone. For years afterward, I'd obediently gone to see Gregor every day, pestering him with questions about whether he had enough victus and clean water or whether he needed me to help clean his shop the way Zel had me cleaning our bakery. It wasn't until I was older that I realized what my father had intended—during my daily visits, Gregor would take care of me. And he had. Without his help, Zel and I would never have survived this long.

And now, I'd destroyed him. I wrapped my arms around my chest as another sob ripped through me. It was all my fault. Gregor, the brewer, the attack on my neighbors.

If I'd never asked for help with the proposal and hadn't involved other merchants in our experiment, this never would have happened. Thankfully, no other lives had been lost in the attack, but all I could think about was Gregor.

I clenched my fist around the rough red fabric and squeezed my eyes shut, rocking back and forth on the bed. Was it so wrong that I wanted to give merchants in Asylia a chance to try something different, a chance to grow and thrive in a way they couldn't on their own? Was it so wrong that Weslan had made the best of his expulsion and found a way to use his powers to build something amazing? Why was I being punished for doing something good?

Tears streamed down my cheeks, the salt burning my worn, raw skin. Was I just supposed to give up now? The bakery stand would either be bankrupted by government fees, or Weslan and I would end up in prison. Gregor was gone forever, and the other merchants would never help us with the petition. What was the point anymore? And yet, how could I give up when so much had been sacrificed already?

Images assaulted me, and I hunched over on the bed, pressing my face into my hands in a desperate attempt to shut them out. The ribbon snake, lifting its head to look at me, as though ready to strike with invisible fangs. The nameless girl's limp hand on the ground beside broken pieces of our lemonburst cake. Gregor's kindly eyes, lifeless, staring up at the night sky as his blood drenched my nightgown.

Once again, I was trapped. I couldn't continue, not without putting us all at even greater risk. But if I gave up, how would we ever escape? Worse, all the death and injuries would mean nothing. I'd be letting the Blight win. Why did they care so much about us, anyway?

I looked at the red fabric in my hand. For weeks now, I'd thought I was going mad, imagining those red scraps and messages. But there was no way I could have known that the Blight would attack shops on our street. The last message had been a promise of reprisal. That meant the message I'd seen on this fabric could not have come from my own mind. It had come from the Blight.

I'd planned to turn the scrap over to the Quarter Guard to help with the investigation—as though they didn't know it was the Blight—but the message in black thread had disappeared. Now the red cloth was blank with no trace of the words I'd seen immediately before the blasts went off.

I thought back over the strange imaginings I'd seen in the last few weeks. How many of them were real all along? What was the Blight trying to do to me? And why did they hate me so much?

If only I could talk to Zel or Weslan about it, but the evidence had disappeared. No doubt they'd think I was regressing, hallucinating after the blast on our street brought back bad memories of the attack on my school.

I scrubbed the tears from my cheeks. Gregor was dead, but I was alive. And until I was dead too, I wasn't completely helpless. I could still do something. And I would.

~

"We have to do it," I said firmly, ignoring Weslan's frown. "We can scrub the names and any identifying measures from the other merchants, but we still have to do it. If the Blight doesn't like what we're doing, then that's all the more reason to proceed, right? It means we're on the right track." I scowled. "Anything that makes the Blight that angry seems like a good idea to me."

Weslan searched my face for something, and I wondered what he was thinking. Finally, he relaxed, though his brow remained furrowed in a small frown. "I'm with you. But I want you to promise something. Stay anonymous, no matter what. Don't let anyone who sees the proposal know you wrote it. They know we're using magic at the bakery, but they don't know we want to change things in the city for everyone. And if you're anonymous, you'll be protected from charges of treason."

I stalled for time, shoving my frustration into the dough I was kneading, turning it and folding it over, then pressing it down with my fists. "If I keep my name out of it, isn't that cowardice? Besides, what if they refuse to consider an anonymous proposal? They have to know I'm serious."

"It's not cowardice, Ella. It's wisdom. If you truly want to win, then you need to stay alive so you can try again if you don't win this time. You can't win if you're executed for treason."

It made sense. As much as I wanted to push forward, no matter the cost, he was right—there would be no victory in my death.

I started as Weslan placed his hand on my shoulder and pulled me around to face him. I stared up at him, smiling inwardly at the smudges of flour on his sculpted cheekbones.

"Now, you answer me this," he said. "How are you planning to get the prince to read the proposal?"

I bit my lip. I'd been putting off this conversation for days.

He bent down so I couldn't avoid his gaze. "If you want me to move forward with this, you need to tell me, Ella. I'm not doing anything else until you do."

"I know this sounds crazy, but the selection ball is coming up in two days." I forced the words out in a rush, suppressing the whirlwind of nerves in my chest. "We need to get the proposal directly into the prince's hands, right? Well, what if I go there, dressed as a Procus lady, and attract his attention? I'll disguise the proposal as a gift or a note or something, and give it to him to read later. All you need to do is dress me up so that I can get in, so that no one else will know that I don't …" I couldn't finish because of the dark look on his face.

"So you want Prince Estevan's attention," he spat. "I suppose if you had *him* on your side, you would be able to do anything you wanted."

"Well, yes, of course." I was confused. I hadn't expected him to like the plan, but I hadn't thought he'd be so angry.

"And you want me to beautify you, as if you were a power-hungry Procus lady, to attract a man with the nickname Beast? A nickname he has most certainly earned, by the way." Weslan's tone took on the sarcastic twist it had often held when he first came to the bakery.

"But I thought he was a reformer."

"Prince Estevan is a monster, Ella. He may be making political and regulatory reforms, but that doesn't mean he's a good man. You cannot trust him." Weslan was looking at me so intensely I thought I might melt under the pressure.

"This isn't going how I thought it would," I said. "I don't care if he's a good man or not. I just want—"

"Oh, really? You don't care. I see."

Clearly, he didn't. I went to the sink, washed the sticky dough from my hands, and dried them on a towel before turning to face him again. "I mean, all we need is for him to listen to our proposal, to see that what we want is what's best for the city. I want him to realize that this would truly change things in Asylia. This is probably my only chance to get the prince's attention. My only chance to get him to listen."

Weslan still looked skeptical. "You want to dress up and go to a ball where the prince is ostensibly looking for a wife, and you want to get his … attention … just so you can talk about regulatory reform?"

I shook my head rapidly. "No. I don't want to talk about it. That would be terrifying. I was thinking … I don't know … I could dance with him once and then put the proposal in his hand and tell him to read it later. Maybe he would think it was a note from some Procus lady. And then he would read it after the ball and realize our proposal makes perfect sense." Why was Weslan was being so difficult?

"Ella." Weslan sighed. "That's not how men think. It's just ... not. He's not going to just think that you're an interesting person who is giving him a note about regulatory reform. He's a womanizer, Ella. He's going to think you want something else."

I scowled. That wasn't my problem. "It doesn't matter what he thinks. All that matters is whether he takes the proposal or not. I only need to get the proposal into his hands and catch his attention long enough for him to realize that we are more than just another group of commoners asking for a favor."

"That's another thing that worries me. If we catch his attention and he realizes how much we can change things, he might decide to ... put a stop to that." He looked at me, and I stared back at him, neither of us willing to budge.

Finally, as though I could pull him over to my side, I reached out and put my hand on his. His warm skin strengthened my resolve. "Weslan, I'm doing this. Please help me. We've made it this far together. This is our one shot for the bakery to survive. If we don't try this, you'll probably be fine. Your powers have grown, and no doubt the mages will want you back when they find out. But this is it for me. For Zel and the girls. If this doesn't work, we're going to have to take our chances in the Badlands or try to get to another city and hope things are better there."

Weslan leaned closer, as though my grip on his hand had pulled him in. The hunger in his eyes made me fall silent. He moved his hand to grip mine, and then ran it up my arm with a gentle touch that had me longing for more, sending goosebumps over my skin. "I'll do it, on one condition. You save a dance for me at the end of the night."

I stared at him, my heart pounding in my chest. Was he serious? He couldn't be. And yet I'd never seen him look more serious. Warmth emanating from his body pressed against my skin, and I fought a strange urge to inch closer to him. Then it occurred to me that we were alone in the kitchen, late at night, and his hand was on my bare arm.

He seemed to realize this at the same time, because he released me and turned away. I watched his shoulders tense for a moment, and then he said, "Just go to bed." His voice roughened, and he gestured to the dough. "I'll finish that. We'll figure this out in the morning."

That night, sleep eluded me. He couldn't be serious. Could he? A mage and a kitchen girl? And could I? A picture of two golden-haired, tan-skinned children flashed before my eyes, a boy with Weslan's cheekbones and a girl with my green eyes. I curled around the sudden pain in my chest.

What was this burning, hungry feeling? It was beyond desire, beyond hope. It was too much. I wanted him too much. And now, I had to wonder. Would it be so bad to be tied to a mage, if it meant I got to be with Weslan? And what if our proposal did set the mages free? Everything would be different. Perhaps ...

I ran my fingers along the side of my face, stroking the wrinkled skin of my scar and doing my best to shove the burgeoning hope back down. It was impossible. Hadn't I learned my lesson by now? I had to stop wanting things that were beyond my reach. I drifted off to sleep with my hand covering my scar, and dreamed of achingly slow dances and perfect, golden hair.

~

A noise came from behind me, and I turned away from reviewing the small, inky words of my final proposal, all cramped on a single page. Zel stood inside the kitchen, a worried look on her face. "I've just been to the front door. Inspector Cyrus came."

My shoulders tensed. "Why did you answer the door? What did he want?"

"I just … I wasn't thinking. I happened to be coming down the stairs when he knocked, and I knew you were busy with the proposal. He asked me a few questions about the bakery and then left. But he seemed so … happy to see me. He didn't mention anything about the tax or setting the trackers on us. But I couldn't shake the feeling that he'd gotten exactly what he wanted. I'm worried we haven't seen the last of him. And now you're going right into the hands of the very people who have the most power to do us harm." Zel's face crumpled. "You're taking much too much risk tonight. It's not worth it."

Of course, Zel would try to dissuade me when my mind was already made up. I took her hands in mine. "Don't you see? Inspector Cyrus is the reason I must do this. He's not going to leave us alone. Now that he's gotten a little bit from us, he's not going to stop. He'll keep demanding more."

I expected Zel to argue with me, to reassure me that everything would be fine like she always did. But this time, she was silent. The encounter with the Inspector had shaken her more than she would admit. I kissed her cheek. "It's time for me to get ready. Can I use your room? I need a full-length mirror."

Zel gave me a small smile. "I suppose."

I climbed the stairs to her room, donned the borrowed black outfit, and reviewed my proposal again. My stomach ached with nerves, and sweat dripped down my back as I hunched over the proposal.

Zel's room was hot and stuffy from a day of baking in the summer sun. The twins thumped around on the roof. No doubt they'd gone up to escape the heat the moment the sun went down.

I'd written and rewritten the proposal so many times that I should have had it memorized by now. Yet I was so nervous I could barely remember any of it. I had included the figures from the bakery and the other merchants, modified to mask our identities, and my forecasts and suggestions. They were laid out for the world to see.

I had attempted to multiply the effect of mage-craft tools in each shop based on an estimated number of similar shops in the city. It was infuriating to take such a big idea and condense it to smeared ink on a single piece of paper. But it wasn't my fault that the petition day was worthless. If the prince wasn't going to listen to me in the official setting, I had to get the information to him another way. Hopefully, I wouldn't get kicked out of the ball. Or worse. I was a commoner who didn't know her place, and Asylia's ruling class would show me no mercy if I were recognized.

Weslan knocked and then entered through the open door. "Ready?"

"I think so." I set the proposal gently on the desk before me. "Let's do this."

He came up behind me as I stared into the mirror, evaluating my appearance. I had set him a ridiculous task. Nobody would mistake me for a Procus lady. What had I been thinking?

My scar, though it had faded significantly, still curved along the side of my face from temple to jaw. My terrible light-green eyes stood out against my skin. My messy dark hair wouldn't stay in its bun. I looked like a common kitchen wench.

Weslan met my gaze in the mirror for a long moment. Could he read all the doubts on my face? He opened his mouth to speak and then shut it. He placed a hand on my shoulder, and a cloud of golden sparkles enveloped me.

I couldn't help the thrill of excitement. Finally, I would get to see myself in one of his designs. The sparkles disappeared. Instead of a long, shabby black dress, I was wrapped in pale blue silk that spilled off my shoulders and hugged my every curve, wrapping around my body in impossible twists and turns, until it spilled onto the floor around me in an extravagant train. The fabric shimmered and glittered with subtle, magical light, brightening the dim room around us. It was the most beautiful dress I'd ever seen.

Not beautiful. Stunning. Striking.

Dangerous.

Weslan's reflection looked oddly ... hungry, but he didn't say anything. Instead, he raised his hand and ran it over my hair with the gentlest of touches. My dark, wild tendrils and loose waves transformed into a pile of sleek, voluminous curls at the crown of my head, with several loose curls hanging down around my face, hiding my scar perfectly. Then a warm wave a magic washed over my face.

I closed my eyes to enjoy the sensation. When I opened my eyes again, my reflection glowed with an otherworldly light. My lips shone a soft pink color. My eyes were lined with something like dark kohl, and my lashes were longer and darker. I blinked. How had he done that?

Weslan stepped toward me and reached around me as though in an embrace.

I met his eyes in the mirror, afraid to move.

He watched me carefully as he ran his hands up my arms. Goosebumps followed his touch, and a pair of white silk gloves materialized, racing up my arms and ending above my elbows. I didn't look like a commoner anymore, that was for sure. I didn't look like a Procus lady, either. I looked like a siren.

Weslan's voice in my ear was husky. "I think you'll get his attention." His hands were still on my arms, and his chest warmed my back.

I ached with the urge to lean into him, but I held myself upright. I couldn't take the chance that I'd mistaken his feelings. "What about the proposal?" My voice sounded husky too. I cleared my throat.

He moved one hand down to my hip, his eyes glinting in the dim light of the mirror's reflection, and the heat of his hand seemed to burn through the fabric of the dress. "There's a pocket," he said. He took the proposal from the table, folded it, and slid it into the secret pocket.

I glanced down. Two scruffy black slippers peeked out beneath the hem of my extravagant ball gown.

"That's right," he said. With a wave of his hand, he transformed my shoes into sparkling glass slippers with delicate heels. They should have felt uncomfortable, but like the dress, they fit perfectly. And they made a difference. The heels forced me to stand straighter than usual, my shoulders back.

I met Weslan's gaze in the mirror again and gave him a small smile. "You're good at this."

He smirked. "I know." But a moment later, the serious, hungry expression returned. "You should go. The ball has started by now."

I faced him, several inches taller than normal, thanks to the glass slippers. I expected him to step back, but if anything, he leaned closer to me. I bit my lip. What was he doing?

His eyes flickered down to my lips and then back up to my eyes. "Ella ..." His voice was as soft as a caress. "I need to—"

"Ready?" Zel's cold voice rang out from the doorway.

We sprang apart, and Weslan ran a hand through his hair. Zel glared at him, but she spoke to me. "Ella, I thought you were planning to be somewhere tonight."

My face burned. What had just happened? "I was about to leave."

Weslan helped me down the stairs.

I watched the ground in amazement as the shimmering, light-blue train lifted and flowed in response to my steps. I wouldn't even have to hold it up.

We crossed the kitchen and stopped at the back door, Zel beside us, a grim look on her face. I peered out the door. There was nothing outside but our worn market cart, sitting forlornly in the dirty alley as the moonlight illuminated its splintery handles. What had Weslan meant by saying that he would handle transportation to the ball? In my manic obsession over the proposal, I had never pressed him for details.

Then he waved his hand at the cart, and gradually, before my very eyes, it expanded until it was the size and shape of a mage-craft fomecoach. Its hood rivaled the luxurious fomecoach that dropped Belle off at the Academy every day. Weslan waved his hand again, and the scuffed wood became sleek, polished white metal with gleaming silver adornments on the grill, wheels, and hood. Then he faltered, leaning heavily against the alley wall.

"Weslan? What's wrong?"

"I'm fine," he said, wiping sweat from his forehead. "It looks like a fomecoach, but it isn't one. Remember that. It only has enough magic to get you to the palace and back. Put your hands on the wheel to start it, but don't attempt to steer it. It knows the way."

I nodded, desperate to prop him up or help him inside.

But he waved me away. "The fomecoach won't last longer than midnight, Ella." He looked at me fiercely, his intense expression at odds with his sagging body as it rested against the wall. "Do whatever it takes to get home by then."

I took one step toward the fomecoach and then another, the train of my dress spilling around me as the glass slippers wobbled on the rough cobblestones of the alley. Apprehension hovered around me like a thick fog. I paused and looked back at Weslan, feeling wild with nerves and uncertainty. "I'll see you before midnight then."

"Don't forget to save me a dance," said Weslan.

I gave him a half smile, fighting against the temptation to forget the whole thing and stay in the bakery with him. "I won't."

I opened the driver's side door and settled into the seat. I swept the skirt inside, closed the door, and looked uncertainly at Weslan through the window. I wanted to fling myself into his warm embrace, to stay with him for the rest of the night, and to give up on this mad scheme. But the fomecoach leapt forward the moment I placed my hands on the steering wheel, sweeping me away from him, zooming down the alley at a breakneck pace.

Chapter 18

I shivered as the wind whipped over my head. This was nothing like the trolley. I gripped the steering wheel tightly, tempted to turn the fomecoach around before we got any closer to the palace. But then I remembered Weslan had created the fomecoach to take me straight to the palace and back. Willing or not, I was going to the prince's ball tonight.

After a harrowing drive through the dark city streets, the fake fomecoach joined the long queue of gleaming fomecoaches that stretched from the gate, down the street, and around the corner. Procus lords and ladies in glittering ensembles sauntered along the footpath toward the palace, laughing merrily as they greeted one another. I looked around for a place to leave the fomecoach. A guard waved to me and directed me over to a spot, and I tapped the steering wheel in the direction of the spot, wondering belatedly how Weslan had instructed it to handle parking. It swung wildly into the spot and jerked to a stop.

The guard smirked. I probably wasn't the only Procus here who didn't exactly drive with the utmost caution. I accepted the guard's assistance as I stepped from the fomecoach and blended into the Procus throngs flocking to the palace gates. Many armed guards lined the steps to the public entrance I'd used on petition day. Black-garbed trackers were sprinkled among them. The trackers and guards stood stiff and unsmiling, as still as the cold palace stones. The Procus families tripped into the palace, not sparing the guards or trackers the slightest notice.

I held my breath as I stepped over the threshold, passing a hand's breadth from the nearest tracker. He kept his eyes straight ahead, ignoring me. I supposed they were on the lookout for the Blight—scenting out traces of suffio, not illicit proposals tucked into secret pockets. Still, it took a concerted effort to breath normally as I passed through the entryway, down the hallway, and up the grand flight of stairs into the ballroom. I'd made it.

I wandered several steps further into the ballroom, gazing at my surroundings in wonder. The chamber was massive. Glowing luminous chandeliers dripped down from the ceiling and lit the room as bright as day, though it was late at night. Elegant tables piled with fruits and iced desserts dotted the edges of the ballroom, and liveried servants wove their way through the crowd, offering crystal glasses of bubbling liquid gold. Chrysos.

Wouldn't Alba be thrilled? It felt like a lifetime ago when she had read the society column to me, back before everything fell apart.

In the center of the ballroom, Procus couples, shining with mage-craft gowns and suits, whirled in a dance I had never learned. Music from the orchestra at the edge of the room echoed off the ornately carved walls, and the spicy, floral scent of goldblossom perfume hung heavy and thick in the air.

The scents, the sounds, the graceful dancers, and the rich clothing were all too achingly beautiful, and for a moment, I couldn't stand it. Too much beauty. Too much luxury. How could they live like this when so many in the city were surviving by choking down cold victus?

What had I been thinking? I didn't belong here. I didn't even know the dances. No wonder Weslan and Zel thought this was a terrible idea. Even after five years at the Royal Academy, I had never felt so out of place in my life.

Suddenly, a tight grip on my upper arm sent a shock through me.

"Ella?" A feminine voice hissed. "What are you doing here?"

~

"I don't know what you were thinking, but tonight is not the night for a prank. Or whatever this is." Belle Argentarius rubbed her silk-gloved hands on her upper arms as we huddled together in an alcove at the edge of the ballroom.

My former Royal Academy classmate looked stunning, every inch the golden Procus heiress. Her dress hugged her curves like mine, but unlike mine, it was practically painted onto her body like a layer of pure gold. Her eyes were magnified in stunning black kohl, and her brown skin glowed as though lit from within. Her skin was perfect, not a single wrinkle or blemish in sight. Had she been healed completely in the hospital or had her mage hidden her scars? I might be dressed as a Procus lady and share her traditional Fenra coloring, but she was far more stunning than I.

"It's not a prank, Belle." I pressed my lips together. Of all the terrible luck. How had she recognized me so easily?

Belle looked around the ballroom, her eyes wide and her face strangely sick. I'd never thought I'd see this, but the heiress to the Argentarius banking empire looked nervous. "Well, I don't honestly care what it is. You shouldn't be here. This is the worst possible night. You need to leave."

I glanced around the ballroom, wondering what she was looking for, but I saw nothing out of the ordinary. "Why? Are you worried I'll distract Prince Estevan from choosing you?"

Belle made a rude noise and looked down her nose at me, recovering her signature arrogance for a moment.

"Hardly. As if I'd ever—" She stopped. "Oh, never mind, Ella. Just leave. Now. You'll thank me later."

"I can't leave, Belle. I came here to see the prince, and I will not leave until I do."

Belle stared at me. Beneath the heavy makeup, her face was drawn, and her eyes were bloodshot. Had she fully recovered from the attack on our school? "Are you well?"

She waved her hand at me dismissively and went back to rubbing her arms. "Of course. Or I would be, if you would just listen to me."

I shook my head. "You're clearly not well, but I've got bigger problems. If you want me to leave, help me get my chance with the prince. One dance, or simply a conversation, and then I'm gone."

Belle shook her head. "I never took you for a girl who'd chase after the rich and powerful."

I narrowed my eyes at her. "I thought you didn't care why I was here. If you want me to leave, help me with the prince. It's that simple."

She drew in a deep breath and let it out, scanning the room yet again as she angled her body as though to shield me from the ballroom. "There," she said, nodding her head. I turned to look where she'd indicated. "He's not wearing his crown. He never does. Tries to mingle with the guests like he's one of us." The disdain in her voice was tangible. "He just grabbed a fresh glass of chrysos. He'll likely slip out on the balcony to drink it in peace before he comes back in. That's his habit, anyway. If you follow him out, you'll get your moment. And then you must leave and not tarry, Ella. Got it?"

"Thank you." I left her in the alcove. I couldn't worry about her now. This was my one chance, and I wouldn't waste it. Belle could take care of herself.

I made my way across the room as quickly as I could without attracting notice, ducking between dancers and chattering groups, and slipped through the balcony door moments after the prince.

I hoped that no one else had noticed me follow him out.

He stood by the edge of the balcony, his hands gripping the rail as he looked out over the city.

"Your Highness," I murmured. When he didn't turn around, I coughed to clear my throat. "Your Highness."

"Yes?" His voice was deep and cold. He kept his back to me.

"I wanted to—"

All my ideas fled from my mind at once. I'd practiced this conversation in my room a hundred times, but now, I couldn't recall a single word of it. What had I planned to say? How did one make conversation with a prince whose nickname was Beast? I stared at his stiff shoulders, my nerve faltering. Somehow, I had to get beyond his cold voice and intimidating demeanor. I had to see his face.

I stepped closer, the blue dress flowing around my feet, and joined him at the railing. The city spread out before us like a sleeping giant with tiny golden spots of glowing luminous lamps breaking up the darkness. The summer air was hot and oppressive even this late at night. I studied his profile. "Please forgive my forwardness, but I had to speak to you."

He laughed humorlessly. "You call this forward?" Finally, he angled his face toward me. He looked me up and down, a little spark of interest glinting in his eyes, reminding me of Weslan's many warnings.

I had to get this over with quickly. "You see, Your Highness, I was hoping to speak with you about something, but not about marriage."

He gave me the slightest smirk. "Is that so? Are you proposing something besides marriage? I'm sorry to say that you wouldn't be the first tonight."

I would have to have been an idiot to mistake his meaning. "I have information for you from … from … a concerned friend," I said, doing my best to keep my voice even.

"Concerned friend? And does this friend have any idea what's happening tonight?" His voice was soft, but his bearing was suddenly tense. He removed his hands from the balcony railing and gripped the sword hilt at his side with one hand.

I took one step back. "I'm not sure what you mean, Your Highness. But this concerned friend has … insights … about our city. And has heard that you paint yourself a reformer."

He laughed drily but didn't respond.

My heart pounded in my chest as I removed the small folded paper from my pocket. I reached for his free hand and pressed the proposal into his palm. I squeezed his stiff fingers once with my white-gloved hand and then let go. "This friend has asked me to pass on some information along with the friend's sincere desire for your listening ear." I curtsied to him as low as I could, my face nearly pressing the ground as my ankles shook and nervousness threatened to overwhelm me. Finally, I rose to go.

Then his arm shot out like a snake and grabbed me, his grip painfully tight on my arm. "Who are you? What are you doing here?" He towered over me, pulling me close, a terrifying expression on his face. "You don't belong here, do you?"

I took a deep breath. "You have nothing to fear from me, Your Highness." I hoped my sincerity came across as clearly as I felt it. "Your friend seeks only the well-being of the city and the advancement of your reign."

His eyes searched my face. He seemed to believe me, for he loosened his grip.

I jerked my arm free and ran. I exited through the balcony door and melted into the crowd. It had grown thicker since I'd been gone.

I'd made it several steps into the crowd when I heard a man shout, followed by a gut-wrenching cry of pain. I whirled around.

Guards in red jackets rushed toward the balcony door where it looked as though someone had collapsed on the ground. Was it the prince? What had happened? I strained my neck to look but could see nothing. I dared not turn back to learn more.

I dodged through the crowd, avoiding the guests as they rushed toward the prince, trying to make myself look as unhurried and innocent as possible. In a crowd of so many, surely I was another faceless girl, another pretty gown. He wouldn't remember me. No one would remember me. I walked with mincing steps toward the door, wishing I had footwear other than the elegant glass slippers Weslan had given me.

Panicked screaming from the guests rose in pitch behind me, and then a guard shouted, "There—in the blue dress! Get her!"

Chapter 19

I had to move faster. I had to get away, or everything would be lost. I bent down and slipped my feet from the delicate glass slippers, and then I clutched them to my chest as I raced barefoot down the hallway and out of the palace.

The guards at the entrance only gave me a passing glance. *Thank you, Weslan, for creating such a convincing disguise.*

I found my white fomecoach and threw myself inside. It jumped beneath my touch, shooting out of the parking spot and speeding away from the palace.

As I reached the corner, I heard the guards at the entrance shout. The word about the girl in the blue dress had spread.

Too late. But there was no triumph in the thought. I kept the steering wheel in a stranglehold. The fomecoach swung around first one corner and then the next, putting ever greater distance between me and the palace. I checked over my shoulder, but no one pursued me. Perhaps they hadn't seen where I'd turned after I left the main street to the palace.

Weslan must have anticipated a scenario like this one. The fomecoach took a circuitous route, sticking to narrow alleys and small side streets. I huddled in the seat as the vehicle raced through the city, hoping desperately that I would make it back to the bakery before the fomecoach ran out of magic.

The coach slowed when it reached the alley behind the bakery. My nerves were shot by the time it puttered to a halt by the back door.

I leapt from the fomecoach, and as my feet touched the ground, I felt a cold wave behind me. When I whirled around, the coach had become the shabby-looking hand cart once more. If anything, it looked even shabbier now, as though it had worn itself out during the trip to the palace and back.

Weslan flung open the bakery door. "Did you do it? What happened?" He strode into the alley, looked left and right, and then put a hand on my back to hustle me into the bakery.

I was inside before I realized the dress had returned it its original black, shapeless form. "Everything's fine, I think. Something happened after I spoke with the prince, but I'm not sure what. And no one followed me here." I paused.

He was staring at my hand with a look of horror on his face.

I followed his gaze to the single glass slipper I held in a white-knuckled grip. No doubt my expression mirrored his. "Oh, no." The other slipper was gone. "Oh, Weslan ... I took them off to run out of the palace, and I must have dropped one in the—"

"FEMALE CITIZENS. ASSEMBLE." A magically amplified voice echoed in the street. Time slowed down.

I crept through the kitchen and into the front room. Toward the voice. It was like wading through deep water. I was dimly aware of Weslan following me and Zel reaching the bottom of the stairs as I entered the front room.

"CITIZENS," the voice said, "You are harboring a fugitive suspected of attempting to assassinate the crown prince. Assemble in the street now. All female citizens aged thirteen to twenty-one will be taken in for questioning now."

I pressed a hand to my churning stomach. "Assassinate? I don't understand—"

"CITIZENS. All female citizens aged thirteen to twenty-one, assemble now, or we will enter and bring you out."

I heard a pattering of footsteps. Bri and Alba descended the stairs with tousled hair.

"Mom?" Bri rubbed her eyes sleepily. "What's going on?"

Zel stood, transfixed, staring through the window at the glittering lights of the tracker fomecoach in the street. For once, she was speechless.

"Zel, I'm so sorry." What had I done? "I never thought this would ... I don't know why they're doing this."

Why would they arrest every female who fit my description? Why not follow me inside the bakery and arrest me alone? If they had enough of my trace to follow me here, surely, they knew who I was. "I'll go out. I'll tell them it was me and get them to leave."

But Zel stopped me with an iron grip on my arm. "Ella, if you go out now, they'll execute you. If you're even suspected of this crime, you'll be executed without trial."

Hot tears streamed down my face and splashed on my neck. "I-I-I don't know what to say. I'm so sorry." I wrenched my arm from her grip and continued toward the door, only to reel back in shock when blonde-headed Bri stepped into my path.

"Stay in here, Ella." Her voice was soft but determined, still hoarse from sleep. That was the last thing Bri said before she walked outside to meet the trackers in the street.

Zel took a painful breath, and then Alba wailed and raced after her sister.

My mind screamed questions at me, and I ran forward to call them back.

Weslan caught me and held me back. "Ella, wait. Think! They're obviously too young to have infiltrated the ball and gotten anywhere near the prince. They'll take them in for questioning, bring them home, and keep looking for the real culprit. This way, no one will come looking inside our house.

That's all that matters. Keep the trackers out. The girls will be home as soon as anyone gets a clear look at them."

Zel stepped in front of me and nodded, though her face was white as a sheet.

I tried to maneuver around her, but Weslan's grip held me in place. "You can't know that! It's too big of a risk!"

"You're a fine one to talk about risk." Zel's voice shook but she kept her body between me and the door. "Would you rather risk your execution, or risk that the twins will be held in the Quarter Guard station for the night?"

I opened my mouth to argue, but the words died in my throat. They were right. It just felt so … wrong. How I wished Bri hadn't taken it into her head to be a heroine. I would rather risk my own execution than have the two girls in danger because of me.

"Hide in your room." She shoved me in the direction of the kitchen. "If they decide to search the bakery for more girls who fit the description, there's a better chance they won't see you."

With slow steps, I complied, feeling numb.

I wiped at the tears coursing down my face, but they kept coming. I left the luminous dial off and locked the door to my room. Pressing my forehead against the window, I strained to see what was happening in the street.

Two figures in white nightgowns, one blonde and one brunette, were huddled together, and more girls from down the street came out to join them. Then the trackers, their gold arm bands gleaming in the light from their vehicles, came over and settled the girls into the fomecoaches.

One voice stood out, and I strained to hear. "I'll take these two." The man's deep, gravelly voice sounded familiar. Where had I heard that voice before? But the view through the glass was too blurry and the night too dark. I couldn't see his face.

I focused on the wavy forms of Bri and Alba as the tracker shut them into his fomecoach and climbed into the driver's seat. And then they were gone.

After the last tracker fomecoach left, I returned to the front room. Zel and Weslan stood at the window, watching the street.

I stopped, frozen at the sight of Zel's face. I wanted to embrace her, but for the first time since she'd come into my life, I was afraid to touch her. I'd betrayed her, utterly and completely. I'd sworn to protect her and her daughters, but instead, I'd nearly destroyed them. I could never take that back. "I'm so sorry," I said again, but the words sounded empty even to me.

"It's not your fault." She went into the kitchen and slumped down at the table as though all strength had left her. "I thought ..." She sighed.

Weslan and I sat on either side of her. "I told them about their father. How he sacrificed his life for me, so I could get away, so I could leave Draicia. I thought if they knew of his love, it would be a comfort. But I—" Her voice broke, and tears welled in her eyes. "I should have known Bri would want to be like her father."

I swallowed and looked away. I'd never known that her husband had died for her. Zel had never spoken of her late husband. I only knew that she'd loved him and lost him. And now I might have cost her the twins too.

Zel kept her eyes downcast, occasionally reaching up to wipe the tears away. It occurred to me that perhaps she was trying to avoid looking at me. My throat tightened painfully. I stood, went to my room, and changed out of the black dress, suddenly unable to stand having it on my skin for a moment longer. I put on my plain work dress and went to the kitchen to make a pot of coffee. I poured three mugs and set them on the table, but then I started to pace. I couldn't relax.

A heavy knock shook the bakery's front door. Weslan patted Zel's shoulder as he got up. "Don't worry, Zel. That must be them now."

Weslan answered the door while Zel and I stayed hidden in the kitchen. We heard a deep, gruff voice, too low to make out the words. Then Weslan spoke, sounding harsher than I'd ever heard him. "What's the meaning of this?" There was another gruff rumble that I couldn't make out.

Weslan slammed the door and returned to the kitchen with a small wooden box in his hands. He stood in the doorway, staring at Zel with a stricken look on his face, and held it out to her.

She stood and took it as though in a trance. She lifted the lid and uttered a tortured noise. "Oh." She clutched the box to her chest, sobbing silently, her breath coming in desperate gasps as though she were drowning.

I sprang forward and then stopped short. "What is it? What's wrong?" I forced the words out, though I was almost too afraid to ask. "What's in the box?"

The sound of my voice startled her out of her grief. She straightened up and squared her shoulders. "Weslan, you'll come with me." She set the box on the table, wiped the tears off her cheeks, and smoothed her hair back. "We will get them home safely, whatever it takes."

Then Zel shot me a fierce, determined stare. "Stay here and stay safe, Ella. I-I forgive you. And I love you like a daughter, no matter what. Never forget that." She held my gaze for a moment as though willing me to believe her words. And then she marched across the kitchen, through the shop, and out the front door.

Weslan watched me from the doorway. "Stay here," he echoed. "I will come back." Then he followed her outside.

Didn't he mean we? *We* will come back?

The door slammed shut behind them, and I finally took another step toward the box. I flipped open the lid. There, in the dusty, grimy interior, were two narrow, mismatched shoes—Bri's worn leather sandal and Alba's soft rose-colored slipper. The shoes they'd been wearing when they left the bakery to cover for me. I picked up Alba's slipper, and a scrap of paper fell out. I held it up to the light with a shaking hand.

YOU LOSE, CINDERELLA

The twins hadn't been arrested. They'd been taken.

Chapter 20

A door slammed somewhere on our street and startled me awake. I lifted my head from the kitchen table, feeling woozy and disoriented. Was it already dawn?

No, the street outside was pitch black. I'd only been asleep for a few minutes. Every luminous in the house was off. The house creaked, and a shutter upstairs slapped against its frame. If only Weslan and Zel and the twins would return.

I was alone in the bakery for the first time since Zel had come to us seeking shelter thirteen years before. And now everything I had ever feared had come to pass. Not only that, I had failed in the only thing I'd ever wanted—to protect my family. Instead, my reckless attempts to change Asylia had resulted in the worst possible outcome.

Who had taken them? Was the message from the Blight? Was it even real, or was I hallucinating again, going mad?

I wiped the drool off my face, dialed up the luminous, and made another pot of coffee. Surely, they would be home soon. All Zel had to do was … Well, I had no clue what the kidnappers had demanded. But why would it take so long?

I poured a mug of coffee and took a sip, but the acid taste curdled in my stomach. I ran upstairs to the bathroom and retched, doubling over and sobbing. Afterward, I washed my mouth out and brushed my teeth, my hands moving through the motions numbly as if they had a will of their own. I stared at my bloodshot reflection in the smudged bathroom mirror. How could this be happening? I was awake, yet I was trapped in one of my nightmares.

Nothing made sense. I shouldn't have snuck into the ball or handed that proposal to the prince. Some might consider that treasonous, but what did that have to do with the Blight? What did it have to do with Zel and her daughters? But it couldn't be a coincidence.

They must know about Zel. In the Blight's hands, Zel would be a powerful, dangerous weapon. And the only thing that could possibly convince Zel to work for them was her daughters.

I pressed my hands against my forehead until my skull ached, wishing I could shove the thought away. But it all fit. The persecution by the Blight that stopped short of harming the bakery. The kidnapping. The shoes in the box to draw Zel out of the house.

I dropped my hands and smoothed my wild hair back into a bun. I straightened my wrinkled dress and ticked off the facts as though they were components to a terrible exam question.

I was alone in the bakery. Fact.

Zel, Weslan, and the twins had been taken or been lured away by someone, most likely the Blight. Fact.

It was well after midnight, and the situation hadn't improved. Fact.

I had to do something. Fact.

~

The night was humid, the moon covered by clouds, but Asylia never slept. I let myself out the back door of the bakery and stood in the grimy alley, listening, in case the front was being watched by trackers or anyone else. Boisterous laughter echoed down the main street in front of the bakery, likely from the pub at the corner. Somewhere, a baby was crying and a couple was arguing, their voices sharp and bitter in the heavy air.

I set off down the alley, my steps hesitant. I still didn't know my destination. Should I go to the Quarter Guard? One of the guards had kidnapped the twins. Could I trust any of them? And yet, who else could I go to, if not the Guard?

I was halfway down the alley when I felt a presence behind me. I whirled around, holding my breath. No one was there. I turned back and kept walking, but the feeling continued to poke at me. I paused again, exasperation warring with terror. Nothing behind me. And then I realized why.

The feeling wasn't in the physical world. It was in the back of my mind. What could it be? Something about it seemed warm and familiar, as though it were … mine. Weslan. It had to be the True Name bond.

I'd tried to ignore the strange spark when we were together at the bakery. I had no need for a tiny spark when I had the real Weslan absorbing more than his fair share of my attention every day.

I faced the opposite end of the alley, where the spark originated, and picked up my pace. I could find them all on my own. Hope fluttered in my chest as I walked, following the gentle tug of our bond. I couldn't let any of them be lost because of me. Not like Gregor. This time, I would do the right thing—somehow, I would get them out to safety. No doubt the Blight had not bothered to take me because I was the only one without magic. But they'd underestimated me.

Weslan's spark led me toward the southern edge of the city. The River Quarter. I followed it as quickly as I could, keeping to the shadows, my head down and my face partially covered by loose strands of hair that had come out of my bun. The sky was beginning to brighten from cloudy black to a deep gray when the pull strengthened considerably.

I was in a narrow, debris-filled street, surrounded by abandoned warehouses. Most likely, these were owned by traders who had closed when the plague hit and never reopened.

Had the pull from Weslan's spark strengthened because he was here, somewhere? I pressed my body into the doorway of an abandoned warehouse. If Weslan was here, that meant the Blight must be too. I only hoped that Zel and the girls were with him. I peered into the darkness. Would I be able to spot any sign of the Blight on the street?

"— a lucky bastard, Silas," said a man's voice. The glow of a small luminous lantern suddenly lit the street and I shrank back. Two dark shapes huddled in an alcove down the street across from where I was standing.

"Luck's got nothing to do with it," came a dark, gravelly voice in response.

That voice. I'd heard it before. Where?

"You're only in a lather because I brought home the winning ticket. Wonder who's getting the next Blight promotion?" Silas said.

I'd heard that gravelly voice at the bakery earlier this evening. The tracker who had put Alba and Bri in his car was standing right here in the River Quarter, not thirty paces from me. He'd kidnapped the twins rather than bringing them to the Quarter Guards' station. A government mage, of all people, was working with the Blight?

I forced myself to inch closer, hoping to catch a glimpse of their faces, even though all I wanted to do was run the other direction and never look back. But I couldn't leave Weslan and Zel and the girls. Not when they were only in this because of me. I crept along the edge of the warehouse until I was almost directly across the street from the men.

"—sick of all this waiting, Si," said the other one.

"We all are," said Silas. "Quit your complaining."

"I joined this thing because I wanted to change things for our people, not sit around night after night standing guard, playing a stricken servant during the day."

Silas leaned back against the building behind them. "Any day now."

"He's been saying that for weeks." The complainer made a rude, scoffing noise. "Any day now. I'm striking ready now. Ready to take those Fenra rats down and make some heads roll."

Heads roll? My pulse raced. Why had I gotten so close to them? I held myself as still as I could, which wasn't hard since I was paralyzed with fear.

Then the door behind them swung open, and the two men straightened. A small square of yellow light lit the darkness until another man stepped into it. "You ladies done gossiping yet? We can hear you idiots inside. You've got a job to do, you know."

"Oh yes, sir. Absolutely. Sorry, sir." The man who'd been complaining spoke, while the tracker only nodded and looked away. The other man glared at them for a moment and then closed the door again. I watched the tracker, feeling as though I was missing something important. The cold, blank look on his pale face had looked eerily familiar, but I hadn't been able to see his face when he arrested the twins earlier. Where had I seen him before?

My eyes adjusted to the dim light, and I squinted at their faces. I held back a gasp. The market. The man across the street was the same tracker who had come to investigate our stand at the market. He'd placed his hands all over our stand. And all over me.

He must have picked up a trace of Zel then. It had been years since she'd worn that dress. And yet, somehow, he'd been skilled enough to catch her trail.

I cringed, wanting to hide but too scared to risk missing some vital clue.

The tracker must have bided his time for days, waiting for the chance to lure Zel out of the bakery and get leverage over her. He'd likely known he stood no chance against her inside our home. But once he had her daughters?

Fury ripped through me. How could a man be so cruel that he would use a woman's daughters against her? How could a man be so desperate that he'd force an innocent woman to act as a weapon? And yet, I knew the answer. They were the Blight.

I joined this thing because I wanted to change things for our people. That's what the other guard had said. They were rebel mages.

A charge went through me as footsteps echoed on the street. Momentarily, I was overjoyed to see a uniformed member of the Quarter Guards walking down the street with a frown on his face. I was so desperate for help that I nearly called out to him, but he waved a friendly greeting to the two men in the stairwell. I held my tongue just in time.

He walked over to shake their hands. "Any day now," he said.

"Any day now," they repeated.

"You hear about the sweet tip I brought in earlier?"

Silas folded his arms and leaned back on the building again, but his partner answered. "Yeah?"

"Some low-level inspector in the Merchant Quarter passed it to me, hoping for a reward. He thinks there's an unregistered mage hiding in the quarter. Even gave me her address."

The man who'd been complaining nodded his head toward the door. "In there now. Get this—she's got the Touch." He chortled. "Bet your inspector didn't realize that, or he wouldn't have been so quick to sell her out."

The guard took a hasty step back. "She's inside? I thought no one in Asylia had the Touch."

"She's not Asylian. She's Draician. And trust me, she's got it." He nudged the tracker. "This lucky idiot confirmed it."

The guard took another nervous step back as the first man grinned at him. "We'll see what happens. Wouldn't be surprised if it's any hour now. An unregistered mage with the Touch? She'll be unstoppable. Better make sure your people are ready." Despite his complaining earlier, the man

193

looked downright gleeful as he boasted to the guard. What were they planning on doing with Zel?

"Uh, we're ready," said the quarter guard. "Just keep the marks coming."

They said a gruff round of farewells and the guard went on his way. When he'd turned the corner, the first man nudged Silas again. "Bet you can't wait to put greasy Fenra bastards like that in their place."

Silas grunted. "You have no idea."

I took one step back. And another. My recklessness had caused Zel to be captured by the very people who had the power to destroy our city, the people who'd been trying to destroy it for years. And now that they'd found an unregistered mage—one with the Touch, at that—whose True Name was not known to the city government, they could make their move at last.

Stumbling back, I caught myself just in time. Thankfully, the men continued to talk.

I edged back along the building until they were out of sight, and then sprinted away, my movements jerky and panicked as though my limbs belonged to someone else. The man with the face of blood in my nightmares had reached his cruel hand right into my life and taken hold of the people I loved most in the world. And now he was going to use them to destroy Asylia. From the sound of it, he intended to return the Kireth mages to power for the first time in seven hundred years. My nightmare would come true for everyone in the city.

I tripped over a loose cobblestone in some nameless alley and went sprawling. My head hit the stones with a painful crack. I sat up slowly, pressing a hand to my head, and looked around. It was dawn. The sky was lightening more every minute.

Running wouldn't solve anything, so what was I doing? I needed to get help. But if the Quarter Guards were being paid off, I had nowhere to turn. I stood, my legs shaky, and straightened my dress. There was only one person I could think of who could help me.

~

Belle's house was at the heart of a massive compound in the Argentarius family estate, smack in the center of the Procus Quarter. I knew Belle's house by reputation. It was supposedly the centerpiece of the compound, the tallest villa, with the golden mage-craft fountain bubbling in front of it.

I looked up at the tall, glass windows and detailed, stone carvings. For a moment, I thought I caught a movement behind the window. If someone had seen me lingering, I had to hurry. I went around to the side and then back, looking for some sort of servants' entrance. When I found the small door, I knocked quietly. Nobody answered.

How strange. Wouldn't her servants be awake at dawn? I knocked again, louder. Perhaps they hadn't heard me in the hustle and bustle of their morning labor. Nothing. I banged my fist on the door and called out, "Excuse me? I have a message for Lady Belle Argentarius!"

Finally, the door swung open, and Belle faced me. "Loud enough, Ella? You're going to get me in trouble."

"What are you doing here?" The very last thing I had expected was for Belle herself to answer the servants' entrance door.

"Get inside. Quickly. And stop making so much noise. There are guards inside."

I darted inside the narrow entryway, and she locked the deadbolt behind me. "I'm here because I—"

"Not here," she hissed. She grabbed my hand and yanked me down the hallway, up a flight of stairs, and down another hallway, turning first one way and then the other. She acted as though she expected someone to discover us at any moment. Finally, she opened a door and shoved me inside, shutting and locking it behind her.

We were in a large, surprisingly dusty schoolroom, complete with desks and a blackboard at the front. The curtains were shut and the luminous dial was off, and she made no move to turn it on. I stared at Belle in the dim light, noticing her appearance for the first time. She still wore her gold dress from the ball. Her hair was a mess of wavy brown curls, all out of place, and her beautiful makeup was smeared around her red-rimmed eyes. "Belle? What's going on?"

She crossed her arms and shook her head, eyes narrowing. "You shouldn't have been at the ball last night. Of all the nights, Ella. I told you to leave."

"I realize that now," I said, annoyed with her tone. "But why? What happened? I swear to you, I did nothing to harm the prince when I met him on the balcony. I simply gave him a harmless note, a ... request for him to consider."

"If it was so harmless, why did you sneak into the ball? Why didn't you go to the petition day, like any normal, law-abiding commoner?"

"Because he doesn't honor the petitions," I said, my voice rising despite my best efforts to keep my temper. "I went to the petition day, and I waited all day but I never got my chance to speak. Besides, he didn't even listen to the petitions that were given. I had to get his attention somehow."

"So you just had to sneak into the ball, did you? Oh, if you only knew."

"Knew what? What happened? You must tell me."

"There was an assassination attempt." Belle's voice was toneless and dry.

"I ... know," I said tentatively. "I heard that. I had nothing to do with that. You must believe me. But the Quarter Guard came to my neighborhood and rounded up the young women, including my stepsisters. My stepmother hid me so they didn't find me."

Belle's stare seemed so empty that I wasn't sure if she'd heard me. Had she not yet recovered from the blast in our classroom?

Then she shook her head and seemed to gain more clarity. "Well, someone tried to assassinate the crown prince immediately after you spoke to him. They timed it as he came through the balcony doors behind you. No doubt your stepsisters will be returned to you as soon as it becomes clear they had nothing to do with it."

"That's the thing, Belle. They never came back." Could I trust her? I wasn't so sure now. The way the men were talking outside that warehouse, they had people on their side throughout the city government. And Belle's family was one of the most powerful families in the whole city. What if she was involved somehow?

Wherever her loyalties lay, she clearly wasn't happy. I had to believe she wanted to do the right thing. Procus heiress or not, she was my only hope. I took a deep breath and plunged forward. "My stepsisters were kidnapped after they were taken by the trackers, and then they kidnapped my stepmother as well."

Belle frowned. "What are you talking about? If the Quarter Guard took them into custody, how could they be kidnapped?"

"Because some of the quarter guards and the trackers are working for someone else." I waited for a look of shock to come over her face, but it never came. Whatever was going on, she must have known something wasn't right in our city. "I followed them."

I might be trusting Belle to help me, but I couldn't risk telling anyone about Weslan's True Name. "And I overheard the man who took them talking. They work for the Crimson Blight. The Blight kidnapped my family, and they're planning to act, to do something big in the city. I don't know what they plan to do, but it could happen any day now. Since they have my stepmother, it could happen any moment."

Belle pursed her lips. "What's so special about your stepmother?"

"I-I can't tell you about that. Just trust me when I say you don't want them to act. They could destroy everything."

"What do you mean, destroy everything?"

"They're mages, Belle."

She raised a skeptical eyebrow.

"They are," I insisted. "I know where they're hiding, and I heard them talking, saying as much. They said they couldn't wait to put the Fenra in their place. I think they mean to return Kireth mages to power in Asylia."

Belle was quiet for several long moments, and I waited on edge for her response. But then she said, "It makes perfect sense."

"Um, what?"

There was no shock on her face. Just calm, bleak acceptance. "I said it makes perfect sense. I've been trying to figure out why my family and the Falconus family are always on the verge of war." Belle paced around the old schoolroom, stirring up clouds of dust with each step. "They're constantly accusing us of being behind the Blight's attacks, trying to destabilize the government so that we can overthrow the crown prince. And my father, for his part, is convinced that Lord Falconus is the one behind the Blight's attacks. He thinks they attacked the school to target me. But if the Blight is controlled by mages, then maybe they're trying to get my father and Lord Falconus to butt heads. But why?"

Then Belle's face paled and she drew in a sharp breath. "I know what they're doing." She swayed on her feet for a moment, and I wondered if she was about to faint.

How long had it been since she'd slept? What was going on with her? "What are they doing, Belle?"

She kneaded her hands together. "My father and Lord Falconus also hold certain positions in government. They're kept a secret from most people for obvious reasons. But if the Blight is pitting them against each other, then the Blight must know who they are."

"They know what? Tell me!"

"They're the true authorities at the Mage Division. Between the two of them, my father and Lord Falconus hold the True Names of all the most powerful mages in the city." She eyed me hesitantly.

I nodded. "I know about the True Names." Hopefully, she wouldn't ask me to explain.

"The rest of the True Names are held in hierarchies among the mages themselves, all the way down to the low-level appearance manipulators who barely count as mages."

I scowled at her offhand remark, but she ignored me. "The entire structure of authority in the Mage Academy culminates with the two of them, my father and Lord Falconus, with the names split between them so no single Procus family controls all the mages, especially not the royal family. It's meant to provide a stable balance of power in the city, and it's worked for seven hundred years." Her voice grew even more tense. "But if they destroy each other in retaliation for these attacks, the entire structure of mage control will fall apart. We'll be at the mercy of the mages once again."

Chapter 21

My head spun with nightmarish images from ancient history class—the horrible abuses inflicted on the non-magical Fenra when Kireth mages first invaded and ruled for three hundred bloody, miserable years. And then my whirlwind of thoughts settled on Weslan—his joy at using his powers, his creativity and skill, and his wistfulness when he spoke of being free to work and live wherever he chose. I'd always thought Asylia's founding families had enslaved the mages for good reasons. They couldn't risk a return to that horrible past, could they? And yet, what new abuses had they inflicted on the Kireth to keep them under control? I remembered Weslan's horrified face the first and only time I spoke his True Name out loud. Should one person ever have such control over another?

And then another thought struck me: "Belle, where is everyone?"

She looked at me bleakly. "My father and brothers are leading an attack on the Falconus compound. My sisters are hiding in their rooms, and all our servants have fled."

I reeled back. "What?!"

"Last night, my father's spies received intelligence suggesting that the Falconus family would make their move against the prince at the ball. That's why I told you to leave—I didn't want you to get caught in the crossfire. When the assassination attempt really did take place, my father took it as a sign that he should move against the Falconus family openly and thwart their ambitions for good."

She shivered. "I wouldn't be surprised if the Falconus family received the opposite intelligence, indicating that my father was about to make his move against the prince. The Blight could not have done this more neatly. If it weren't so horrific, I'd be impressed."

I shook my head. Only an Argentarius would be impressed by the calculations of dangerous fanatics. "We have to tell someone. Prince Estevan. He must know. There's no one else we can trust, and besides, he's likely the only one who can force your father and Lord Falconus to call a truce. Can you get me an audience with him?"

Belle laughed incredulously. "Just how do you think this works, Ella? I might be rich, but that doesn't mean I'm on casual speaking terms with the crown prince."

I glared at her. "Then what do you suggest? We've got to see him somehow."

Belle ignored me and turned toward the window, her face as cold and bleak as a stone statue. I would never have known her father was involved in a private war. She looked untouchable. But then she sighed. "I hate to say this, but you're right. We have to tell him. The thing is, the prince will never see me, especially if he's still recovering from last night's attack. My father is not exactly his favorite Procus lord. The best I can do is take you to the palace gates and use my name to get you inside. From there, you'll have to find someone who believes you, someone who can get you to the prince."

I blew out a long breath. A few hours ago, the conspirators had come to my home to arrest me for the attempted assassination. Could I walk back inside the gates of the very people who wanted to execute me and ask them to believe me? I balled my fists at my sides. It had to be safer than turning myself in to the Quarter Guards. If I was at the palace when I was arrested, there'd be less chance for someone in the Blight's employ to intervene.

Would Zel do this for me? No question. She would do it without a moment's hesitation or doubt. Would Bri or Alba do this for me? The very thought of those two tousled heads, one light, one dark, bent together as they waited beside the tracker's fomecoach, made my eyes burn.

They'd already done it for me. The least I could do was try.

~

The splatter of blood on the footpath was my first sign that something was wrong.

I followed closely behind Belle and stepped around it as she did. The morning was growing hotter, but we both wore jackets and hats pulled low over our faces, hers glittering and ornate as befit a Procus lady, mine the plain, clean black of a household maid. We turned on Procus Avenue, and Belle stopped so quickly I nearly ran into her back.

"Turn around," she said quietly, taking several quick steps backward. "Go!"

I took in the scene on the street at a glance. Guards in the deep navy and gold uniforms of the Argentarius clan clashed in the street with guards clad in the black and orange liveries of the Falconus family. At least a dozen bodies lay in the road around them. I retreated in a hurry.

Belle shoved me into an alcove—a servants' entry on the abandoned street—and we huddled there, both breathing heavily. She shielded her eyes with her hands for a moment before she resolutely straightened. "Do you still want to do this?"

I stared at her, still seeing the bloodied bodies lying about the street in my mind's eye. "What?"

Belle grabbed my shoulders and gave me a shake. "Ella. Do you still want to do this or not?"

I swallowed. I had to be brave. For Bri. For Alba. I had to be stronger than my fear. If nothing else, I had to get into the palace, throw myself on the mercy of the guards, and beg for their help. That was something even a coward like me could do. "Yes. I … I still want to do this." The words came out barely above a whisper.

"Then we'll take another route. Come on."

Belle led me in the direction of the Royal Palace, slipping down back alleys and side streets to avoid the main avenues. We could still hear the shouts and screams of men fighting, and even the occasional boom of an explosion. But we kept our heads down and hurried from street to street. Finally, we came out of a narrow alley between two stately government offices. The Royal Palace was straight ahead. We'd made it.

But the shouting wasn't coming from the fighting we'd left behind. It was between us and the palace gates.

~

After all our twists and turns to avoid the fighting in the street, the sun had risen high over the city by the time we made our way to the palace. Somewhere nearby, a clock tower's bell rang ten times. The bell's clanging made my head throb as worry coursed through me. I'd gotten back to the bakery just before midnight, which meant Zel, Weslan, and the girls had already been in the Blight's grasp for almost ten hours. It had taken me far too long to reach the palace, and now we faced further delays. What if I was too late?

Belle pulled off her hat and her jacket and handed them to me. Then she fussed with her hair. With her straight bearing and glittering gown, she looked regal enough to be a princess despite her wild hair. "Stay close behind me, Ella. Don't allow yourself to be separated, even for a moment. Got it?"

I nodded mutely. I couldn't believe we were doing this. We hid in the alley and peered around the corner.

The mob in front of the palace wasn't made up of guards from the Procus families. They were commoners, attacking each other, screaming curses and slogans. As far as I could tell, they all thought something different was going on. Some shouted slogans in defense of the Argentarius family, the scions of open trade, while others cried out in support for the Falconus family, the patrons of the arts who abhorred dangerous, plague-inviting trade practices. Some had placed themselves by the gate, as though to defend the Royal Palace. Others railed against the Procus families and the royal family, shouting about greedy leeches and coming to blows with those they suspected of supporting any Procus family.

Inside the tall gates, a squadron of armed guards stood and watched, but they made no move to bring order to the mob. And Belle was planning to walk us right through the madness.

"Belle, are you sure about this?"

She'd already taken one step toward the mob. She paused and eyed me over her shoulder. "I'm sure if you are."

I bit my lip. "If we don't get to the prince, the Blight will win. We don't have a choice."

She had the nerve to roll her eyes at me. "Then what are we waiting for?"

She squared her shoulders and charged toward the crowd, and I hurried along in her wake. She aimed for the part of the mob with the most Argentarius supporters. As she approached, nose in the air, the first few people recognized her and stood back.

"Out of the way, there," said one man, shoving some of his comrades back to make space for her. I followed as closely as I could behind her.

Belle gave him a regal nod. "Thank you, kind gentleman. My maid and I are needed at the palace. Perhaps you could help us clear a path?"

He nodded eagerly, and began to shout, charging before us and shoving his buddies none too gently out of our way. Sweat dripped down my back. People jostled roughly against us as we steadily worked our way through the crowd. We were halfway to the palace gates when the Falconus supporters realized that the Argentarius heiress herself was in their midst.

"Traitor!"

"Get her!"

But the Argentarius supporters shielded us as we pushed toward the gates.

Belle showed no sign of fear, remaining ice cold and imperious, as though the commoners who jostled against her were too far beneath her to notice.

At the end, we were pressed up against the palace gates. The crowd surged behind us and the iron bars of the gate dug painfully into my chest. We had to get through soon, or the mob would crush us even if the Falconus supporters didn't find us first. Belle called out to the guards standing several feet from the gate. "Hello, there! Fellows! I've a matter to discuss with the prince. Might I and my maid enter the gates?"

A guard took one hesitant step forward, sweat beading on his upper lip. With his closely shorn hair and nervous eyes, he looked younger than either of us. "And who are you?"

"Lady Belle Argentarius," she said, as though announcing that he'd won a pot of gold marks. "Let us in, and I'll explain."

"We ... we're not supposed to open the gates for anyone," he said shakily.

From my profile view I could see Belle clench her jaw, but she maintained a stately smile for the guard. "I'm sure His Majesty is grateful for your loyal and faithful service. However, he may not take too kindly to you turning away a Procus lady, especially in a ... well, a scene like this."

The guard looked around. His fellow squadron members shrugged at him, seeming more worried about the growing mob than the lady at the gate. "Fine, then," he said. "Inside, and be quick about it." He swallowed and glanced at her. "That is, if you please, my lady."

He unlocked the gate and opened it the slightest crack, and Belle grabbed me by the hand as the weight of the crowd pressed us through. We fell in a pile of skirts as the guard shoved a few commoners back and slammed the gate in their faces, locking it again with shaking hands. I got to my feet and helped Belle to hers, and we looked around. We'd made it this far. Now we had to convince someone to let us see the prince.

"What are you idiots doing?" A red-faced guard charged out of the nearest entrance to the palace.

The guard who had let us in swore under his breath, and then stood straight, his feet together. "Sir. The lady … ah, Procus Lady Belle Argentarius, she said she needed to see His Majesty."

The red-faced man halted a few inches from the young guard's face. "And exactly what part of 'let no one in' did you find it difficult to grasp?"

"N-n-no part, sir." The guard's eyes flickered to us. "Should I …?"

"Get them out of here, you imbecile." The man in charge took a moment to glare at us before he about-faced to march back to the palace.

"Wait!" Belle glanced at me. "My maid … she has information for the prince." She prodded me.

But I was frozen. I had no idea what to do.

The man stepped forward with a frown on his face. "What kind of information?"

"About the assassin," I said, my voice raspy.

He smirked at me. "We know where she is, sweetheart. Quarter Guards will bring her in any minute now." He nodded to the guard. "Get rid of them."

He was leaving.

I looked at Belle and swallowed. If we went back into that mob, we'd never get this close again. We'd be lucky if we survived it a second time. This was my only chance. "It's me." The words came out thick and dry, practically a whisper. The young guard eyed me strangely, but the other man kept walking. I cleared my throat. "It's me!"

He returned, skepticism coloring his face.

"I'm the girl you've been looking for. Me. I'm here."

There was an awkward pause, and then the young guard dove at me. The next thing I knew, my face was pressed against the stones on the ground as he twisted my arms behind my back.

I gasped at the pain. "I'm here to help," I said. "Yes, I was there, but I wasn't trying to assassinate the prince. I know who is. I'm here to help, I swear it. Please, just let me talk to the prince!"

Someone wrapped something around my hands, fixing them behind my back, and then the older guard hauled me to my feet with a bruising grip. "A traitor like you, see the prince? You'll be lucky if we wait until tomorrow morning to execute you."

He yanked me toward the palace, and I wrenched my head around to look for Belle. The young guard was pulling her back toward the gate. She tried to pull her arm from his grip, but was rewarded with a stronger yank that nearly brought her to her knees. "Belle! Wait, please! Let her stay inside, it's not safe out there!"

"Get her out of here," said the guard holding me.

I tried to pull back but he shoved me forward, and I fell to the ground. As he hauled me to my feet, the younger guard opened the gate and pushed Belle through the opening. The last thing I saw before the mob swallowed her was the look of horror on Belle's face, her eyes wide, her mouth open in a silent scream.

Chapter 22

I landed hard on my knees on the ice-cold stone floor of the cell before I lost my balance and fell on my shoulder. My arms were still bound behind me so I couldn't catch myself. The door slammed shut with a clang, and my captors left me.

As the guards had dragged me inside to the top of a flight of stairs, I'd cried, screamed, and begged to be taken to the prince. I'd told them the Blight was planning to move against the prince. They'd silenced me with a heavy cuff on my head, and I'd cowered, numb with shock, as they dragged me down the stairway and into the dim dungeon, lit by a single luminous on the ceiling.

I lay on my side in the cell, my cheek pressed against the horrible-smelling straw, and squeezed my eyes shut against the vision of Belle's last moments. She was one more person lost because of my failure. One more person who had paid the price because I couldn't fix this mess. But what else was I supposed to do? And I would be the next one to pay.

The heavy thump of footsteps grew louder as someone approached my cell, and I knew it was time. They would execute me, and the knowledge of the Blight's location and of Zel's dangerous power would be lost with me.

I'd failed everyone. Not just Zel and her daughters. Not just Weslan and Belle. I'd failed the whole city. Perhaps it would be better this way. I wouldn't have to see the ugly future that my failure had brought about.

The door swung open, and I struggled to a sitting position, forcing my wobbly legs to stand. A tall, heavily muscled guard in a black uniform stood in the doorway, staring at me with an inscrutable expression on his face. I'd never seen a uniform like his before. Older than the other guards, he had a scruffy beard along his jaw and a suntan on his cheeks.

I squared my shoulders as best I could and looked him in the eye. If he worked for the Palace Guard, he'd execute me soon enough. If he was the Blight's man, he'd seize the chance to kill me now. But I was dead either way, so what did it matter who did the job?

I had failed everyone else, but at least now, in my last moments, I could be brave. If only I could be sure he wasn't in the Blight's employ. But I had to try. "Before you kill me, I beg you, please send a guard to an abandoned warehouse in the River Quarter. You'll find the Crimson Blight's headquarters and a woman they plan to use as a weapon against the prince." My voice shook, but I'd said the words. I'd tried.

The new guard only watched me.

"The woman is my stepmother, Zel Stone, and she is an unregistered absorbent mage with the Touch. They also have her two twin daughters, who are mages as well, and another mage, Weslan Fortis, held captive."

At the sound of Zel's name, he flinched. At the mention of Bri, Alba, and Weslan, his shoulders bunched up for a moment and his brow tensed as though he were in pain.

What did that mean? "I believe the Blight's leader is a mage, and most of those working with him are mages. They plan to end Fenra rule in Asylia and return the mages to power. Please, I know you're going to kill me, but this is bigger than me. You have to stop them!"

He pressed a hand against his forehead, staring at me so intently I wondered if he was seeing me or something else. After a beat of silence, he snapped into action and stepped inside the cell with me.

I flinched backward, but where could I go?

He grabbed my arm and leaned close to my ear. "Not another word of that until we get to the prince," he whispered. "Play along with whatever I say."

He hauled me out of the cell, his grip tight on my arm, and dragged me back down the hallway to a point where two uniformed guards stood at attention. "We need answers out of this one. Taking her to the Sentinels for interrogation."

One of the two guards, the red-faced man who had ordered the younger guard to throw Belle to the mob, frowned and opened his mouth, but the guard holding me cut him off. "I know you've got your own tools, Lupus, you blood-thirsty rat." He squeezed my arm so tightly I knew it would leave a bruise. Of course, that was the least of my worries now. "Let's just say we've got better ones."

I didn't have to fake the terrified wail that came out of my mouth at his words. Was he one of the Blight's men, trying to get me away from the real guards so he could kill me? Would he torture me?

Lupus glared at us before he followed us up the stairs in silence. At the top of the stairs, he stopped and watched us go.

The guard holding me led me down a long, empty passage and then another one before he stopped. He looked over his shoulder and then opened a small closet that held only a shelf with folded cleaning rags and a large broom. "In here." He gave me a quick shove inside and shut the door behind us. The room went dark.

I felt his arm reach around me, and I hastily stepped backward, hitting the side of the closet.

He opened a door in the back wall. "This way." He ducked through the small door and paused in the doorway, the dim light coming from further down a hidden passageway. "You're safe," he said. "At least, for now. Come with me."

Feeling woozy, I swayed for a moment before following him through the door and into the narrow passageway. I stayed close behind his back and stumbled along in the dim light, my balance thrown off by the tie that still bound my hands behind me. We walked in the near darkness for several minutes, twisting and turning, going down narrow staircases until I couldn't have said which way was which.

He stopped and tapped on something.

Bright light flooded the passageway, blinding my eyes. Panic built in my stomach again. His tall, broad form blocked the light for a moment as he stepped through the doorway. And then, wondering if I was walking into my own execution after all, I followed him.

The room was well lit, but small and cramped. It held only a large wooden desk, piled with papers, and a faded couch with a man reclining upon it.

"Your Highness," said the guard beside me. He knelt on the ground and bowed his head.

I gaped at him and then dove to the floor, copying his pose. It was no easy feat with my hands still tied behind my back. That man on the couch was Prince Estevan? What was he doing here?

"Rise," came a tired-sounding voice. Where was the cold, arrogant voice from the night before? I rose slowly, eyeing the prince. A clean, white bandage covered his side, but the couch where he lay was stained with blood. His face was pale and drawn, his hair stringy with sweat. "What is this, Darien? Is this the girl?" He coughed roughly and then groaned, his hand hovering over his side. "Doesn't look like her."

"Your Highness, this is the one accused of being involved with the attack on your life last night. She's also the girl who gave you that proposal."

And the prince's haggard face lit with the slightest of smiles. He lifted a small sheet of paper crumpled in his fist.

My proposal. It looked like I'd gotten his attention after all, for what it was worth.

Darien nudged me. "Speak, girl. Tell him what you told me."

"Your Highness, I am so sorry … I didn't know that someone was seeking to take your life. When I sought you out on the balcony, I thought only to give you my note and beg you to consider changing the regulation on mages. When I heard the commotion as I was walking away, I knew something had happened, and I was worried I'd be wrongly blamed for it. I ran home. But the trackers found my home. Instead of arresting me, they called for all the girls my age to come in for questioning."

I shivered. "At the time, I thought they had simply tracked me to my street but didn't know which house I was in. My two stepsisters—"

My voice broke at the word, but I kept going. "My stepsisters went outside to protect me, even though they are only thirteen, and obviously far too young to be mistaken for me. A tracker took them away, but instead of going to the Quarter Guard station, he took them to the Crimson Blight." I glanced up at the prince.

His eyes were on me, but his face was indecipherable. He waved a weak hand for me to continue.

"My stepsisters were kidnapped by the Blight for a reason, Your Highness." I glanced warily at the guard, but he nodded at me. "They were taken because their mother, my stepmother, Zel, is an unregistered mage. She has the Touch."

The prince glanced from me to the guard beside me. "I'm guessing she's the one?"

Darien only grunted and prodded me to keep going.

"Um, yes, Zel has the Touch, Your Highness," I went on. "But I promise you, she is the gentlest, kindest woman I've ever known. In Draicia, she was forced through her True Name to work as an assassin. But she escaped, and she has been in Asylia for thirteen years, caring for her daughters, harming no one. No one!"

I was babbling, but I couldn't seem to stop. Never, in all my worry-filled nightmares about exposing Zel's secret, had I imagined spilling it to the crown prince himself. "I'm telling you, she never—"

Darien folded his arms across his chest. "Tell him what you said about the Blight."

"The Blight. Well, not an hour after the twins were taken, someone came to our bakery with proof that they had the girls, so Zel had to go with them to get her daughters back. She told me to stay home, but I followed her." I swallowed, feeling guilty.

I couldn't risk telling them the truth about Weslan's True Name and digging myself any deeper. "I followed them to an abandoned warehouse in the River Quarter. And while I was there, I overheard two of the Blight's men talking. Both were mages. I recognized one as the tracker who arrested my stepsisters. I'd seen him before at Theros Street Market. There was a quarter guard too. They were saying that since they had Zel, they would be able to make their move any hour now. They said they couldn't wait to get rid of the Fenra."

I took a deep breath and met his eyes. "Your Highness, I believe the Crimson Blight is made up of mages with people in the government, including trackers and quarter guards, under their employ. They are planning to overthrow the Fenra and bring Asylia under their rule."

I gasped as a thought struck me. What about Belle? I'd been so wrapped up in my own impending death, I'd forgotten about hers. "The Blight's attacks seemed random to me, but my friend … well, my classmate, Belle, believes they have chosen specific targets to convince the Argentarius clan and the Falconus family to go to war against each other. If they destroy each other, the mage authority structure will collapse. She said the Blight tried to kill you last night, Your Highness, but her father and Lord

Falconus each thought the other was behind it. In fact, Lady Belle Argentarius, she was with me when—"

"She's fine," said the prince, with another wave of his hand. "They stopped the fighting. She's home safe."

I sagged with relief. Belle was fine. Maybe there was hope for the others who hung in the balance because of me. "Your Majesty, please, if you send guards to the warehouse, you could rescue Zel and her daughters and the other mage, Weslan. You could stop the Blight from making their move, and no more lives need be lost—"

He broke out into another painful-sounding cough, cutting me off. After a moment, he lifted himself up into a reclined sitting position against the side of the couch. I expected Darien to go to him and help, but he remained by my side. The prince stared at me with that piercing gaze, and though his face was slick with sweat and tight with pain, the arrogant, cold man from the other night was visible enough. "Let me be sure I've got this right. You've been harboring an unregistered mage with the Touch, a known murderer and assassin from Draicia, for thirteen years."

He held up one finger as if to keep count. "And she has two daughters"—his eyes flicked to the guard and back to me—"who are most likely mages as well. All three of them have been hiding, unregistered, for over a decade in my city, thanks to you.

"There's also the other mage you've been sheltering, a Weslan Fortis, who is apparently far more powerful than he ever let on until now." Three fingers.

"Then there's the bakery stand you've been running which profits daily from illicit use of magic in almost every aspect of its operation." Four fingers.

"And the fact that you snuck into my selection ball, which commoners are not allowed to attend, caught me alone, and handed me a supposedly anonymous proposal to free my most powerful enemies, a proposal that many in this city would consider outright treason. A proposal that has involved secret collaboration with other merchants who should have known better." His balled his fist and rested it on his knee.

I felt as though I'd sink right through the floor.

He watched me with an icy gaze as he spoke, "And there's more, isn't there? You distracted me—knowingly or not—enough that an assassin's knife found its target in my back for the first time in years. When my guards would have arrested you, you resisted and ran. And then you came to the palace gates, demanding to see me, and nearly got a young Procus lady killed in the process. I'm starting to think you're running a dangerous rebellion of your own, Cinderella."

Chapter 23

I bowed my head. "Your Highness, I'm so—"

"I'm not done." He grunted and lifted himself up a little further, eyeing me with a strange look on his face. "I've had the chance to do some research since I last saw you, you see. You were also the first child from a common family to win a scholarship to the Royal Academy, where you were at or near the top of your class in every subject. You survived an attack by the Blight in your own classroom, an attack that scarred your face and robbed you of your graduation, and then, rather than give up, you launched the most successful shop our city has ever seen, in a location that many had been too afraid to visit, thanks to the Blight.

"When you realized that the regulations were against you, you found a solution—a change in the regulations that would benefit not only you, but the entire city—a change that could lift this city out of the plague years completely. And, even though you knew the guards would likely kill you on sight, you came to the palace to warn me when you found out about the true threat."

I dragged my gaze up from the floor and back to his face. What was he saying?

"My father would have killed you, Ella, on principle alone." His face took on an intensity I had never seen before.

"But I am not my father." He glanced at the guard beside me. "Darien, get your team together. Sounds like it's time. And get this girl something to eat and drink. She's about to fall over."

The guard nodded. "Will do, Your Highness." He unbound my wrists and left the room, this time from the main door, not the small passageway we'd come through.

I stared nervously at the ground, darting the occasional glance at the prince. I couldn't believe they'd left me alone with him.

He relaxed his head against the couch for a minute and then lifted it again. "You may be wondering why I'm lying here, injured, without a healer to attend me."

I nodded slowly.

"My father, before his death, was convinced that the mages were against him. He believed that even though the mages were under True Name control, they could still find ways to harm us. He allowed no mages or mage-crafts in the palace, save for a few loyal trackers, the suffio, the luminous supplies we get from the common markets, and the occasional Procus event. Even then, all mage-crafts are confined to a single room. I've never seen a healer, and though I'm not the paranoid bastard he was, I likely never will. Can you imagine what a powerful expellant mage like a healer might do to me if they had even the smallest desire to harm the royal family? I can't risk it."

"But if you believed the mages were rebelling, why didn't you stop the Blight sooner?" I asked bluntly, and then bit my lip as I realized how accusatory that sounded. He'd been beyond gracious to me so far. Would my question push him over the edge?

He laughed, then he grunted and grabbed his side. "I think you're overestimating my power. Not that I don't appreciate the loyalty, but I'm not omniscient. We had no intelligence suggesting with any certainty that the Blight was made up of mages, and we've never tracked them to one of their hideouts. Until now, that is." He eyed me curiously. "We've been preparing, however. You'll see."

The door swung open, and Darien stepped back into the room. "Ready, Your Highness. Ella, I'll need directions and details, as much as you can give me. If I may, Your Highness?" My stomach dropped. Directions? Of course. There was more than one abandoned warehouse in the River Quarter.

The prince nodded, and I curtsied before following Darien out the door. I could hear deep voices in conversation further down the hallway, and occasionally a shout of male laughter rang out. But Darien led me into another small room and shut the door. Inside, a dark-haired woman waited at a table. She was dressed in a black uniform that matched Darien's with the addition of a gold armband around her upper arm. I noticed for the first time that, unlike the Quarter Guard and the Palace Guard, their uniforms held no symbol or identifying mark at all.

"Sit," said Darien. "Let's be quick about this. Tell Raven here everything you can about the location."

I pulled out a chair and joined the woman at the table. She shoved a plate of bread and a glass of water in front of me as Darien joined us at the table. I stared at the bread, my stomach turning. I was desperately hungry, and so thirsty my head had been pounding for hours. But how could I eat and drink when everyone I loved was in danger?

I looked away from the food and focused on Raven instead. "I … well, it's in the River Quarter. I know that much. The warehouse was dirty on the outside. Maybe had a few broken windows, I think. And … there was a small entrance. A door. That's where I heard the Blight's men talking. I think they were standing guard."

Raven raised a cool eyebrow. "That's it?"

"Um …" I closed my eyes and tried to replay the scene from hours earlier. "I'm sorry, it was so dark before dawn, and I just …" I'd been too terrified to pay attention to little details like street names, but I didn't feel like admitting that in front of this woman now.

"Did you see your stepmother or stepsisters, or this other mage, at the warehouse?"

"No, but the guards said—"

"But you didn't physically see any of them?"

"No ..." I glanced at Darien who was frowning at me.

"Then how do you know they're there?" She looked at Darien. "I thought you had vetted her."

My heart jumped in my chest. They had to believe me. I couldn't come all this way only to fail now. "I know they're there." I swallowed. "I know it, because I know the True Name of Weslan Fortis, the mage who was with my stepmother. I didn't follow them. I waited for them to come home, but when they didn't, I realized I could track his location in my mind with the bond. I didn't know what else to do, so I decided to try and find them on my own." By the end of my confession, I was whispering. I glanced between Darien and Raven when they didn't respond.

Raven's expression was cold and inscrutable, despite the slight widening of her eyes, so I watched Darien run a hand over his face. Finally, he spoke. "I understand why you didn't tell us, Ella. But you should've. If we'd gone in with hazy directions, we could've lost any advantage we might've had."

The corner of Raven's mouth lifted. "Yes, you could have told us. What's one more count of treason, after all?"

I swallowed against the painful lump in my throat. "I'm sorry ..."

And then, to my surprise, she laughed, the warm sound at odds with her cold face. "You're something else, Cinderella. And it sounds like you'll be coming with us."

~

The long, black fomewagon jostled us as it took a corner, and I clutched the seat to remain upright and avoid bumping into Raven again. We sat near the front so I could give directions to the driver as I felt the bond pull me. Outside, the day was hot and the sun high. It had to be nearly midday.

I glanced toward the back. The men of the Sentinels were packed into most of the remaining seats, a small army of black-clad muscle. I'd learned that they reported directly to Prince Estevan and had trained for years to fight one terrifying threat—mages turning on humans.

The Sentinels laughed and joked as though they weren't about to meet the Blight head-on for the first time since the attacks began. They were a mismatched bunch, some tall and broad, some wiry and small. Some were dark, and others light. Some had closely shorn hair, and others had wild hair and long, streaked beards like badlanders.

To a man, they were powerfully built, even the wiry ones, and they carried themselves with an air of quiet power that I'd never seen in the Quarter Guards before. Three female mages rode with us, one of whom was Raven. The guards were rough and jovial, cracking jokes and pretending to fight with each other. But the mages were stoic and distant, with an absence of emotion that seemed more painful than a frown or scowl might have been. Something in their demeanor reminded me of Belle, as though each one had looked evil in the face and lived to tell about it.

I shivered and faced the front. "Up there. To the right." The fomecoach swung around the corner, and I felt the inexplicable pull get a little lighter. "We're close." My words were soft, but everyone in the coach quieted. I squeezed my grip on the seat. I'd felt nervous before, in exam time, when I wasn't sure if I'd studied sufficiently the night before. This was nothing like that feeling.

I closed my eyes and focused on the pull as we went deeper into the River Quarter. "Take the next left." I opened my eyes as I felt the fomecoach turn. The warehouses looked familiar. We were in an old, dusty part of the River Quarter, far from the hubbub that surrounded Riverwalk Market and the many tenements near it. Here, there were only old buildings, leftover from another time when wealth poured into Asylia like a flood from the West.

The pull grew weaker. I knew this street. I'd tripped and fallen right there, after turning the corner and successfully getting out of view of the two mages I'd spied on. "Stop!"

The fomecoach jerked to a stop, and the driver frowned at me.

"It's right around the corner." My voice felt far too loud, and the words echoed in my head. I glanced behind me again, my eyes unconsciously seeking out Darien's, looking for what, I didn't know.

How many of these men and women would be lost today? What could a bunch of magic-less soldiers, three female trackers, and a kitchen girl do against the Blight? Against the bloody man from my nightmares?

"Then we're up," Darien said.

There was a general grunt of acknowledgment, and the soldiers filed out into the street, weapons at the ready. Raven and I jumped out after them, and Darien looked to me expectantly. "You'll have to show us, Ella."

I nodded and led them around the corner, letting the pull confirm that Weslan was still in the same warehouse I'd found before. No one stood at the narrow basement entrance this time. I looked up at the dusty warehouse. It must have been grand in its time, for the warehouse was massive. Now it was nothing more than a dirty, broken shell.

And then I felt it. The pull was getting weaker. I glanced around wildly. Weslan was there, but he wasn't staying in place. He was moving farther away. "They're moving," I told Darien. "Getting away. They might be moving within the warehouse, or maybe there's another door on the other side. I don't know. I won't know until we're inside."

He nodded. "Then we're going inside now."

Darien gave some sort of signal, and three of his team split off and approached the narrow door.

I kept looking for any sign of the Blight, his men, or his captives, but I saw no one.

Then the door swung open, and the three men disappeared inside. A moment later, one appeared at the entrance and signaled Darien. He nodded to me, and the rest of the group headed for the door. Would any of us come out of this warehouse alive?

The warehouse was oppressively dark inside, and it was baking in the stifling summer heat. It took several moments for my eyes to adjust. I stopped inside the door as the guards searched for any sign of the Blight and focused on that little spark, wondering where the pull would take me. The pull drew me across the wide warehouse, past the empty pallets and shelves. There, on the far side to the right, a cluster of doors led to offices of some kind. I gestured to Darien and pointed to the doors.

He nodded and sent a few guards toward the doors. We followed. The rest continued to search through the warehouse, working toward the doors as well.

My legs shook as we walked, and I was thankful my old shoes made almost no noise on the warehouse floor. Weslan had to be behind one of them—the pull was undeniable.

Darien gave me a questioning look and gestured at the doors.

I shut my eyes to concentrate. Where was Weslan? I focused on his familiar pull, concentrating on how it felt to be with him. I thought of the quiet moments we had worked together in the kitchen, each knowing what the other needed before a word was spoken. In my mind's eyes, I saw his golden hair, falling into his eyes again and his big hands, coated in flour as he kneaded the dough beside me. I had always been tempted to lean in to the warmth of his shoulder, but never—

I opened my eyes and pointed to the door on the far right. It was that one. I was sure of it.

A guard edged forward and tried the door handle, but it was locked. The rest of the guards approached the door, swords out and ready. And then, with a single powerful kick, he took the door down.

The next few moments were a blur of screams, crashes, and the deafening sound of my own heartbeat in my ears. The other guards rushed the door, and Darien left us to join them.

Raven held me back. "You're with me."

I couldn't tell who was screaming, but the screaming wouldn't stop. My breath came in rapid gasps.

A shout issued from the room, "Raven, we need you!"

She glanced from me to the door, clearly torn.

I shoved her forward. "Go! I'll be fine." My voice shook. But if she was needed, I couldn't be the one to keep her back.

She disappeared into the room, and I waited, sweat dripping into my eyes. I wiped it away and strained my ears, but still couldn't tell what was happening inside. Should I stay safely outside? Or should I go inside to see what was happening?

And then I felt it again—that little weakening of the bond. Weslan was moving away. While the Blight's men were fighting the guards, someone was taking Weslan, and maybe Zel and the girls, out of the warehouse. And the pull led right through that room. I had to find them.

I dove into the room and huddled behind a desk. The fight was pure chaos. I couldn't tell who was winning. All I could see were bodies locked in close combat, knives and swords darting through the air. The wounded and dead sprawled on the floor.

But there was no trace of Weslan or Zel. I made myself as small as I could behind the desk, hoping no one would notice me there. I focused on the little spark again. Where was Weslan going?

There were two doors in this room in addition to the one I'd entered from, and the pull drew me toward the door farthest away. He must be there.

I peeked around the edge of the desk. There was no clear path to the door. I'd have to run for it and take my chances that the Blight's men would ignore me. I crouched and took a deep breath. The pull was getting farther away. It was now or never.

I shot from behind the desk and dodged two men fighting right beside it. I wove my way between the fighters until I was at the door. A hand gripped my ankle, and I fell to the floor. With one kick, I was free. I rolled to my back and struggled to my feet. But the large man tackled me, squishing me against the floorboards. We were face to face. His forearm pressed against my throat, and I gurgled in protest. Was he going to kill me? I couldn't have come so far only to die now.

His face was bloody and twisted with anger, his eyes wild, and it took a moment to recognize him.

"Professor Jace?" My words came out in a strained gasp. I shoved with all my might against his arm and only managed to budge it a hair's breadth.

He bared his teeth at me, looking nothing like the refined Procus teacher who'd hated me so much at the Royal Academy. "You little traitor," he growled. "You don't know when to listen, Cinderella. Didn't the Blight tell you to give up? He's won."

"Why ... why would you help them?" I croaked the words out as I wriggled under him, desperate to relieve the pressure on my throat. "The Blight is going to enslave everyone. That includes you."

He pressed harder. "I only seek order, not that you would understand." Spittle flew from his mouth as he spoke. "Mages are superior to humans in every way. They're the true rulers of this city. Mages, then Procus families, then commoners at the bottom. That's the natural way of things. We can't have grasping commoners like you trying to upset the natural balance."

My head felt as if it might explode. I wasn't getting enough air, and soon, I'd be done. As hard as I pushed, there was no way to budge him. He was too much heavier and stronger than me.

Hot wetness covered my stomach. Had he also stabbed me? Why did I feel no pain?

Then his arm weakened against my throat.

I wasn't the one who'd been stabbed. He was. And he was bleeding out, right here on top of me.

Professor Jace glared at me. "You'll never stop him. The Blight is too smart, too powerful. You were an idiot to think you could ever control a mage. You and every Fenra in this city."

I waited until his grip weakened again, and then I shoved with all my might, rolling in the same motion. He flopped over with a grunt of surprise, and I staggered to my feet.

He lay on the ground, staring up at me. "I'll die with honor for the Blight," he whispered, his hand falling slack at his side. "You'll never—"

His words were lost when I plunged into the dark hallway behind me.

I raced forward, stumbling over boxes and debris that lined the walls. I focused on the little spark, letting it guide me. The sounds of fighting receded as I rushed through the warehouse. The pull got stronger. I was close.

Finally, the hallway ended in an open bay where fomewagons used to load goods in the days before the plague. I stumbled to a halt. I'd found them.

Chapter 24

A group of men in black hoods and red masks stood across the bay with their backs to me. Just steps away, a shabby black fomewagon waited to be loaded. Weslan and the twins were at the edge of the loading ramp, gags over their mouths and bindings on their hands and feet. But Zel—

She was free. She stood beside a tall, golden-haired man, the only one not wearing a mask. Where were they planning to go?

They moved toward the fomewagon and, without thinking, I raced toward them. "Wait! Zel! Wait, it's me!"

I skidded to a stop as they all faced me. There was nothing I could do to stop them. All I'd done was give myself away.

Weslan strained against his bindings, shouting a muffled warning that I couldn't heed. It was too late to run away.

"Zel." My voice sounded pathetic and small in the massive shipping bay. "I brought help. Prince Estevan's men are here. I mean, they'll be here soon."

I'd meant to sound confident and assured of victory, but instead, the words came out shaky and high.

Zel stood beside the blond man and stared blankly ahead, her lifeless visage a stark contrast to the warm, kind woman I'd known since I was a child. I was too late. She was already under his control. Beyond her, the twins' stricken faces streamed with tears.

One of the men in the red masks grabbed my arm, his grip painfully tight.

Sick with trepidation, I dragged my gaze to the unmasked man beside Zel, and his laugh chilled me. I hated to meet his smiling gray eyes. Dread pressed upon me until I wasn't sure I could breathe. I knew him. That face. Those features. I'd seen him before. Where?

The man I assumed to be the Blight's leader laughed again. "Cinderella, Cinderella. Here you are. After all our little shared moments, I'd started to miss you."

Cold sweat dripped down my forehead and back. The man from my nightmares. But not just my nightmares—the attack. The blood-red face in the door of my classroom. The man who'd waited until I'd seen him before setting off the bomb. He'd wanted me to know him.

A high-pitched noise came from the back of my throat, and the shipping bay swam around me. The daily imaginings and attacks had appeared and disappeared until I'd thought I was losing my mind. I'd been haunted by the feeling that someone was there in the kitchen with me. It was real.

He was real. He was here, unmasked, not five steps away from me. He held a single glass slipper in one hand. And he was smiling. "Call me Flavian. It's so nice to meet formally, isn't it? I chose you the day you won the scholarship, and I bided my time. Who knew I had selected such a prize? You led me to your stepmother. I couldn't have asked for more."

Zel didn't even blink.

Flavian waved his hand, and a red ribbon materialized out of thin air in front of my face. It darted through the air and nipped sharply at my face and arms, cutting my skin like a small, sharp knife.

I didn't recognize the sound of my own sobs.

Then he waved his hand again, and the ribbon dissolved into tiny pieces before my eyes, rematerializing in his hand. "A mover can't create things out of thin air, darling

Cinderella. But we can get awfully close." He moved toward me, and Zel followed on his heels, like a pet. "I'm glad you're here. It didn't seem right to do this without you. You were my muse, after all, Cinderella." He stepped closer. "What, no response? Tell me I haven't waited all these years to speak with you, and you're speechless."

My guard gave me a shake. "Speak, girl."

I'd know that gravelly voice anywhere. Silas. The tracker who had destroyed our lives held me with an iron grip. My skin crawled, and I shivered uncontrollably. I forced my mouth open. "I-I don't …" My voice was tinny. I sounded like someone else. Someone who knew she was about to die. I swallowed. "I don't know what you want from me."

Flavian's expression changed from mockingly warm to ice cold in an instant. "You don't know? How sweet. How innocent." He loomed over me, his tall body terrifyingly close to mine. "You greedy little commoner." He grabbed my already-bruised throat and squeezed. "How dare you? I was livid when I read that disgusting article in the *Herald*. A stinking, grasping kitchen girl, forcing your way into the Royal Academy when you had no right to touch their books, much less attend their classes. To think that a commoner like you might one day work in government and hold power over mages—your superiors, in every possible way?

"Unthinkable. Unacceptable. When I stopped you, you dared to enslave a mage in your own kitchen. A mage! In the kitchen! Serving commoners, as though he were beneath them."

I struggled in his grip, but Silas held me fast. There was no way to move back. I heard muffled screams from Weslan's direction, a loud crack, and then silence. "I don't think he's beneath them," I babbled. "I don't. I just wanted to help him. I wanted to help everyone. I swear it! I want to make it so that mages don't have to work only for the government or the Procus families, but can be free to choose what they want to do. I want mages to be free! Please, you have to believe—"

He cut off my words along with my breath. "You want mages to be free, hmm? Well, so do I, Cinderella. You filthy, pathetic Fenra have enslaved us long enough. It's your turn." He released my throat, and I collapsed against the guard holding me, gasping for breath.

"Imagine my delight when my tracker discovered that the very girl who had vexed me so many years was also harboring the woman who would be the key to our rebellion. The dress, my dear. The faintest of traces. You hid them well, but Silas here's one of the best. He found traces of a woman with the Touch and two young female mages—one absorbent, one expellant. Hiding, against all odds, in plain sight, smack in the middle of the Merchant Quarter."

Flavian turned to Zel, who stood docile and silent by his side. He ran one hand slowly down her back, making my skin crawl at the sight, before turning back to me, his smile growing wider. "Delight doesn't even begin to capture the emotion I felt at his news. And then he found the same traces on a glass slipper left by the foolish girl at Prince Estevan's selection ball, and the city's greatest weapon practically fell into my lap. We're going to kill every Fenra who's ever held power over a mage in this city, beginning with the crown prince and his Procus lackeys, and we won't stop until you Fenra are firmly under Kireth boots once more." He gave me a shallow bow, and I fought to retain control over the anxious, gasping breaths that threatened to overwhelm me. "So thank you, Cinderella, with all my heart."

Flavian put one hand on his chin and frowned, a look of mock concern coming over his face. "Does it hurt, knowing you've singlehandedly brought our rebellion success? Knowing all the suffering we're about to inflict on this forsaken city could have been stopped if you'd kept to your place in the order of things?" Then he dropped his hand and smiled again. "I thought it might. That's what makes this whole moment so satisfying. You've truly been a wonderful muse."

He stepped away and then returned to me, as though he'd just remembered something else. "Did you know, Cinderella, that some of the most beautiful things can come from death? I've learned that. There was a time, when you were a small, grimy child, that the plague set me free. The mage who held my True Name died, and for two glorious days, the idiots who ran this city forgot to replace him. I tasted freedom, thanks to his death, you see. And once you give an enslaved man the taste of freedom, you can never truly enslave him again." His smile remained, but his face was like dark ice, cold and hard.

"All it took was planting a few seeds—a well-timed word, here and there, to my new master. That there might be certain exceptions to the 'do no harm' command. That I should be able to harm no one except commoners who might occasionally stand in the way of progress. That I should harm no Procus families save those who had enriched themselves through trade, risking the plague all over again with their reckless imports."

Flavian brushed an imaginary speck from his sleeve. "Of course, I shared my methods with other mages who chafed under the yoke of slavery. When you wormed your way into the Royal Academy, I knew it was time to begin putting a more destructive plan in place. I couldn't in good conscience allow the slavery of mages to continue, not knowing that one day, a commoner might control their chains." He reached toward my neck again, and I flinched.

He drew his hand back and tapped his cheek. "I know what we need," he said. "A little something to get things started." He looked at Zel, whose beautiful face was calm and blank as she waited beside him. "Rapunzel, my dear, kill her."

Chapter 25

His words rang in my ears, punctuated by the muffled sobs of Bri and Alba. Weslan must have regained consciousness. He screamed, too, his words too distorted to understand.

I tried to rip my arm from the guard, but he held me fast. My feet scrabbled against the ground as my terrified body decided to try to run anyway, unwilling to give into its fate. But my mind was locked on Zel as she advanced toward me, her graceful movements so painfully familiar.

I watched her face desperately, hoping against hope. And yet, wasn't that the whole point of the True Name? To wrap a mage's will in your own? Flavian controlled her now. There was nothing she could do.

She raised her hand to deliver the killing touch just as Darien and Raven shouted from the hallway behind me. The Sentinels were here. It was too late for me, but not too late for them. I stopped fighting and sagged with relief.

Zel, the twins, and Weslan would be rescued. The Blight would be stopped. Zel would kill me, but she needed a future. I had to make sure she would be able to move on. It wasn't much, but it would have to be enough.

I stared into her hazel eyes and ignored their blankness. Zel was in there, somewhere. I had to try. "Zel, I forgive you." I echoed her own words back to her. "I love you like

my own mother. No matter what. Never, never forget that."
I forced myself to keep my eyes open as I waited for the end to come. I wouldn't leave her alone in this. I would show her, right up until the last moment, that I forgave her, that I loved her. That she wasn't alone.

She froze.

I stared in amazement. Her face was no longer completely blank. There it was—the slightest tightening around her eyes. Was she resisting Flavian's command?

My enemy must have wondered the same thing. "Rapunzel," he hissed, and this time I could practically feel the controlling magic that dripped from her True Name. "Kill her. Now!"

But Zel's hand hovered near my throat. There was a heavy, terrifying pause, as though the whole city was holding its breath at once.

Then she snapped. One second she was in front of me, and the next, she was gripping Flavian's throat instead of mine. His mouth gaped open as her absorbent Touch took over. Before I took my next breath, his body was gray and parched, utterly drained of life.

Zel dove at the tracker holding me, and then he was gone. She took out the other guards in the same way, moving gracefully and rapidly, like a spider pouncing on her prey before they knew what was happening.

The Blight's men were lifeless, gray heaps on the ground. Zel stood among them, not even the slightest bit tired.

A shock of silence followed.

"Zel Stone," Raven called, "by order of the crown prince, you're under arrest. Come peacefully, or die now."

Chapter 26

The silence of the bakery unnerved me. I sang to myself to fill the silence as I worked on my hands and knees, scrubbing the kitchen floor. The soft, haunting melody from Alba's fabulator crystal came unbidden to my mind.

Asylia, the City of Hope,
you never sleep but always dream.
I know you love those who love you,
no matter how hard you may seem.

I sang the words under my breath, off-key, wishing I could hear Alba's sweet, clear voice instead.

Seven full days had passed since Zel killed the Blight leader. Seven days of scrubbing and cleaning, polishing, packing, and humming to drown out the hurt and loneliness, to fill the emptiness around me.

I'd sold the bakery. I couldn't keep living here on my own, not when memories of Zel, the girls, and Weslan lurked in every corner of the shop and living quarters. At noon today, I would hand my ring of keys to the new owner and move the few possessions I hadn't sold into a modest studio apartment over on Thrush Street, several blocks away in the Common Quarter.

After Zel's arrest, we'd all been shuttled to the palace and hustled into the Sentinels' offices for debriefing. I'd spent hours pacing alone in a small room, wondering what was happening to everyone else. When a guard finally came for me, I was ready to burst. And then I'd followed him out into the hallway, only to see Zel standing there, unbound, with the twins tucked under her arms and an impossibly wide smile on her face.

They'd rushed forward and hugged me, and we'd rocked back and forth in a tearful, happy, eight-legged mess. Finally, the twins got tired of being mashed between us, and they ducked out of our arms.

I pulled back and looked at Zel's lively face. "How did you do that? I don't understand! I thought you were going to—" I stopped speaking as tears filled her eyes.

She swallowed and shook her head. "I almost did. I—" Her voice broke, and she pressed her palms against her eyes.

I rubbed her shoulders. "But you didn't. Somehow, you didn't."

She moved her hands away and smiled at me through her tears. "I thought it was possible—even when I was a little girl locked in that tower—that I might be able to resist my True Name. I always thought that one day, if I was just strong enough, stubborn enough, I'd be able to escape control and never be someone else's weapon again."

"But how?" I asked.

She shrugged. "I did my best to practice, even at the bakery. But it's like training your muscles when you have no weight to lift. I had no idea if I'd ever be able to resist. But I had to try, because I couldn't go back to that life."

All those times she'd been cloistered on the rooftop, working quietly in her garden, she must have been practicing. I'd occasionally thought it odd that a powerful absorbent mage like Zel would dedicate so much time and effort to growing plants—it seemed like something more suited to an expellant mage, like a grower or creator. Now, it made sense.

Zel shivered. "And then, when Flavian ordered me to kill you, all my resistance and training meant nothing. My hand moved forward, no matter how I fought it. That's when I realized I'd been thinking about it all wrong. The key wasn't to resist, because that channeled all my energy against my True Name. The key was to focus my energy on remembering who I am, to take my True Name and make it my own again." She smiled gently. "And I know who I am. I'm your mother."

She folded me into her arms, holding me tight and rocking me for a moment like I was a small child again. Then she pressed me close one more time. "Sell the bakery," she whispered in my ear.

I pulled back from her, shocked.

The softest hint of sadness touched her eyes. "We're not coming back with you. Prince Estevan has given me a place at the Mage Division, but because of ... well, everything ... I'll be confined to the division." She glanced over her shoulder. "Still, it's far better than it could've been. Bri and Alba will go to the Mage Academy, and life will be better. I know it."

Her secretive smile confused me.

I followed her gaze instead. She was right. The girls would love it. They would be so excited to be around their peers. How wonderful it would be for them to have the chance to meet people, to roam free and explore, the way young women should. I forced a shaky smile onto my face. "I'm happy for you, Zel. For all of you." I didn't know what I would do without them.

"I owe you an apology, Ella." Zel swallowed. "I've told you how I grew up hidden in a tower in Draicia. Well, as horrible as my life was there, I think I got so used to staying hidden that I ended up doing the same thing to you and the twins. I turned that bakery into a tower. And yes, it kept us safe, but there was a price. You paid the price for us. And I'm so very sorry."

I shook my head. Why was she apologizing? She'd had no choice. "What else could you have done?"

She took my hands. "I love you, sweetheart. But you can't stay there anymore. It's not your prison anymore, got it? Sell the bakery, and the funds will be enough to tide you over for a while until you decide what to do. Find something for yourself. Promise me."

My throat threatened to close. "I … I'll try." I forced out a laugh to ease the tension.

"I'll take it," she said.

I said a tearful farewell to the twins, and then my stepmother and stepsisters were led away by Darien, the same guard with the scruffy beard who had believed my wild tale.

After that, I met Weslan in Prince Estevan's small, messy office in the Sentinels' headquarters. He'd called us in together after Zel left and sentenced us for all our various crimes against the Crown. We had to close the bakery, for now, but he would cancel our fines, leaving us with a tidy sum of profits to divide between us. We had to work off our crimes as laborers in the work of the prince's choosing.

Prince Estevan smiled when he announced that we would serve our sentences on a research committee to explore reformation of the regulations on mage employment in Asylia. "You had the right idea," he said. He had significantly more color than when I'd seen him last. "Now do the same thing, but legally this time." He gave me a sharp look. "And with more test subjects."

I couldn't help but grin.

Weslan and I left the prince's office, and then paused in the hallway when the door shut. His perfect face was now marred with horrible bruising, his once-clean shirt ripped and covered with dried blood. He'd never looked more handsome to me. He stared down at me with a faint smile on his face, like he couldn't tear his eyes away from me, and I had to wonder if he was thinking the same thing about me.

"Shall we …?" I suddenly felt nervous. I'd never lived at the bakery without Zel and the twins there. "Shall we take the trolley back?"

His face shifted into a frown, and he leaned back on his heels. "I'm not going with you, Ella."

"What?" I felt my heart beat uncomfortably at his words. He wouldn't—

"I'm going back to the Mage Division. Since Prince Estevan rescinded my expulsion, I have to go see my family, my friends. I can't stay with you anymore, Ella."

I didn't trust myself to speak. My throat felt like it was being squeezed in the Blight's iron grip again. I nodded and then lifted a hand in a small, awkward wave. What was I doing? "Good-bye," I whispered.

I rushed away, following the guard who waited to lead me through the maze of corridors and out to the palace gates.

I'd expected Weslan to call after me, perhaps to give me some sort of farewell embrace, but he'd let me go without a word. No doubt he'd seen all that I felt on my face, and in the fact that I had rushed off like a heartbroken fool. I'd humiliated myself with my show of emotion, and he'd said nothing.

I had no one, now. Not Weslan. Not Zel and the girls. Not even Gregor. My chest gave the usual painful clench when I thought Gregor's name, and I had to stop scrubbing for a moment and wait for it to fade. I'd spent my whole life taking care of other people, and now, all I had was myself.

My face grew hot at the memory of my last moment with Weslan, so I scrubbed the floor even harder, wishing I could scrub the embarrassment away. To distract myself, I thought of my new apartment on Thrush Street—its high windows that let sunlight stream in and brighten the room without any need for a luminous and the quaint nook in the corner by the main window where I planned to sip my morning coffee and read the *Herald*.

From the *Herald*, I learned that Flavian had been a high-ranking mover mage in the Transportation Ministry. He'd been close to the top of the mage authority structure. If he'd succeeded in his plot to use Zel to assassinate the human leaders over him, he'd have been able to do unimaginable damage to the city.

The paper related that the surviving Blight fighters had been arrested and were being questioned to find out the names of their collaborators in Asylia. I could only hope the Sentinels would relentlessly follow every lead.

I had to believe this was over. If nothing else, the man who had stalked me so relentlessly for so long was gone. Perhaps Asylia would never be a truly safe and peaceful haven, not with so many mages and humans packed within its walls. But this time, at least, we had won.

~

The next day, I spread the bright white coverlet over my bed, pulled it tight, and smoothed it with my hand. I'd slept soundly during my first night in the new apartment with not a single nightmare to plague me. It was strange to wake feeling so rested and relaxed. The room smelled of lavender and shone with the early morning sunlight. From east-facing windows, I could see all the way to the Theros River, glittering like a fat, lazy snake on the other side of the city.

I splashed cold water on my face and put the kettle on for coffee. Then I dressed in my new sky-blue house dress. For once, I left my hair down, brushing it into soft waves that spilled over my shoulders. I glanced in the small mirror in the creaky old bathroom that was tucked into my apartment.

I looked different, somehow. Only two months had passed since the Blight attacked my classroom during final exams, yet I felt years older. I was still fearful, sometimes. There were moments when I thought I glimpsed a scrap of red out of the corner of my eye, and I whirled around, heart pounding, wondering if somehow he was back.

But the fear wasn't quite so overpowering anymore. At times, it hovered like fog over me, thick and heavy, but like fog, it didn't control me anymore. And, like fog, it would dissipate. I'd looked my nightmare in the face, felt his hand grip my throat, and heard him order Zel to kill me, but instead of dying, I'd survived. I'd watched him die instead of me. I wasn't Cinderella anymore.

Tomorrow, I would report to the new committee on mage regulations. Today, I planned to explore my new neighborhood in the Common Quarter and go to Theros Street Market to see how Master Marus was getting along without us.

I'd seen him once, last week, after everything. He'd been disappointed to hear that Weslan and I wouldn't be back, and he'd bemoaned the fact that I'd be busy with the committee for the coming weeks and months. "I could use someone like you at my side," he'd said with a hearty slap on my back.

I'd left, promising to visit again, but then I'd wondered. What if he had need of an apprentice? He owned several small markets around the Common Quarter, besides the one at Theros Street. Perhaps he might hire me after my sentence had been completed.

Footsteps creaked on the stairs, followed by a gentle knock at my door. "Ella?" It was Mrs. Florence, the sweet, motherly landlady who lived on the first level and rented out the other levels. She'd hung bunches of dried lavender in my apartment and invited me for coffee when I'd first arrived.

"Come in," I said.

She opened the door with an uncharacteristically mischievous grin on her face. "You have a visitor, dear." She stepped aside to reveal Weslan. He wore a crisp white shirt, tailored slacks, and a nervous expression.

My heart tumbled in my chest. What was he doing here?

Mrs. Florence looked from me to Weslan with obvious delight. "I'll leave the two of you to it, then." She stepped back reluctantly and went back down the stairs, looking over her shoulder so many times I worried she might fall.

Weslan lingered on the landing outside my door, looking uncomfortable.

"Well, come in, then," I said, hating how breathless I sounded. But why should I be embarrassed anymore? I'd shown him my feelings. What did I have to lose? I gave him my warmest smile as he entered, and was shocked to see his ears turn pink. I smiled wider. "Would you like coffee?"

"That's—" his voice cracked strangely, shooting up an octave, and I couldn't restrain a giggle. He ran a finger underneath his collar. "Ahem. No, thank you. I'm ... I'm fine."

I nodded slowly. "Would you like to sit?"

"Actually, I just ... I'm here because ..." He ran a hand nervously through his hair, sending the perfectly combed strands into disarray.

Never, not once in the two months we'd spent working together, had I seen him look this uncertain. "You're here because?" I prompted him when he didn't speak.

A blush crept into his tan cheeks. He thrust a hand toward me. "This is for you," he said in a rush.

I stared down at a bouquet of pink rosedrops. He must have been hiding it behind his back. I took them, pretending to admire them to hide my confusion at his strange demeanor. "Thank you. They're beautiful." The words came out like a question.

He cleared his throat again, and I looked up. His face was bright red now. "Ella, I have to—" He broke off. "I'm in love with you, Ella."

You could have knocked me over with a feather. I didn't dare to breathe.

He spread his hands, palms up. "I haven't done many things right in life. Well, anything at all. And I love you, and for once, I want to do this right, with you. I want to court you, and marry you, one day, if you'll ... if you'll have me."

I couldn't have spoken if he'd begged me. All I could do was stare at his flushed, familiar face in awe, storing up his words so I could hold onto them forever.

"I left you at the Sentinels' because I wanted to give you some space before I asked this." He stepped closer. "I know it's asking a lot from you. To tie yourself to a mage, to live with uncertainty and constraint, not knowing if mages will ever be free. But I'm going to ask it anyway. I've lived my whole life under someone else's control, Ella. But I saw what Zel did. I won't be controlled again. I hope the regulations change, I do. But even if they don't, I'm my own man. I always will be. And I love you. Whatever the future holds, I want to spend it with you."

I couldn't wait any longer. I raced across the room and leapt into his arms, wrapping my arms around his neck as his warm hands gripped my waist. I pressed my lips against his ear and whispered the words that fear had silenced too many times: "I love you too."

Then his mouth found mine, and I lost myself in the warm, persuasive pressure of his lips.

"Find something for yourself," Zel had said.

I pressed in closer, unable to get enough of him, and was gratified when he shuddered and held me even tighter. Him. I wanted him. Whatever happened in our wild city of hope, he would be mine, and I would be his. And it would be enough.

AFTERWORD

Thank you so much for taking the time to read Ella and Weslan's retelling of the Cinderella story. I hope you enjoyed this story as much as I enjoyed writing it. If so, please make my day and leave a quick review! Reviews are often the best way to get the word out about indie books like this one.

There are so many familiar clichés in Cinderella, aren't there? Stepmothers are cruel. Stepsisters are jealous and selfish. Beautiful girls are helpless victims, and only a handsome prince can save them.

But real life is a bit more complicated.

Sometimes villains have battles of their own to fight, and victims are actually heroines just waiting for their chance to rise. And sometimes the man you fall in love with isn't the rich, powerful prince—it's the man who would do anything for you, the man who makes you feel beautiful.

Craving more of Ella and Weslan? Sign up for my new release email list at http://smarturl.it/torn-freebie and get the free prequel novelette *Torn*, a short story set two years before *Fated* begins.

ACKNOWLEDGEMENTS

Thank you so much to my beta readers, Michelle, Natasha, and mom. Your candid feedback and encouragement made this book what it is today—no question!

And thank you to the many dear friends who believed I could do this and cheered me on the whole way, especially Jenn, Katy, and Megan.

Extra special thanks to my amazing editor Kathrese for seeing the core of this book and putting in incredible work to help it become what it had the potential to be. I don't know what I would have done without you!

Thank you to my parents, who always think I can do anything I set my mind to. Your confidence means the world to me.

Thank you to my sweet, fearless, strong-willed daughter— my very own princess. You gave me a reason to write a different kind of story about a different kind of fairy tale princess.

Thank you to my husband, for going above and beyond to make sure I get my writing time, and for embracing my nerdiness with only a modest amount of teasing. Love you, babe.

Most of all, thank you to Jesus, the Author of the greatest story in the world and the Creator of creativity itself. I would be nothing without You.

ABOUT THE AUTHOR

Kaylin Lee is an Army wife, mama, and white cheddar popcorn devotee. She lives in the Pacific Northwest with her real-life hero husband and sweet toddler girl. After a lifetime of staying up too late reading stories, she now wakes up too early writing them. It was probably inevitable.

63670039R00140

Made in the USA
San Bernardino, CA
19 December 2017